ZENITH presents the best science fiction being written in Britain today. Startling, entertaining, stimulating and inventive, these twelve imaginative excursions into the unknown demonstrate that creativity and good writing are alive in this country as never before . . .

David Garnett is the author of several science fiction novels, and his own short fiction has been nominated for both the Hugo Award and the British Science Fiction Award. He is also the editor of *THE ORBIT SCIENCE FICTION YEARBOOK*.

ZENITH
The Best in New British Science Fiction

Edited by

David S. Garnett

SPHERE BOOKS LIMITED

SPHERE BOOKS LTD

Published by the Penguin Group
27 Wrights Lane, London W8 5TZ, England
Viking Penguin Inc., 40 West 23rd Street, New York, New York 10010, USA
Penguin Books Australia Ltd, Ringwood, Victoria, Australia
Penguin Books Canada Ltd, 2801 John Street, Markham, Ontario, Canada L3R 1B4
Penguin Books (NZ) Ltd, 182–190 Wairau Road, Auckland 10, New Zealand

Penguin Books Ltd, Registered Offices: Harmondsworth, Middlesex, England

First published in Great Britain by Sphere Books Ltd 1989
In Translation copyright © Lisa Tuttle, 1989
Time of the Tree copyright © Robert Holdstock, 1989
Death Ship copyright © Barrington J. Bayley, 1989
The Traveller copyright © Colin Greenland, 1989
Cinema Altéré copyright © Andrew Stephenson, 1989
The Pleasure Giver Taken copyright © Storm Constantine, 1989
White Noise copyright © Garry Kilworth, 1989
Gardenias copyright © Ian McDonald, 1989
Feminopolis copyright © Elizabeth Sourbut, 1989
Days in the Life of a Galactic Empire copyright © Brian W. Aldiss, 1989
Skyrider copyright © William King, 1989
The Bridge copyright © Christopher Evans, 1989
All other material in this collection copyright © David S. Garnett, 1989

1 3 5 7 9 10 8 6 4 2

Printed and bound in Great Britain by
Richard Clay Ltd, Bungay, Suffolk
Filmset in Monophoto Ehrhardt

CONTENTS

ACKNOWLEDGEMENTS

I would like to thank Martin Fletcher of Sphere Books, whose idea this anthology was, for giving me the opportunity to edit it. And thanks also to everyone who sent me a manuscript—or most of them . . .

D. S. G.

FOREWORD
AND FORWARD

by
David Garnett

Short stories are the very heart of science fiction.

The majority of 'big name' SF authors began their careers writing short fiction for the magazines. It is almost inevitable that most new authors start out by writing stories and then progress to novels, but they often do their finest work at shorter lengths. Magazines and original anthologies such as this one produce the best in science fiction: new stories by the genre's most famous authors, and new stories by the latest talent in the field.

And in *Zenith* you will find twelve of the best new sf stories available anywhere. This isn't simply a collection put together on the strength of the authors' names. The fiction is more important than the writers, and that is the only criterion by which the stories were selected for inclusion. They have been written by authors who were first published in the fifties, sixties, seventies and eighties. Some of the writers may be unfamiliar, but amongst them are those who will be the 'big names' of the nineties and the next century . . .

The next century is only eleven years away. (More or less, depending on whether you believe it begins in 2001 or 2000.) But that date marks more than the start of a new century. We are almost in the third millennium. Such was my idea when I set about compiling this anthology: what I wanted were 'stories for the next millennium'. It is a paradox that nothing becomes so rapidly outdated as certain types of science fiction, the forgotten futures first created only a few years ago. With *Zenith* I hoped to present fiction which would be as relevant in the future, and to the future, as it is now.

I also intended to produce a cross-section of modern British SF, a mixture of themes and treatments, of new authors and more established names – and in this respect I know I have succeeded.

All the authors in this book are British, but they include one who was born in the USA and another in Venezuela. The majority of the others are English, although Ulster, Wales and Scotland are all represented. Science fiction in the eighties has become almost totally Americanized. Most of the SF books on sale in Britain (and the rest of the world) are by US authors; the contents pages of most American magazines and anthologies are made up of American authors. This isn't by design, simply the way it is: there are more of them than us.

I enjoy American science fiction, and I also enjoy British science fiction – but the latter has been in very short supply recently. It is often said that American SF is more 'optimistic' than its British counterpart. (Archetypal British SF is supposedly the 'disaster' novel in which humanity is defeated by some external force.) It is also claimed that British science fiction is too 'literary' and thereby suffers a lack of 'traditional story values'. But American authors can be as 'literary' as any Brit; and the Brits can produce 'rattling good yarns' the equal of any written by an American. *Zenith* provides stories across the complete spectrum of science fiction.

Zenith is an all British anthology, but not through a deliberate anti-American policy. If I had not found enough good fiction by British writers, I would have invited other authors to submit stories for possible inclusion. There was no need, however, as there is an sf renaissance on this side of the Atlantic.

It is no coincidence that the lack of new British authors during the late seventies and early eighties came at the same time that there was no science fiction magazine published in this country. New authors need outlets within their own territory, reflecting their own national – and international – obsessions and interests, passions and politics. A whole new generation of British science fiction writers is now emerging, encouraged by the magazine *Interzone* and anthologies such as *Other Edens*, edited by Chris Evans and Rob Holdstock. *Zenith* is a part of this explosion of fresh talent: two of the authors included here are at the very start of their careers.

4

At a time when the science fiction shelves are packed with interminable fantasy trilogies, mindless horror books and sf novels which are far too long – and probably the first part of a series – *Zenith* presents the real thing: the true core of the genre, the best in contemporary SF short stories.

In the end, the only reason for an editor to write an introduction to a collection such as this is to say: I enjoyed these stories, and I hope that you will.

I did, and I do.

IN TRANSLATION

by
Lisa Tuttle

Lisa Tuttle, unlike everyone else in this book, came to Britain of her own free will. A Texican, she has lived in Harrow since 1980. The following year, she won the Nebula for her short story 'The Bone Flute' – and became the first and only writer to refuse the award. She is the author of the novels *Familiar Spirit* and *Gabriel* (and co-author, with George R. R. Martin, of *Windhaven*), the collections *A Nest of Nightmares* and *A Spaceship Built of Stone and Other Stories*, and the non-fiction books *Encyclopedia of Feminism* and *Heroines*. She is currently not writing her next novel.

Jake Bourne was twenty-two, happily married, and working as a clerk for the Texas Department of Public Safety when the aliens came. Overnight, everything changed. He was still married, he had the same job, life went on and the bills had to be paid, but none of it seemed important. For the first time in his life, Jake was driven by a pure and unwavering desire: to see the aliens, to meet them, know them.

But the aliens were a very long way from Austin, Texas. They were in Severnaya Zemlya, Pulau-Pulau Banggai, the Gobi Desert. They might as well have been on another planet, Jake thought. He wrote letters to Washington, offering his services, in any capacity, on any project connected with the aliens. He saved his money. He joined one of the local groups devoted to studying the aliens. As time passed, more aliens arrived, in more places. They visited Managua, Khartoum, Vancouver, Helsinki, Miami ... Who knew but that they might not one day come to Austin? Jake dared to hope. Then they began to settle, always in distant, inhospitable landscapes – Siberia, Baffin Island, the Great Sandy Desert – but right from the start each settlement had its quota of human inhabitants. Visitors were sometimes allowed. Jake made calculations, and planned a trip to Australia. And then one evening he saw on the news that a group of aliens had arrived in New Mexico. According to their translators, they intended to establish another settlement there in the desert.

New Mexico! A long day's hard driving, and he could *be* there. Jake stared at the televised aliens as their images flickered and shattered into amorphous shapes of swirling colours and incomprehensible shadow. Soon, he thought, he would be able to see for himself what they looked like; he would no longer be dependent on the distortions of film and tape, on the descriptions of others. Long after the news had ended, Jake went on staring at the television screen, seeing his own pictures as his dinner cooled unnoticed beside him.

Eventually, he looked around for his wife, wanting to share his excitement, but she had gone out, or maybe she hadn't come home. He couldn't remember. When she did come in, near midnight, Jake was pacing the floor impatiently, his suitcase packed and waiting near the door. He was tensed for an argument, but she surprised him.

'I thought you would have left already,' she said. 'I thought it as soon as I heard them say "New Mexico" on the radio. I'm surprised you waited.'

'Where were you? Of course I wouldn't go without telling you,' he said. 'I'll be back next week. Could you phone the office in the morning . . .'

'Why come back next week? Why not stay? You could probably get a job there. It wouldn't matter much what it was: you'd have your aliens nearby to keep you going. That's what you want, isn't it? That's what you really care about. Why should you come back here?'

'For one thing,' he said, 'there's you.' He embraced her, but she was as unyielding as a wall. 'Hey, come on, honey. I'm not talking about leaving you, you know. You know how I feel about the aliens – but it doesn't have anything to do with *us*. Look, why don't you come with me? It could be a vacation for both of us. I'd like that.' Although it was difficult, having keyed himself up to leave, he made the concession: 'We could wait until the weekend.'

'I don't want to go to New Mexico. What kind of vacation would that be? I don't want to go to the desert and hang around hoping to see the aliens. I don't *like* the aliens. I think they're creepy. I don't want to know anything more about them. You do, OK, fine, go to them, but don't you try to come back to me afterwards, because I'm not going to be waiting.'

'What do you mean, what are you talking about? You're talking like I'm going to see another woman.'

'Oh, no. I could cope with that. This is worse. You're obsessed with those creatures. They're more important to you than anything . . . and you can't even see how strange that is . . . I'd rather you were in love with another woman than with them.'

He stared at her. 'You're crazy. This is probably the most significant event in the whole history of the human race. Contact with another species! Of course I'm interested – I'm fascinated! – anyone with any intelligence would be! But not you. I can't believe it. You think there's some comparison . . . There is more to the world than us, you know; more things besides our relationship.'

'I don't care what you say. If you go now, don't bother to come back. That's all.' She walked past him, into the kitchen. He could hear her getting something out of the refrigerator.

Briefly, Jake was caught by the feeling that he should defend himself, and by the belief that, given a few hours, he could convince his wife that she was wrong and he was right. And yet, as he thought about it, he wondered why he should bother. Their values and interests were completely at odds. They hadn't really been a couple for a long time. How could he, why should he, go on living with a woman who found the aliens fearful rather than fascinating? She was wrong to compare his relationship with her to his curiosity about the aliens, and yet it was true, after all, they had become the most important thing in his life . . . far more important to him than she was.

Others made the pilgrimage to the New Mexican desert, so many others that Jake had no difficulty in finding the alien settlement. The heavy traffic carried him along relentlessly in the right direction, until he could go no further, and had to park his car among all the other cars, trucks, campers, trailers and tents. It was a huge, makeshift camping ground, which reminded Jake vaguely of a music festival – one of Willie Nelson's picnics – or maybe a religious revival. Biblical, he thought, that was what it was; all the strangers gathered in the desert to receive the tablets of the Law, or to find God in a burning bush.

As for the aliens, Jake could see no sign of them, no proof that this was an alien, and not purely human, settlement. But there were the rumours which kept rippling through the crowd, keeping them all in a state of barely suppressed excitement, of incipient celebration. Rumours that an alien had been sighted, that someone had touched or been touched by one. Individuals would begin, suddenly, to vocalize, making incoherent, yet sometimes weirdly beautiful noises: 'sounding' it was called, and it was the mark of a translator. Some people had an innate talent for communicating with the aliens, it seemed. The ability could not be taught or understood, and as yet no one – no group, individual, or computer – had managed to generate any other means of understanding or communicating with the aliens. Jake had dreamed of becoming a translator, although he wasn't entirely sure if this was a fate he longed for, or feared.

Where were they? Jake kept staring around until his eyes were cloudy and his head ached with the sheer effort of looking. He walked restlessly, avoided other people, and tried not to hear their comments: 'Like looking in a mirror that keeps moving and fragmenting.' 'Just like a person, really, that's all . . . only, you *know*.' 'Just a feeling, kind of like a smell in the air, like before a storm.' 'Like a person . . . a human, you know, but much bigger, and the *angles* are all wrong . . . and the colours . . . I can't explain it.'

He didn't want his experience second-hand. When he saw his first alien Jake wanted really to see it, for himself, through his own eyes, undistorted by imagination or expectation or the experience of others.

There was someone – a really big man – just in front of him – and Jake made to walk around him, glancing sidelong – he was really huge! – as he passed. Huge – Jake stopped. The air was shimmering around the . . . giant? Like a person, yet not a person. The air sparkled and fragmented into flares of swirling colour, the way it sometimes did on television, and then the colours reformed into a not-quite-solid, larger-than-life-sized, almost-human figure. Jake stared and stared. Sometimes he thought he saw it, and sometimes not, but he never could quite get a fix on it, on its boundaries, or how big it was. But it was there. It undoubtedly was there.

And then it was gone. Jake heard a small sound of loss. He thought it might be his own voice, until he turned his head and saw a girl with hair as yellow and soft as an Easter chick and a tanned, skinny, nearly naked body. She had seen the alien, too. They had both seen it. It was real. Their eyes met, and suddenly Jake felt happier than he had in a long time.

Three weeks later Daphne and Jake were sharing their new life in a one-room apartment in Albuquerque. They both wanted to work for the Alien Relations Agency, but didn't even make it to the interview stage. Both tested as translators – this meant another close encounter with an alien – but neither of them manifested the talent. Daphne got a job as a receptionist/typist for a real estate agency. Jake couldn't do any better than the Burger King, despite his age and experience. Albuquerque, less than three hours' drive from the alien settlement, was flooded with people looking for work and a place to live.

Daphne was sunny and accepting, and more easily satisfied than he. She was given to counting their blessings. 'We've got work, so we've got money, and we've got an OK place to live, and we've got each other, and we've got your car, so every weekend we can go out to the desert, and sometimes we'll see the aliens!'

Jake did not miss his wife, his job, or his life in Austin at all, but he was bitterly aware of how far he still was from what he wanted. He'd failed to get a job that would bring him in contact with the aliens, and he lacked the talent to be a translator. He made the obvious suggestion.

'Let's apply to go in anyway. As their guests.'

She gave him a look. It was a look that reminded him of his wife.

'Well? We've tried everything else. Why not?'

'You know why not.'

'If I did, I wouldn't ask.'

'Jake, you can't be serious.'

'I left my wife for the aliens, I quit my job, I moved here . . . Why stop now? I thought they meant as much to you as they do to me.'

'They do! Of course they do! But I have my self-respect. I won't go and whore for them.'

Anger flared up in him. She was as blind and as wrong as everyone else. 'Why do you say that? Why do you call it that? You don't know.'

'Everyone says it . . .' She couldn't meet his eyes.

'Oh, everyone! And what does everyone know? How can anyone know, who hasn't gone inside? Who says they're whores? Who says what they do in there is sexual? What a stupid thing.' He had heard the same rumours. Somehow everyone 'knew' that there were only two types of people who went inside and stayed: there were the translators, and there were the whores.

'It's stupid,' Jake persisted. 'How can you have sex with something that isn't a person . . . something that isn't even male or female? People who say that are just scared, and jealous of the people who aren't scared to go inside. So they try to make it into something contemptible. "Whores" they say. They're not. They're the aliens' guests.'

'And why do the aliens have guests? What do they want with them?'

'I don't know. Nobody knows. You can't know unless you take a chance . . .'

'And once you find out, you're inside, and it's too late.'

Jake looked into her eyes and saw the fear, the fear he felt himself. He loved the aliens for their strangeness, and feared them for the same reason. He wanted to know them, but maybe they were unknowable. He was teetering on the brink, wanting to jump but afraid to let go.

He put his arms around her. 'OK,' he said. 'We won't go. Maybe something will happen.'

'We can still go out to the desert every weekend. You never know what might happen. Things might change.'

But things did not change, and the longer he relied on luck and fate, the less satisfied Jake felt with his life. He had to get closer to the aliens. He had to know more about them. If that meant leaving Daphne behind, if that meant becoming a whore . . .

Was it sexual, his feeling for the aliens? That seemed too small, too narrow a definition for the most overwhelming thing in his life. What he felt for the aliens was not anything he'd ever felt for another human being. It was like love, and like religion, and curiosity, and need, and obsession – maybe sex was part of it, although no one knew what sex meant to the aliens.

One day, without telling Daphne, he took the bus out to the alien settlement, and applied for admission. If he was refused, she need not know about it. If they accepted him, he'd send her a postcard before he went inside. It needn't say much; he already knew what she would think of him for taking this final, desperate step. But he was desperate.

The bus took him far into the desert, a long, silent journey. There were others on the bus, but no one spoke. Some of them might have been translators, returning from a brief leave period; but most of them must have been like himself, driven to offer themselves for some unknown fate, not knowing even if their offer would be accepted. The only sound inside the jolting, air-conditioned vehicle was the muffled thump, boom and blare seeping out of half a dozen personal sound-systems.

Jake stared out at the dust and the sunlight, lacking even the cushion of music to protect him from the unknown. In the distance the huge concrete block, 'the human compound', glimmered palely, like a mirage. It looked more like a prison than a whorehouse. It didn't look like anywhere he wanted to live.

Enter of your own free will, he thought. He was trembling.

Men in uniforms showed him the way to go. No eye-contact. The examination was all by machine and remote control. He was interviewed via computer, tapping in his answers to questions as they appeared on a screen. A disembodied voice gave him instructions: 'Remove your clothing. Walk across the room. Lie down on the table. Put your head in the helmet and remain as still as you can for thirty seconds. Stand on the scale. Look at the screen. Say the names of the colours you see there.' Were aliens watching? Or was he being judged by humans, or machines?

It lasted for several hours. Finally, he was told to dress himself and go to Reception.

'Am I in?' he asked. 'Have I been accepted?'

The room was silent. The voice had nothing more to say.

Instead of the uniformed guard he had expected, there was a woman waiting for him in Reception: an attractive young woman with pale, freckled skin and copper-coloured hair, her body a mystery enveloped in a long, loose grey robe. Her wide, light-coloured eyes met his, and she said, 'Welcome, Jake Bourne. I'm Nadia Pecek. I'll be your translator during your visit here.'

No, he thought.

'That's the way it's done,' she said gently. 'Surely you didn't think you could talk to them directly.'

'I didn't really think about talking,' he said. 'There are other ways of communicating.'

'Of course. But if you *could* communicate with them, you'd be a translator yourself. You wouldn't have had to come here like this.'

He hated her for having succeeded where he had failed, and for knowing he had failed.

'Look,' she said. 'It's not a contest. It's not a matter of training, or will, or intelligence. I don't know how I do it: I'm near them, and I say what comes into my head. I *sound* or I talk. When I sound, I don't know what it means; when I talk, I don't know where the words come from. I don't know if I'm really translating, or *what* I'm translating. I'm not sure they know, either, or if it matters to them. Maybe it doesn't have anything to *do* with communication or understanding. Maybe it's an art-form. Maybe it's a game. Maybe it's a meaningless physical response. The worst thing — fortunately it doesn't happen often — is two translators with one alien at the same time, both of us responding and *saying different things*. And we don't know, we never do know, which of us was right, or if either of us was, or if they know or if they care.' She stopped. She was panting slightly, a light sheen of perspiration on her pale face, looking at him with entreaty in her eyes. She had been nakedly and unnecessarily honest with him, forcing an intimacy he didn't want.

Deliberately, he looked away.

After a silence she said, 'You can ask me any questions. You'll have a room of your own — I'll show you there now — and you can come and go as you like. But once you leave the compound — as I'm sure you've been informed — you can't come back, without applying for re-admission and being interviewed and examined all over again. And just because they let you in once, there's no guarantee they'll do it again. You're not a prisoner — you can always leave. You're a guest — and they might not have you back. There are food-slots in all the rooms, and a computer terminal. You can ask for anything you need — books, tapes, clothes, toiletries. Most requests are granted, although there are limits, some of which may seem — may *be* arbitrary. It's a little like "Beauty and the Beast", you know, the invisible hands laying the table . . .?' She paused.

He remained silent. She sighed. 'It's better if we can be friends. If you want to change your mind later, I won't hold today against you. I understand how it is.'

'You don't.'

'Of course I do. That's why you hate me.' She shrugged. 'Come on. Let me show you to your room. You can do it your own way. Ask me questions if you like — that's what I'm here for — but if you don't, I won't force anything on you.'

She left him at the door of his room. Unattractively institutional as it was outside, the rooms were surprisingly pleasant. Jake had expected something like a dormitory room or prison cell, but although his room was simple and barely furnished, it was unexpectedly large, and the colours, the proportions, and the light made it beautiful. He felt his heart lift as he stepped through the door, and he realized that, besides his excitement about being here, he was also, quite simply, pleased by his new home.

But although he was glad to be alone, here at last, he was also nervous. He almost wished he had asked Nadia how long it would be before he saw an alien, but he'd felt it was important to establish his distance from her right from the start. He spent the afternoon and the night and the whole of the following morning in his room, getting coffee and juice and sandwiches from the food terminal, playing around with the computer, napping, too restless to concentrate or stay still for long, yet afraid of leaving in case he was wanted.

Late in the afternoon, Nadia and an alien arrived.

Nadia and a shadow, he thought. A tall shape, darker than darkness, yet occasionally lit up so that he could see familiar shapes: the curve of a bare shoulder, a protrusion that was a knee . . . He had the sense of something female, and there was a faint smell, as of leaf-mould, with something slightly citrus. He saw eyes – dark, gentle eyes looking at him. In the alien presence Nadia seemed very small, almost invisible in her grey robe, and she kept her gaze downcast.

Jake looked and looked. He felt almost dizzy with anticipation. Now, now it would happen. Jake waited. His eyes and head ached with the effort of trying to see in something more continuous than those lightning-brief flashes. He tried to catch and hold the gaze of the other but could never be certain of success. Were those great, round eyes looking at him or through him . . . looking with curiosity, with desire, with disgust . . .? He was in agony. He couldn't wait any longer. He had to know. He appealed to the translator.

'What should I do?'

Nadia's eyes closed. After a long moment, she threw her head back and began to utter sounds. It was not quite singing, but it couldn't be recognized as anything else – certainly not speech. Although he had witnessed this phenomenon often enough on television, and a few times in person, this was the first time his own words had ever been offered in translation, and the strangeness and the importance of it – he was speaking to an alien, at last! – made him shiver.

Then it was over. Nadia opened her eyes. The alien did not move or make a sound that Jake could hear, but Nadia said, 'She asks you to take your clothes off.'

Fear and desire shot through him, too closely interwoven to separate. 'She?'

Nadia did not respond, and Jake suddenly understood that, in some sense, Nadia was not really there: she was not there for herself, she was not there for him; she existed, for the moment, only as an extension of the alien, a living mode of communication.

Jake took off his clothes, fumbling, almost falling over as he climbed out of his jeans. He felt more naked, more exposed and vulnerable, than ever before in his life. Despite his fear, he had an erection. And what did the alien make of that? What *would* the alien make of that? He wondered about its sexual organs. Nadia had said 'she'. He was glad of that.

He waited. The waiting went on and on. No one moved. He began to feel cold, although the room's warm temperature had not changed. He lost his erection. 'What . . . what does she want me to do? Can you ask her that? What am I supposed to do now?'

Nadia closed her eyes and produced a short burst of sound. Then, eyes open, said, 'You may do as you wish. She is glad to see you. She hopes you will be happy here.'

'Is that all?'

'She is going now. She has enjoyed this time spent in your presence, and hopes that the enjoyment was mutual.'

'Wait – Can't we talk, or –'

But the alien was already gone. The room chimed like a bell with emptiness. Without a backward glance, Nadia walked out. Jake watched the door close, and then he put his clothes back on. He was trembling with frustration. He had been ready for almost anything, he thought, but not for nothing.

*

The next day he kept to his room, and the next, feeling bored. He grew tired of playing computer games, reading and listening to music; he felt bloated with egg-rolls, potato chips and beer. Nothing happened to interrupt his solitude. 'You may do as you wish,' he muttered to himself, and so, on the following morning, he went exploring.

He was hoping to see some more aliens, but if there were any currently visiting the human compound they were hidden behind the doors of the private rooms, inaccessible to him, or invisible. There were none to be seen in any of the public areas – the library, the gym, the restaurant, the bars, the galleries and meeting rooms all were occupied, although sparsely, by humans. Jake ignored them all. He had no wish, now, for any of the complicated business of friendship. And yet, when he caught sight of Nadia reclining in a large chair and leafing through a glossy magazine in one of the common rooms, his heart lifted, and he made straight for her, as if it were she he had been looking for all along.

'Hello.'

'Oh, hello.' She sat up straight and put the magazine face-down in her lap. 'How are you? Are you all settled in?'

'This is the first time I've come out of my room. I was waiting – I don't know what to do, you see. I don't know what I *should* do. If I knew when the alien was likely to come back – if I knew what to expect – it would be easier. Maybe you could tell me what usually happens?'

'If you have to know what to expect, it'll never be easier. Things don't work like that here. Look, why don't we go have a drink? We can talk in the bar; I'll tell you what I know.'

'It's not even ten o'clock . . .' He saw her grin. 'Oh, I see. That doesn't matter – time works differently here, too.'

She nodded. 'People fall into the rhythms that suit them. There's no consistent outside demands. It's best to be adaptable, to take what comes. Time works differently for the aliens, that's obvious. But I haven't been able to figure out *how*. If there's a pattern, I can't see it. And believe me, I've looked.'

She took him to a small, dimly-lit room furnished with a

22

bar, small tables and rather uncomfortable chairs. There was no one there. Nadia went behind the bar, opened a bottle of red wine and, without asking him what he wanted, poured some into two glasses. The idea of wine in the morning did not appeal to Jake, but he sipped to keep her company.

'How long have you been a translator?'

'Nearly two years. Baffin Island, before here.'

'Always with the same –'

'No. Various lengths of time with various aliens, sometimes back to one I've been with before, sometimes several different ones in a row, none of whom I ever see again . . . If there's a reason for the changes, or a pattern to them, I haven't been able to see it. Maybe because it's on a time scale too big for me to comprehend yet. The way it happens is . . . well, that's different, too. Sometimes one of them comes to me, in my room, and I follow him – or her.'

'How can you tell if they're male or female?'

She exhaled sharply, irritated. 'I can't. Nobody can.'

'But the one the other day, in my room – you said "she".'

'I said whatever I said because of the alien. I wasn't thinking about it; I wasn't talking for myself. I wasn't talking at all; I was translating. I thought you understood that much, at least.'

'I'm sorry. Go on.'

'Well.' She poured more wine, sipped it thoughtfully. 'What was I saying?'

'Sometimes they come to you.'

'Yes, and sometimes I go to them.' She was wearing a fine gold chain around her neck, and she pulled it out now to show him what was on it: egg-shaped, no bigger than a finger-nail, made of something like smooth, cloudy glass. 'It gets warm, it kind of vibrates . . . When that happens, I start walking. It guides me somehow, I don't know . . . It goes dead again when I get to wherever I'm wanted. Sometimes it stops as soon as I set eyes on a particular alien; sometimes it stops when I get to a particular place. Then I wait in that place until one of them comes for me. It could be two minutes; it could be an hour. Once, I waited nearly eight hours. I never did know why. Maybe there was some reason that made sense to them, or maybe it was just a malfunction.'

'Couldn't you ask?'

'I can't ask them anything. Not for myself. I can only ask questions for other people. I'm a translator. They don't talk to me – they talk *through* me. Don't you like the wine?'

'It's fine.'

'It's better than fine. It's a very good wine, indeed. I know something about wine. I used to be a restaurant critic for *New West Magazine*. And I did an in-depth piece on the vineyards of California. I was going to expand it into a book. And then . . .' She looked melancholy. She was still holding the little egg-shaped thing between thumb and forefinger, sliding it back and forth on the chain. 'I was engaged to be married. Well, sort of engaged. People don't get engaged anymore, do they? Not grown-ups, anyway. I guess we said "engaged" mostly for our parents. He didn't actually give me a ring or anything like that, but he really meant it. He wanted to marry me. And I meant to marry him. I really loved him.' She let go of the necklace, picked up her glass and drained it.

There was no need to ask what had happened, Jake thought. She had become a translator. 'Did he – your fiancé – was he interested in the aliens?'

'He wasn't obsessed. Neither was I, although I was flirting with it. We talked about them a lot, read about them, bought videos . . . I guess like a lot of people. Well, how could you not be interested? But it wasn't the main thing in our lives. We certainly wouldn't have packed up and moved, changed our lives just to be near a settlement.'

'How did it happen?'

'By chance. I was out shopping. In a mall. I'd bought some make-up and stuff for my skin, and I was going to the record store when I saw . . . it was crazy; I thought I saw my grand-mother. I loved her better than anyone in the world, but she'd been dead for five years. Yet there she was, by the fountain, looking at me and smiling a little bit, the way she did, and – I was going to say her name. I opened my mouth, and then . . .

I felt as if something had been poured down my throat, something thick and warm and sweet ... and like I was being stroked ... and I dropped whatever I was holding. I felt sunlight on my face. I realized at the same time that it wasn't my grandmother. That it wasn't a human being at all. And that didn't matter. I could hear myself making noises ...' She compressed her lips, and then let out her breath in a long sigh. She was looking at nothing. 'I don't remember what happened next. Except that I must have followed the alien out of the mall. And the next thing I knew, there I was in one of those embassies, with a lot of professionally *caring* people asking me what I wanted to do ... And, well, it was like I'd had some kind of fit, or passed out and just woke up ... I was horrified. No, of course I didn't want to go to the translators' school and be trained to work with the aliens; I wanted to go home, back to my real life. They were surprised and disappointed – I guess that's not the usual response! – but what could they do? They called my fiancé and he came and got me. He treated me – well, we both did – as if I'd been sick and was convalescing ... but as if what I'd had was a little embarrassing, so we wouldn't talk about it. I didn't want to talk about it. I just wanted to forget it as soon as I could.'

She poured the last of the wine into her glass and stared as if hypnotized at the red liquid. 'Except I couldn't. Everything had changed, and it couldn't ever be the same again. So finally, even though it wasn't what I wanted to do, I realized it was what I *had* to do. What I was meant for.'

'You hate the aliens.'

Startled, she met his eyes. 'No. No I don't. That would be pointless. Silly. Like hating the world. Hating myself. Hating reality.'

'Plenty of people do.'

'Not me.' She smiled. 'I had to change. I've accepted this life. I make the most of it. There are pleasures here, too.' She looked at the empty bottle and then at him again. 'Would you like to go back to your room?'

He stood up, the suddenness of his movement rocking the

small table. 'By myself,' he said, and left without waiting to see how she took the rejection.

It was two days later when he saw her again, in his room, with another alien. At least, he had a feeling that it was a different alien, although he couldn't be sure. He wondered resentfully if *she* knew, if she could recognize them as individuals.

As before, they entered and said nothing. Jake remembered Nadia had said that time worked differently for the aliens, and although he wished he'd not had to hear this from *her*, he decided to make use of that insight, to try to adapt, to try to experience things on alien terms, rather than pushing it with his human questions, forcing it into translation and altering its reality, making it seem more like his, and false.

So Jake stood there and said nothing, as the alien said nothing, and as the alien looked at him, Jake looked at the alien. He tried to look without effort and without expectation, seeing sometimes eyes, sometimes skin, sometimes a sharp, bony ridge or a face like a carved mask. He tried not to worry about what he really saw and what he only imagined. He tried to keep his mind still, until the air of the room buzzed around him, and his own body seemed to recede, as if he were observing from a position about six inches above his own head. As he thought this, he suddenly wondered how his body was still managing to stand, and then he felt himself wobble, and before he fell over he had to back up and sit down rather heavily on the bed.

There was a shimmering of the air, and then the alien was gone. Nadia turned to go.

'No, wait! Don't go! Ask it – ask it if –'

But of course it was too late, and he was left alone again behind a closed door, tears of frustration burning unshed in his eyes.

The next time – how many days? Jake tried not to know. If he could have stopped counting, he would, but he was trapped in his obsession. There was nothing else to think about, nothing else he cared about for distraction. All he could do was to try to think about the aliens in different ways.

The next time, when Nadia and the alien entered, Jake smelled again leaf-mould and citrus, and his heart beat double-time. He felt certain that this was the first alien returning, and both the return, and the fact that he had recognized it, seemed deeply significant. He felt light-headed, almost drunk with excitement.

'I want to know you,' Jake said. 'Please, I want to touch you . . . I want you to touch me. Let me know you. In any way that I can. I'll do whatever you say. Please give me a chance.'

Nadia made her chilling, beautiful, eerie noises, and then she said, 'He says, you may do as you wish.'

'He! I thought this one – last time – why did you say "he" when it was "she" before? What does that mean? Nadia?'

But Nadia wasn't there, it seemed. She gazed serenely ahead as if she had not heard him. It had to be a con, he thought. She was pretending. Deliberately ignoring him. Probably mad at him. 'Can I ask him questions?' Then, impatient: 'All right, ask him; ask him if I can ask him questions, dammit!'

'You may ask him questions.'

'Is that you talking? I didn't hear you ask him.'

'You may do as you wish.'

He could do as he wished, and here he was, wasting his wish, like the fool in a fairytale. 'Are you . . . have we met before? Are you the same one who came to see me before?'

This time, Nadia sounded. Then she replied: 'He says, this is his first visit to you. The other time, another visited, one who is like him, yet is not him.'

Jake stared, trying to match reality to memory, trying to see, now, not likenesses, but differences. But there was nothing to see. A shimmering, like a mirror. Light flashing out of darkness. A pair of eyes that might have been his own, might have been Nadia's, might have been only a memory, or a fantasy. And yet there was something in that darkness. Something solid, something real, if only he could reach it.

'May I touch you?' He closed his eyes while Nadia translated

27

his words. He tried to imagine what it would feel like to have those words coming out of him, out of his control.

'Put out your hand,' said Nadia.

Into the fire, thought Jake. He opened his eyes and stretched out his hand towards the alien. He felt something beneath his fingers, something smooth, hairless and warm. Gently, holding his breath with excitement, Jake stroked it. Perhaps human skin would have felt the same beneath his fingers; Jake wasn't sure.

'Would you like to touch me?' Jake asked. 'Would you touch me now? Should I take off my clothes?'

Nadia said nothing. Jake was about to repeat his question when he realized there was no need. He already had permission.

Now he was naked before the alien. He looked at Nadia, the conduit between them, and her body was hidden, enveloped in that shapeless grey robe she always wore. It wasn't a uniform; other translators dressed differently; she must have wanted for some reason to look like a nun.

'I'd like the translator to take her clothes off, too,' he said.

Her grey eyes met his gaze; disconcerting after the previous careful avoidance. Then she reached up and began to undo a set of buttons along her shoulder-line.

'Wait a minute – aren't you going to tell him what I said?'

She didn't reply, not even by a nod or a headshake. Because she couldn't? Or because she thought the answer was obvious? Maybe the alien had told her what to do. Or maybe the rules were she had to do what he said – or what *either* of them said. Or maybe she just wanted to take her clothes off. He remembered how she had looked at him just before he left her in the bar.

She had a good body: stomach a little flabby, but such lovely curves. He would have thought it impossible to be more aroused than he was already, and yet the sight of her breasts, and the pale slope of her naked hip, kicked him into a higher gear. His longing for the alien became even more confused and inextricable from a hard, hot, immediate sexual need.

Without losing its urgency his desire embraced her and blurred, spilling across boundaries, as if she and the alien were somehow the same. Did he want them both in different ways? How could he want them both at once? Yet his need seemed indivisible. Maybe she *was* the alien in human form, at least in a sense, if they spoke inside her head, spoke through her; could he not perhaps know the alien through her human body?

Nadia's face took on a distant, listening look, and when she spoke, she was translating. 'You may mate.'

The shock of it, expected though it was, went right through him, and he tried to make light of it, sneering, 'Mate? I've never mated in my life. Is he going to expect offspring in nine months?' He had not expected a reply, and did not get one. He looked at Nadia, who was still waiting, as if listening for further instructions. 'Will he stay?' he asked. 'Ask him, will he stay – will he watch?'

She looked at him, and she was with him here and now, no longer listening to the alien – if she ever had been, if that had ever been more than a con, he thought. 'They always do,' she said. 'If you want them to. And of course you do. Otherwise, what's the point? You want *him*, not me. You're not interested in me at all, are you? You won't let yourself be.'

'Look, don't take it personally, but I didn't come here for that. I have a girlfriend, you know. I didn't come here to find another one. I came here for something else.'

'So did I. We're not so different you know. We both want the same thing. We want something impossible. So why not . . .' she made a helpless little gesture with her hands, 'comfort each other? Maybe we can't have exactly what we want, but . . .'

There was something very appealing about her, and because he wanted her sexually he was inclined to be generous, to give her what she wanted, if only in words he would later deny, but he suddenly thought of her saying, 'They always do,' and instead of anything kind, he said, coldly, 'You've done this a lot. How many men?'

'That doesn't matter. Yes, a lot! It comes down to this so often: sex with me as second-best, as a last-ditch effort to make contact, through me, with one of *them*. But it doesn't work, Jake, that's what I'm trying to tell you. It just doesn't. It never has, it never will. You're smart enough to know I'm not lying. You don't have to be like all the others. It could be different with you and me. I felt that, as soon as I saw you. Tell him to go away now, and I'll stay with you.'

Jake could not bear to look directly at the alien, as if, like the sun, it might burn his eyes. 'I don't want him to leave. That's the last thing I want. It's all right for you, you with that thing around your neck. They'll call you back, they'll find you again – they've got a use for you. But not for me. I don't know what they want with me at all. I just have to keep hoping I'll find some way of connecting. I'm not interested in you. They're all I care about.'

He saw the hope die in her eyes. 'OK, fine. But I want to tell you, you can't get to them through me. Making love to me won't make any difference. You won't know any more about them, or be any closer to them. And it won't actually make any difference to *him* whether you mate with me or tell me to put my clothes back on. So why don't you just ask him some more questions?'

'You're not here to tell me what to do,' he said. 'You're the translator.' It occurred to him that if he was unkind to her maybe she would not stay with him; maybe her mind would move to that place where she was in touch with the alien, and somehow, through her . . . 'Are you going to get on the bed, or shall we do it on the floor?'

She moved reluctantly towards the bed. He pushed her down on her back, felt between her legs, laughed, because she was as ready as he was, and then thrust roughly inside her.

She caught her breath and put her arms around him, pulling her legs up higher. 'Oh, Jake.'

'No! Don't talk to me, talk to *him*. Ask him – ask him how his people mate. Ask him *why* they do it. Ask him, ask him is it only to reproduce, or do they spin fantasies about it, do they

30

expect more, do they imagine it's one of life's great experiences – ask him, ask him!' He gasped, his mind spinning, but the words gave him some sort of control.

'I can't.'

'You're lying.'

'I can't.' There were tears at the corners of her eyes.

'Why can't you? I don't believe you. It's what they all want, isn't it? Go on, ask him! Talk to him, damn you, it's what you're *for*!'

'I can't,' she whispered again, but weakly, and she closed her eyes. He knew she had given in; he felt the change in her even before she began to sound. And as the noises came swirling and spiralling out of her, he came inside her, fiercely, helplessly, unable any longer to resist the demands of his body.

Afterwards, he hated himself. He knew he had failed, somehow, and he felt the most terrible fear.

'What does he say? What's the answer?' he demanded of Nadia. She made a sound.

For a moment he did not understand; then he did. He raised himself up enough to look around. The alien was gone. They were alone in the room, and the woman beneath him was weeping, giving voice to his sorrow.

TIME OF THE TREE

by
Robert Holdstock

Robert Holdstock's first novel was *Eye Among the Blind* (1976), and since then he has written over twenty more books – some of them even under his own name. One of these was *Mythago Wood*, which won the World Fantasy Award as best novel in 1985. A companion volume, *Lavondyss*, was published in 1988. He claims to be the co-editor of *Other Edens*, whatever that is.

Tundra

All the signs are that the long winter is coming to an end. The great expanse of tundra, with its strange bluish hue, still shimmers and shivers in the biting winds of early morning. Yet to the south, below the swollen hill with its deep lake, Omphalos, there are signs of green. I am certain that a fresh and vibrant grassland is beginning to spread across the land. From my fixed point of observation it is hard to see so far to the south, but sometimes the cold and stinking winter wind, the stench of the foetid tundra, is replaced by the scent of new meadow and flowers.

I no longer feel so cold.

As the day advances, the tundra dries slightly. Its slick shine fades and I imagine that the air is filled with the buzz and hum of insects. The lake, though, remains full. I have abandoned my game of emptying the pool. The water is rich and ripe. If I could see clearly enough I imagine it would be scum-laden, dense green growth feeding on the stagnancy and the dead life that falls into its murky depths. But as further evidence of the coming of the spring, there are rushes at its borders. Again, seeing in any detail is hard, but the tiny growth is evident, and the wind from the caves in the north takes the tall rush-heads and blows them wildly.

I suspect that a migrating bird-life has already settled at the shores of the lake. To see this would be too much to ask. One thing, though: I have sensed a darker movement on the swathes of tundra, in the shallow valley between the Pectoralis hills. Since this is closer to my point of observation, and my lens is more effective, I can say with certainty that the shadow is *separate* from the land. It may be nothing more than that:

37

the shadow of cloud. But I think I may have witnessed the first migrating herds of some bovine species, perhaps reindeer. My dreams are often filled with the eerie cries of the wild.

The Birch Accession

The first forests are beginning to appear, and with their growth they bring with them a strange sense of pain, and a new sense of time. I realize how much I have been living by the time of the empty plains; those centuries of silence, save for wind and water. How slow that time has been, following the retreat of the ice from the north of the land. Time has been as stagnant as the standing water on the peat. Time has been in suspension. Sunrise to moonrise, the land has whispered and shivered, and dried and become wet, but there has been no change. The bursting life of the forests had remained asleep below the skin of the land, the cells as quiescent as the marshes.

Suddenly that life has begun to erupt, and now at last I begin to live by the time of the tree. Now there is *vibrancy*. There is a *swaying* feel to time, a wind-whipped and vital sense to time, as if time is being *stretched*. It hurts. It brings a strange discomfort to the land, and to the perception of the land. The forests strain to grow. The trunks thicken and reach out and up. They spread, they expand, they quiver at their tips, and in their roots. They suck the memory of the forest from the cells below the land, draining the genetic code, feeding hungrily upon the mass of silent chromosomes.

Silent? Silent no longer. *The tree in the man*, that forgotten part of history, that unacknowledged presence of the primordial plant, has taken root upon the man himself, and the swathes of birch begin to spread. They are in the Pelvic Valleys; they cover the slanting length of the Man-Hill. They reach across the Thigh-Ridge Mountains, down almost as far as the sharp Bone-Ridge of the Calf-Plain. They reach across the Pelvic Plain as far as the lake in the navel itself. Omphalos.

The water gleams with a new and enticing light. It is silver, now. The smell has gone. When I dip my finger into its depths, the taste on my tongue is sweet. All foulness flees before the surging spread of birch and spruce.

I am living by the time of the tree, yet I have no conception of how that time compares with the time of the world outside the land. For me – observing from the north – a day in the passage of the world seems to be . . . how *many* years, I wonder, in the time of the forest? Two hundred? Three?

Each day the winter woodland stretches north, surrounding the lake, covering the hollow of the Solar Plexan Plain, spreading up the Sternal Valley and over the Pectoral Hills, even surmounting the flattened mounds (like the barrows of some forgotten civilization) which top the knolls. Hard to see, these winter trees, yet their roots are like spikes into the flesh. They are like thorns. It is a thin forest, this, struggling for life in the cold air, consuming and taming the acid land that for so many centuries has covered the skin.

It is a long time since the ice retreated. Sharing time between that of the tree and that of the land, I begin to forget the accident that precipitated the glacial movement. The Ice Age is fading from memory, just as is the event that started all of this. I struggle sometimes to hold these unreal images in my mind: the 'cold room' at my University; the high-tech lab where I worked on Primordial-DNA, those sequences of genes that retain memories of the primaeval environment, codons that contain bizarre echoes of a world long since lost; the sudden alarm in the cold room; my own surprise, then slip; the slamming of the door across my body; the sensation of ice building up across my face and shoulders.

I know I was dragged from the freezer room, but I have no memory of that rescue. I know that ice had coated me from head to chest, a millimetre of ice, which slowly melted, a glacial advance that was thwarted but which somehow activated the hidden memory in the land below . . .

This is how the forest came into being. It is unbelievable to contemplate. Now, though, all that matters is how it will develop!

The Coming of the Wildwood

A milder climate envelops the microcosm of the land. Outside my room it is cool and raining, a typical early summer's day. Inside, a dry, pleasant heat occupies that volume of space that has become the woodland micro-environment. The birch forest still occupies the high land to the north, but there is much pine, now, and its scent is *wonderful*.

The bristles cover me completely. They itch where they enter the softer skin below my chin. When the hairs of the human land dropped away they left me sensitive. I wonder, sometimes, if the trees have grown from the follicles of the hairs themselves. The tree-line ceases below my lips, but spreads slightly to cover my cheeks. My crown is quite bald, and is cold to touch, as if winter still holds sway there. When I brush my cheeks I wonder what damage I might be doing, but through the lens and in the mirror I can see the proud stands of pine, still extant after the brutalizing touch of the Giant, on whose corpse this world is starting to evolve.

The tallest tree rises from the skin by no more than a fraction of a millimetre. In profusion, though, they make my body shimmer green; the canopy is dense. But around the lake of Omphalos, and below, across the Pelvic Valleys and the stump of the Man-Hill, down across the ridges of the thigh, the forest has become softer; it gleams like velvet, and is gentle on the fingers. The wildwood, the deciduous forests, have replaced the scrawny evergreens. Now the trees crowd and fight for light. The elms and the oaks can be clearly seen. Round the Omphalos great stands of alder crush together. Over the flank of the land a stand of hazel has a touch like emery paper. The Scar of the Appendix is covered by a coarse thornwood, painful to the touch despite the minuteness of its size. Where the land grows colder, above the Line of the Eleventh Rib, a battle for supremacy occurs between the pine and the gleaming ranks of hornbeam and ash. But the wildwood is spreading north, and in the lower valleys it is dense and rich, the trees tall, some of them giants, rising higher than the canopy, the great standard oaks and elms that grow where destruction has occurred around them.

Sometimes I pass my hands above the land, letting darkness fall. I pour water over my skin; great floods. I moisten myself for comfort: showers of rain, sometimes storms. I wonder how the forest perceives these actions. I have ceased to sweat. My skin exudes the scent of sap, of undergrowth. I am in no discomfort. The creases in my body flow with water, small streams, rivulets, supplying the root needs of the body forest. I eat from cans. It is sometimes painful to walk. There is no growth upon my back, which remains a pristine, unconquered realm. When I lie, I lie supine, legs apart, arms to the sides, and in this position, like some slumbering god, there is a wonderful sense of peace.

Below my chin, below the relaxed face of the world, a terrible struggle for the light ensues. The sounds of the wild-wood occupy my mind, the cries, the screams, the creaking, twisting growth of trees. These are the first sounds of the world. Among them I can hear the shrieks of birds, the howls of wolves, furtive movement in the dense, dank undergrowth.

At dawn all is silent; from Glottal Mound to the Phalangeal Rocks in the far south, the land is a rich and vibrant green, catching the light. The land rises and falls with peaceful steadiness, a gentle wind blowing across the virgin swathes of forest, catching the branches of the giant elms that reach so high above the canopy; watchtowers; guardians of the hidden world below.

The Elm Decline

There is a smell of woodsmoke in the air, just a hint, penetrating the pungency of the rotting food and unwashed bedding of my room. I am used to the smells of my own decay, and so this new odour is sharp to my nostrils. In the slanting sunlight from the world outside I can see the tiny drifting coils of smoke.

Pain! Sharp pain, that takes me by surprise. It comes from the area around the lake. Through the lens I can see that it is from here that smoke is unfurling. The pain is a tiny focus, like a pinprick, a prick of fire.

There can be only one explanation . . . *The forest is being cleared!*

It is hard to make out detail. The clearing is being made on the shores of the lake, which is brim full and brilliant in the dawn sun. Now I have a decision to make: do I extinguish the fires? But that might risk destroying whatever or whoever is burning the forest. If I leave them, however, they may bring barrenness to the land.

There are other fires. As the day in the real world advances, so coils of smoke drift up from my right groin, from an area in the dense mass of wildwood over my belly, and from two locations on my right leg. The pricks of pain are tolerable. I wonder if the communities are related?

They have begun to fell the great elms. Through the lens I see one of them topple, a tiny shard, no bigger than a trimmed whisker, yet majestic for all of that. I suppose that whoever is clearing the wildwood is also building the first settlement lodges.

The First Totems

In my dreams I can hear the ululations and strange chanting of the forest clearers. At night, they sing and dance around the smouldering fires of the day's clearing. They are dressed in the raw, red hides and heads of beasts. The people by the lake are the Clan of the Spiny Boar. Their youngest and fittest male wears the carcass of an immense wild pig; his body is impaled with sharpened tusks, and he dances and screams his invocation to this ancestral creature. They are called *Kalokki*. In my dreams I feel the presence of forty or more individuals. They shelter in lodges made of bone and wood, whose roofs are branches sealed with lake mud. They hunt at dawn. They are building crude boats and I sense that the mist-covered lake is a place of worship to them. They drift across the lake and throw huge wooden carvings into the water. It is here, when they are on the surface of Omphalos itself, that the sound of their voices is loudest.

All sensation of hunger seems to have gone from me. The forest itself sustains me, drawing nutrients from the air, from the light. A fine mist fills my room. The sounds of the outside world have faded. There is no light, no heat, save that which streams through the window.

Creatures move on the floor of the room, among the debris. Sometimes I hear thunder, but it passes: people at the door, friends perhaps, or colleagues, but I cannot move to answer them. Time is too precious. The body forest is too fragile.

The dwellers by the lake fight for survival. A Wolf Clan has attacked them. I dreamt the pain. They burned a lodge, then were driven away. But the Wolf Clan is hungry and restless and hovers in the wildwood, watching the clearing on the lake shore, biding its time.

All of this is in the form of glimpses, half seen, half felt scenes in my restless sleep. During the night the land heaves. No doubt it disturbs the Kalokki.

If only I could communicate with them. If only their words could be heard . . .

I pass my hand over the lake. I hold the lens toward them, peering through its rounded glass. Perhaps they see my face. What manner of heavens do they witness, I wonder.

The Temple Builders

Over the weeks, dust and dirt, the grime of my room, has settled on the cleared land, and fallen in and among the dense wildwood.

I have been sensing the deliberate movement of these great stones for some time, now. The Clans are organized. They drag the monolithic particles of dust from the forest edges and

43

shape them, working by day, by night, chanting to the instruction of the priests. They are erecting the massive sarsens into a great circle, on the very edge of the lake itself. A mightier stone circle has never been created. By fire they dance within its ring. Travellers have come south, from the cold woods of the Sternal Valley, to witness this great construction. They have journeyed north, from the now-desert land below the Plain of the Patella. Even in those dark communities, where the forest flanks the edge of the world itself, even there they have heard of the Great Stone Ring of Omphalos. And in my dreams I hear the crying and the singing of votive dedication. They are singing up the gods. They are dancing up the powers of the forest, and the lake. And they are planning a sacrifice . . .

Ritual Sacrifice

Her scream of fear alerts me. In a half dreaming, half waking state, I feel the pounding of her heart. It is dawn in their world, and a heavy, cold mist hangs above the clearing and the lake. Bone horns are being sounded, and bone rattles, and skin drums, beaten with a ferocity that makes the whole lakeside shiver with anticipation of the murder to come.

She is very young. They bind her with willow wood, arms behind her back, legs crooked behind her, tied to staffs of wood. Her neck is bent back. Creeper and ivy entwine her body. She is trussed and helpless, laid in a boat on a bed of leaves. They strike out into the water. A young male voice calls for her. The drums thunder, the bone horns blast eerily through the dawn fog. Water laps at rushes against the shores of Omphalos.

Soon I sense the stillness in the centre of the waters. Something is whirled around a head, and it creates a strange humming sound. Voices drone. The girl struggles, but is held so tightly that she cannot even flex a finger. A thong is tied around her neck. It tightens and her heart screams for help. The blood thunders in her head. A blow by oakwood to her skull and the water is reddened and enriched. She is placed, face down in the lake, and sinks by weight of stone to its bottom.

I feel her enter me. She is sublime in her dying. She trails her life vertically in a coil of warmth to the surface of the lake where the small boats bob and the priests watch for signs of acceptance of their sacrifice. When she settles in the debris of the navel, her eyes are closed. Something slips into my mind.

She seems to have risen from the corpse and is running . . .

Journey to the Underworld

Where is she running?

She seems to be in a moondream wood. The trees gleam white. They grow from the roof and sides of a great winding passage. Where is she?

The moonforest is all around her. She expands to drift among the moonbright branches. Moonlakes glimmer. She floats above them. She travels through the caverns of the underworld, round the spiral tracks, into and out of dark caves, where the land heaves and shifts, like the pulsing body of some great creature.

And in this way she spreads to the north, to the place where the ice had once lain so heavily upon the rock, scouring the soil, feeding upon the seeds below. Here is a place where the trees hum and fire burns, great streaks and flashes of fire, running through the roots and branches. Here is a fire-forest where the voices of the ancestors sing loudly, where faces peer, bodies shift, and a whole world of image echoes through the crowded wood.

She is in the fire. She spreads herself to sink into the fire-trees. She spreads through the forest, stretched thin, touching the coils of the seeds, where the forest co-exists with the creatures of the past, where the codes snap and fold, twist and replicate.

Our Lady of the Chromosomes

The Boar is threatened by the Wolf.

She means that war between the Clans is killing her people. She drifts there, in the seed-codes of the forest, enveloped by nucleotides, fed by ribosomes, arrows of RNA winging from her spectral presence. What do I say to her?

MAKE A FIRE THAT IS HOTTER THAN YOU KNOW. MELT ROCK. SOME ROCKS FLOW. WHEN THE ROCK FLOWS IT WILL HARDEN INTO BRIGHTNESS AND CAN BE SHAPED INTO A BETTER KNIFE THAN BONE OR FLINT.

I must return to the lodges of the Boar. I must return from the wasteland. I must take this vision back to them.

How do I help her? She is a ghost in the man-forest-machine that lies upon its bed in a rancid, rotting room. The forest above has disposed of her, thinking her dead. The forest within is a place of spectres and she is a ghost.

FLOW INTO THE RIVERS OF THE WORLD. FLOW INTO THE SAP. I WILL GUIDE YOU BACK THROUGH THE CAVERNS. I WILL GUIDE YOU THROUGH THE CAVERN IN THE MAN-HILL. YOU WILL RETURN TO YOUR PEOPLE IN A GREAT FLOOD FROM THE OTHERWORLD.

She dissolves from the roots of the fire-forest, flows into the blood, and drifts into the channels that drain sap from the tissues and the organs of the land. I feel the building of the flood, and the rising of the Man-Hill. By the lake, the Kalokki watch the skies in awe. An immense shadow is across the land. The cave that opens at the head of the mountain gushes. The lake is filled. The Kalokki escape the flood by climbing the giant trees. The naked goddess returns to them, ghostly white, floating above the waves, bringing her vision from the dark and fiery wastes of Hell.

I have slept for too long. Much time has passed, and I wake to great pangs of hunger. And yet hunger had been banished from me, and thirst too. The forest had sustained me, as all forests sustain the land. Why, then, hunger now?

The Kalokki have gone. They ceased to be in my dreams. With their passing came a time of resting and sleep. I have let the world on my body grow and flourish in its own, inexorable way.

Now, though, there is a great itching. I am swathed with the cracking, crusty signs of eczema. My skin seeps a thick and stinking exudate. What has happened? Great swathes of the Pectoralis valley, and the belly plain, are barren. The wildwood exists in patches only, small, amoebic spreads of green in the orange and yellow wasteland. And even through that greenness I can see great lines and tracks of red, roadways, perhaps, although what travels along them is too small to see.

A heavy smog hangs above the groin. It is an impenetrable smoke, oily to the nostrils, and sulphurous . . . The air of the room is filled with a distant buzzing, like machines. Even as I watch I see the edge of the forest shrink a little. The itching increases. There is pain in my bowels.

Someone is drilling deeply into the world. Seeking for what, I wonder?

I have slept too long. I have let too much time pass. I cannot stand the itching. Whilst the pain of the Kalokki's forest clearing had been a pin prick, suffered to allow them to establish their presence upon the world, this eczema is too much.

I smear and squeeze, scratch and smudge. I blow away the smoke from above my groin. I scratch at the soreness and the hard scabs of the cities. A black and tarry residue fills my finger-nails and I scrape it out between my teeth.

Soon there is stillness on the land. And peace.

I will have to find food for a while, but the grasslands will soon be re-established upon the world. Then, the first seeds of the forest will germinate and the wildwood will return.

And once more I will dream by an ancient light.

DEATH SHIP

by
Barrington J. Bayley

Barrington J. Bayley's first SF story was published in 1954, and his first novel was *The Star Virus* (1970). Since then, he has published twelve more novels and two collections of short stories. Several of these books were issued by one notorious publisher, and Bayley is famous for having taken them to court for non-payment of royalties – and winning. (The moral of which is always to deal with a trustworthy company. Such as the publisher of this volume . . .)

At breakfast Thiessen's sense of frustration was only increased by his son's tears. Fourteen years old, and crying!

Throughout the daily ritual of watching the morning bulletin from the front, the school report had lain unopened on the table. The boy had plainly been nervous, staring blindly at the displayed maps, at the tracking shots through the deep trenches and the glows and flashes of a night engagement. When it ended Thiessen leisurely ate his bread rolls and drank his coffee. Only then did he open the envelope and quickly scan the sheets, holding them up in front of his face.

It was as bad as he had feared. He did not even try to hold back the storm of recrimination. His son's cheeks burned, his head dropped, and in the end he began to blubber. Thiessen left the table in disgust and made ready to leave.

His wife read the report wearing her sorrowful frown. She dutifully approached him as he stood by the door buttoning his coat.

'He *does* have some very good results, dear. In –'

'Don't give me that,' Thiessen interrupted. The boy had ideas about being a graphic artist. That put Thiessen in a fury. 'Artists and degenerates of that kind are no use to Europa Leader. He needs technical men. The boy is to be a physicist, like his father.'

'But he hasn't the aptitude!' she murmured distressfully. Thiessen stiffened and held his arms by his sides. 'Are you criticizing my genes?'

'No dear, of course not,' she said hurriedly, looking away. Thiessen jabbed a finger at his terrified son.

'There are correction camps for people like him. One of those will put some iron in his soul.'

He left without waiting to see their shocked looks. In the corridor his car had arrived to take him to work. He settled in the single seat, grieving with the pain of having an only son who showed signs of being a failure.

In today's world there was only one kind of work for a *real* man – the work of *science*, of *technik*. From the beginning he had tried hard to influence Peter in the right way. He was dismayed and shamed by the soft, feminine traits the boy seemed bent on developing. What he wanted in a son was a first class research scientist, one who could stand before Europa Leader confident of his services to the race.

It takes three generations to make a genius. That was one of Europa Leader's sayings. Thiessen knew in his heart that he was only on the first rung of that ladder. His own parents had not been scientists. He had got where he was by sheer application and hard work. On the technical front he was perfectly sound – that was undeniable. But he was only a work-horse, 'a steady member of the team', on the theoretical front. From his son, with all the help he had been given, he had the right to expect more.

The nonsense would have to be knocked out of the boy. Even if it did mean a spell in a correction camp. Meantime he would instruct Peter's school to remove him from all 'arty' courses.

He struggled to compose himself as the car wound its way through the underground city known as Karkhov Keepsafe. When engaged on work of vital importance to Europa, personal problems should be put aside. The thick steel shutters guarding the entrance to Physics Project No. 9 trundled aside to let the car through. Minutes later he was in his white gown and had joined his colleagues in the test bay: Ferguson, head of the design section consisting also of Marais, de Kruiff and Anhokin; Revaux, whose main job, with Thiessen, was to liaise with the engineering crew. Academician Zamyotov, the project leader and its chief theoretician, had not yet arrived.

They clustered together under the metal-ceramic hull of the bullet-shaped vehicle they had, between them, created. It rested on rails at the entrance to a tunnel. *The Death Ship,* they called it privately, though officialese for it was future-ship. The first test had been scheduled for the tenth of the month of Lenin, but if Over-Minister Cleves' rumoured visit came about, the big day would no doubt arrive sooner than they had thought.

The chamber's speaker suddenly coughed. A measured announcer's voice spoke.

'Attention, comrades. Europa Leader has issued the following message to all citizens of class four clearance and above.'

A continuous musical tone followed his words, stopping abruptly after a few seconds. Into the silence came the gruff, thrillingly confident voice of Europa Leader, heard only occasionally. The screen over the speaker remained blank. They rarely saw his face.

'Fellow citizens! Comrades in blood! It is my duty to bring you news of import in the conduct of the war. In his attempts to break the stalemate at the front, the enemy is reported to contemplate the use of third and perhaps even fourth-grade weapons. Should he thus break the unwritten rule, be assured that our response will be in kind.

'Meantime, all notified personnel who have not already done so are to take up keepsafe residences.

'Let there be no alarm – we are too mighty to be overthrown. In the end, the object of the war will be gained: we *shall* recover the Siberian territories. Nothing can prevent the triumph of our will, for the white race's right to the north of the world is inalienable. Comrades, pay heed to my words.'

Briefly the musical tone resumed. Europa Leader's closing injunction was his invariable way of signing off, and no one said anything for a while. Thiessen guessed the Leader was conditioning the public to expect large-scale casualties from the front, rather than attacks on population centres as he had intimated. The higher grade weapons – gas, germ, high-yield nuclear – would almost certainly be restricted to the battle zone if they were used at all. Even then, judging by past experience, they would quickly be relinquished. Both sides had learned before this how costly such an exercise could be.

'He didn't mention the penetrator system,' Marais remarked suddenly.

Thiessen shrugged. 'Because there isn't one,' he said. It was the old nightmare: a rapid succession of hydrogen warheads targeted on the same spot, tunnelling their way through a keepsafe's rock cover and protector lid. It was always assumed that the first side to perfect such a system would launch a full-scale assault against the other; only the Leader-Keepsafe, lodged far under the Swiss Alps, could be guaranteed proof against it.

In practice, the problem of maintaining the required stream of missiles in the face not only of defensive measures but also of the disruptions caused by preceding detonations was well-nigh insuperable. Thiessen did not expect to see an effective penetrator system, ever.

Lean, saturnine Zamyotov, himself a Siberian exile, entered. 'It's true,' he said. 'Cleves is coming. He'll want a clear exposition of what we're doing.'

De Kruiff leaned against the death ship and grinned. 'Now we're for it. How do you explain non-idempotency to a bureaucrat?'

'Why bother?' Thiessen replied sourly. He rapped his knuckle on the death ship's cold shell. 'Metaphysics is all right, but in the end it's only talk. *Technik* is what counts.'

Idempotency: the concept went back to Aristotle. Quite simply, it meant that a thing is identical with itself – a fact so obvious that a layman would never think to state it. Put in terms of mathematical logic: the intersection of A with A equals A, and the union of A with A equals A. Otherwise known as the idempotent laws.

At Physics Project No. 9 they believed they had answered a question that had perplexed mankind throughout history: did only present time have a physical reality, or were the past and the future also, in some way, real?

The future, at any rate, they now knew to be real. But it differed in one important respect from the present.

The future was non-idempotent.

Nothing there fully equated with itself. Identity was undifferentiated. It was hard to say whether discrete objects properly existed in it at all.

And they had established that it was possible to travel into the future state – 'future absolute' they called it, to distinguish

56

it from 'future present', namely the materialization of tomorrow's events. Nobody knew yet what such a translation would be like. But it all depended on one trick: you only had to lose idempotency.

Some trick. Personally Thiessen distrusted the entire 'metaphysical' (as he called it) underpinning of the project. Although expressions for idempotency were involved in the mathematical theory, Thiessen had pointed out that the physical apparatus they had constructed did not depend on it. He compared the concept to Faraday's lines of force – descriptively useful rather than a statement of reality.

What the real state of future absolute was they would find out when they got there.

Over-Minister Cleves, head of the Ministry of Technical Innovation, arrived an hour later. Thiessen studied him surreptitiously, fascinated by such personification of power. Here was a man who could do what he pleased with any of them. He was large and muscular, his face round and remarkably smooth for his age, almost boyish, with small, cold eyes that never seemed to move behind old-fashioned pebble lenses. He carried with him a sense of controlled ferocity which Thiessen had noticed before in senior ministers. It was part of the political ethos of the state of Europa.

They sat in the small conference room, Cleves at the head of the table. There fell to Zamyotov the unenviable task of explaining the progress that had been made. He began nervously, and to Thiessen's satisfaction did not attempt to give an exposition of idempotency.

'We can think of time as being like an hour-glass,' he said. 'The sand in the upper reservoir represents the future, a reservoir of potential events. The future exists as a real state, coterminous with the present as it were, but it is indeterminate as regards to events and entities. Now if we think of the neck of the hour-glass as being very narrow, so that only one grain of sand can pass through it at a time, then we shall have some idea of what the present moment consists of. Events become single instances, and sequential, as they flow into a past equally as homogeneous, in its own way, as the future.

'We can never travel into the past. It is fixed and unchangeable, and therefore cannot be penetrated. The future is a different matter. There is nothing to impede an intrusion from our world, if the special conditions of the transient present can be cast off.'

Zamyotov's voice had gained confidence as he spoke. Cleves' small eyes narrowed. Thiessen wondered how much all this meant to him. To become an over-minister he would have to possess a nimble intelligence and a quick grasp of facts. But his mind would be focused on what he saw as the *real* world – the only one visible to the idempotent senses.

'And the future, therefore, can be *influenced*? *Directly* influenced? And through it, so can *future present*?'

'Exactly, Minister. That is our hope.'

And there it was. The reason why all necessary resources would be put into this project. The dream of the state's being able to control the future directly, without having to struggle to attain its ends through the evanescent present, with all the trials and failures which that involved.

Cleves nodded. He was silent for a short while. When he spoke again his voice was quiet, but clipped and insistent.

'And what,' he asked, 'of the *death* aspect?'

Zamyotov hesitated. This had been mentioned only in the informal reports.

'Some of us,' he answered slowly, 'are of the view that future absolute is the death state. That is, at the death of the physical body human consciousness –' He caught himself. Thiessen knew he had been about to say that consciousness became non-idempotent. '– is released into the future condition of potentiality. Admittedly this is hard to envisage. On the project we privately call the future-ship *the death ship*. Because it might enable us to voyage into the realms of death.'

The Over-Minister was silent again, a compelling silence he imposed on them all. 'Europa Leader is extremely interested in death,' he intoned eventually. 'If your claim should prove true, you can expect a signal honour: to be presented to him personally.'

He looked at each of the scientists in turn, meeting gaze after gaze. Thiessen fell into a reverie. He was thinking of his son again. If the state could achieve its aims by manipulating future absolute, why could not he personally? He had tried and tried to direct Peter on to the right path, and so far he had failed. What if it were possible, instead, to reach out and *shape* his future directly . . . ?

The accelerators were warming up at this moment. Cleves had been promised he could witness the first manned test run, however much the team would have preferred to keep to its own schedule. Anhokin and de Kruiff had been selected for it

Afterwards, if the project proved its worth it would be expanded, and there would be no further chance for Thiessen. He would be relegated. A furious sense of urgency began to mount in him. He saw himself lean forward earnestly. He heard his voice speak. 'I wish to volunteer as a test subject in the coming exercise.'

'Please be quiet, Thiessen,' Zamyotov said with an irritated frown. 'That's already been decided.'

Thiessen ignored him and rounded on Cleves. On an inspiration he moulded his features into the melodramatic and slightly ferocious cast that displayed the Europa ethos – the look that Cleves himself so often wore. He spoke passionately, almost savagely. 'I am better qualified for this than either of those selected, minister. My colleagues all have finer theoretical minds than I – no one will quarrel with that; I myself accept it. So should the experiment end in tragedy, I will be less of a loss to the team. Hence I demand, minister, *I demand* that I be allowed to offer my life in the service of the race!'

While Zamyotov and the other team members looked on appalled by his behaviour, he added more calmly, 'Also, I liaised with the construction team and know the equipment better.'

Cleves regarded him. Thiessen could almost see a thought going through his mind. *Often these science types are too spineless and compliant. Here at least is one with some guts.*

'Very well,' the Over-Minister said. 'I approve.'

Thiessen leaned back, trying, not quite successfully, to suppress his sigh of triumph.

*

The padding of their body – brain monitor suits made Thiessen and de Kruiff seem unnaturally bulky. They stood in the test bay by the door of the death ship. Involuntarily Thiessen looked into the dark mouth of the tunnel down which it would travel, and for the first time a shiver of fear went through him.

The tunnel ran down the centre of a one-hundred-kilometre-long particle track. The reason why Project No. 9 was located in Karkhov was that it was here, using the gigantic Karkhov Accelerator, that protons had for the first time been disintegrated into their component quarks. The Karkhov machine was, in fact, the only one in the world capable of performing such a feat.

Along with the successful accomplishment of proton disintegration had come the reason why quarks had proved so elusive. They were fuzzy with respect to present time, not proper particles at all but quasi-particles, hovering around the intersection of the future and the past – the neck of the hour-glass – the first stage of differentiation from the non-idempotent future. They became fully idempotent only when confined in the present-instant particles, such as electrons, protons and neutrons, that they combined to form – hence their spectacular binding energy.

And hence the feasibility of a future-ship. Proton disintegration created a quark flux, a shift out of the present moment, a door into the future absolute. The arrangement was stunningly simple.

Zamyotov's voice came from the wall speaker. 'It's time. Get aboard.'

Thiessen looked up to the control room window. A row of faces was there, watching, Cleves in the middle. An impulse seized Thiessen. He turned his face to the bureaucrat and raised his arm in a salute. His voice rang out, carried to the control room by the wall microphone.

'Tell Europa Leader, Minister, that we go to solve the twin mysteries of time and death!'

De Kruiff went first, reaching up to haul himself through the doorway. Thiessen followed into the small cabin. Two seats were bolted side by side before the instrument panel. They settled in these, strapping themselves in and plugging the short umbilicals dangling from their suits into the black box recorders.

There were no controls. Zamyotov himself would throw the switch accelerating the vehicle to six hundred kilometres per hour – the whole trip would last only ten minutes.

The death ship trundled on its rails into the tunnel and leisurely took the long curve that would move it through ninety degrees and into the dead-straight hundred-kilometre flux tube. Thiessen found that his heart was racing and his breathing was ragged. He fought to suppress his panic, trying to draw strength from the unflappable de Kruiff beside him.

What would they experience? What would they find? For his part, Thiessen knew what *he* was looking for.

His son. His future son.

Having passed through the vacuum lock and into the quark track, the death ship paused. The two proton accelerator rings, each eighty kilometres in circumference, were now hurling opposing jets of protons into the collision chamber, at velocities very close to the speed of light. The resultant free quarks were racing down the track to the collector at the far end – where they would seek one another out and recombine into protons once more. At Zamyotov's command, the vehicle suddenly surged forward with a howl of its motor, slamming the two men against the backs of their seats. The bullet-shaped craft hurtled down the tube ensheathed in quark flux.

After about a minute the pressure ceased, the acceleration over. Early experiments had placed fixed objects in the path of the flux; it had floated them free of the present moment, but they never transcended the quark haze. The answer, it transpired, was to accelerate them relative to the surrounding rock. Their motion was translated into futureward impetus, giving hope that the future absolute might prove navigable.

De Kruiff was looking at one of the instrument dials, the one that was supposed to tell them where – *when* – they were. 'According to this we are on the upper edge of the quark region. Do you sense anything unusual, Thiessen?'

'No.'

'One and a half minutes into journey,' de Kruiff intoned

into the recorder. 'No unusual sensations.'

But Thiessen *was* feeling something.

At first he wasn't sure. It reminded him of dreams. But then he realized that de Kruiff had caught on too and was looking around him.

'There's something funny about this ship,' de Kruiff said.

There was something funny about de Kruiff too. Thiessen peered sidewise at him. The firm idea came into his mind that de Kruiff was, so to speak, like a book with countless leaves. Each leaf was a de Kruiff. He could have ripped one off and thrown it away, could have ripped off any number – and there would still be an infinite number of de Kruiffs left.

This ship. It could go anywhere and leave itself behind. And it seemed larger than before. Or was it smaller?

Non-idempotent. This must be what it's like, he thought dimly. *Zamyotov and the others were right.*

The instrument panel had controls after all. A joystick jutted up from the board. The ship was steerable.

He reached for it. The future-ship lurched as he swung first to the right, then up, climbing at a steep angle.

Suddenly de Kruiff was unfastening his seat belt. He stood up, pulling out his umbilical cord as he did so. Then he lumbered to the rear of the cabin. Thiessen's gaze followed him. As de Kruiff moved, he left himself behind. A solid mass of de Kruiffs made a column behind him, slowly fading.

The end member of the de Kruiff series stepped to one side and turned to face Thiessen. From somewhere inside his suit he took a gun.

So they gave de Kruiff a gun, Thiessen thought sourly. His death shipmate was staring at him closely, his expression uncertain. 'Stop jumping around like that. I can hardly see where you are.'

'I'm not jumping around,' Thiessen told him calmly.

'Of course you are.'

Thiessen sat as immobile as he could, carefully watching the other. 'Why the gun? This isn't necessary.'

'Zamyotov thinks you're unbalanced. I'm supposed to shoot you if you go crazy.'

'But what harm could I do?'

'Try to open the door, perhaps, while we're in vacuum.'

'But don't you see, we're not on the track any more. We've left the quark region behind – this is future absolute. We are flying in the upper quadrant.'

De Kruiff came closer, peering at the dial. 'It doesn't say that.'

'Of course it does. The indicator is off the scale.'

They had gone further than they ever could have believed possible. Thiessen was sure of that. As he sat there, the walls of the ship seemed to become transparent. Beyond them stretched a vista, which his eyes struggled to understand. Here, he reminded himself, there was nothing which was contained within its own identity. Hazy glowing lights, like vague patches of colour, approached and receded. He thought he saw shining cities, great blocks of buildings sliding past.

He seized the joystick again and moved the death ship in a wide circle. He was searching, aimlessly of course, but he had it in mind that if he *tried* he would somehow find Peter.

And if he did, could he change anything? Perhaps mental will alone would suffice, he thought, in this strangely immaterial region . . .

In its circling the death ship encountered something, a barrier or membrane which it seemed to penetrate. First it had been the walls of the ship which had become transparent; now it was his skull, the walls of his brain. The scenery outside was entering his mind; there was no longer any separation between them.

It was true about idempotency.

And something else was true. Nothing that was idempotent could be changed.

A person's life, for instance.

He saw himself lying in a hospital in Berlin Keepsafe, seventy-four years of age, an embittered old man due to die of angina before the next nursing shift took over. He was remembering – or perhaps witnessing, an under-idempotent observer – his life. It was like looking at a standing wave made up of events and experiences. With regret and anguish, he saw how he was to continue to bully and direct his son, forcing him on to paths for which he was wholly unsuited. Peter was finally to commit suicide at the age of twenty-three, utterly unable to fulfil his father's demands and expectations.

Thiessen couldn't change anything. Not for himself, not for Peter. Europa Leader would never be able to change anything. Not for Europa, not for anybody. What was going to happen would happen. It had already happened. There was a plain reason for it. It was part of idempotency.

This was the worst news. With a cry of horror Thiessen threw off his restraining belt. He leaped to his feet and turned to de Kruiff who was still at the rear of the cabin with the pistol trained on him.

'We've misunderstood everything, de Kruiff! Yet it's implicit in the theory, we could have realized it! We see everything upside down – cause and effect, that is. The cause of our lives lies in future absolute. That's where we come from. *We did this to ourselves.*'

'Stay where you are,' de Kruiff told him.

'This isn't a death ship! We aren't in the afterlife! Future absolute is the authentic universe, non-idempotent, alive, in a state of freedom we can't imagine. *Death is idempotency*, what we call present time. *We were already dead when we were born*. We condemned ourselves because of something awful we did –'

The truth was like a panorama. Those religions had even guessed it which were forced to admit that life was insufferable. But now he knew why. Some ghastly mistake had been made, some terrible wrong, some sin, causing those who committed it to become trapped in idempotency – in sequential time, in the fleeting present, without any hope of release. That was how 'time' had been created; and with it the whole horrid story of human history.

The fleeting moment of present time was not even real, but an illusion. Because one never escaped one's life. One was always in it, always enacting it as if in a play that ran every night for eternity.

Neither was there any past. They had debated what its status might be. They had come to no firm conclusion except that it was unvisitable. Thiessen would now be able to report that it did not exist at all. Time was not an hour-glass. It was more like a jar of water being poured on to a landscape and forming still pools, each pool a period of history. Every so-called past event was indistinguishable from a present event. It carried its own 'present' and continually re-enacted itself.

'We must tell Europa Leader,' he said thickly, his voice sounding blurred to his ears, 'that nothing can be changed, because we are trapped in our own self-caused suffering. The course of the war is predetermined: Europa will be destroyed.'

'Get back in your seat, you damn fool,' de Kruiff ordered. His voice also was blurred. 'We'll be decelerating shortly.'

Thiessen suddenly became alarmed. 'We have to get back on the track!' he said. The cabin filled up with the shapes of the two men as they moved to their seats and strapped themselves in. Thiessen worked the joystick. The floor tilted under him; somehow he was confident that even flying blind he could find the rails and land the ship like an aircraft on a runway.

Sure enough he soon felt the satisfying bump of touchdown and the ship went speeding on its rails. Thiessen began to ponder on how the idempotent world would cope with their sojourn in indeterminacy. How would it manage to remain unchanged, faced with knowledge of the future? Would it bend in some fashion and eliminate that knowledge? But then, the scientists of Europa would certainly continue their explorations of future absolute.

While he was trying to resolve the paradox Thiessen abruptly realized that he was sitting on de Kruiff's right, whereas a few moments earlier he had been on his left. He looked to the other man. Sitting there was not de Kruiff. He saw himself, as though reflected in a mirror. Or rather, he saw not himself but Thiessen. For he, he reminded himself, was de Kruiff.

No, he was Thiessen. He was both. The multiplicity of being comprising the two had got smeared, interleaved and shuffled like a pack of cards. He saw with two pairs of eyes, thought with two minds.

The exercise was instructive, for de Kruiff, he learned, had made his own contribution to the sum total of human misery. He was conducting a passionate affair with a young party worker. He had contrived to get his wife and two daughters out of the way by having them transferred to a small, bleak town barely a hundred kilometres behind the front. They were to be killed, slowly and horribly, when the Asiatics overran the settlement.

But de Kruiff, as de Kruiff, seemed unaware of their impending fate. Indeed he seemed not to know that his companion shared his identity. For a different thought altogether was uppermost in his mind.

This lunatic Thiessen has got to be taken off the project. He's as crackbrained as Europa Leader himself.

A most interesting opinion of our head of state, Thiessen thought acidly. He was wondering how to use the knowledge against de Kruiff when the onset of deceleration hurled them against their seat restraints, and at that moment their smeared identities separated. Thiessen, hanging dejectedly in his harness, reflected bitterly on all that he had learned.

His son a failure. An early suicide. Peter, on whom he had pinned his ambitions. The ship was slowing, and as it slowed it was changing shape around him. For a while he was sure it was a pleasure boat floating on the Danube. He was back nine years in time, seated on a floridly ornamented deck with his wife and young child – no more than five years old then – watching the sunlight shimmer on swirling water, talking and laughing: a transient happy episode.

How pleasant it was to be here. He relaxed, thinking once again of the paradox he had discovered. Was it really true that nothing could be changed? Surely knowledge of the future was bound to influence it in some way? How, he wondered, would Europa Leader react to such a message of gloom? Would he meekly accept the predetermined nature of events?

Never! He would never cease to fight for Europa. He would confront the very universe itself, idempotent laws or no!

A new mood came over Thiessen. So it would be with him. He would use his knowledge to tear destiny to pieces. He would save his son. Even, he promised himself, if he had to abandon thoughts of a scientific career for Peter.

66

Then it came to him. How he had confused himself. Yes, it was idempotency that made a man's life unchangeable. But the future-ship was a way to break out of idempotency. It had smashed the prison of unalterable reality. There *was* hope. For Europa, for Peter, for himself.

He rejoiced. The pleasure boat flowed, altered, became the future-ship once more and slowed to the pace of a tram in one of Karkhov Keepsafe's main concourses. Shortly afterwards it entered the far terminus, where it would wait briefly while the titanic cyclotrons were depowered, meantime swinging round on the turntable in readiness to shuttle them back to the despatch bay and debriefing.

As the ship ground to a halt de Kruiff surprised Thiessen by unbuckling his restraint and leaving his seat. Casting him an unfriendly look, he gestured for Thiessen to follow him and made for the door. Fazed, Thiessen obeyed, lowering himself from the doorway. Once on the floor he became even more confused, for this was not the terminus but the test bay from which they had set out. How could he have failed to notice when they made the return journey? Looking up, he saw faces staring down from the wide control room window, Over-Minister Cleves occupying the central place.

Zamyotov's voice came from the wall speaker. 'It's time. Get aboard.'

At those words an irresistible impulse seized Thiessen. He raised his arm in a salute and his voice rang out.

'Tell Europa Leader, Minister, that we go to solve the twin mysteries of time and death!'

De Kruiff went first. Thiessen reached up and hauled himself through the doorway. Once they were strapped in, the death ship trundled into the flux tube, and within a minute the bullet-shaped craft was hurtling down the track ensheathed in quark flux.

During the journey the two spoke little except to ask if either felt anything. Every minute and a half de Kruiff intoned a terse report into the recorder. Ten minutes passed.

They were at the terminus.

Wearily, de Kruiff sighed.

'Well, that's it. Nothing.'

Thiessen's disappointment was like a physical pain. He had thought, somehow –

'We *have* been in 'future absolute', according to the instruments,' he pointed out. 'The same as in the unmanned tests.'

'What use is that if we don't *experience* anything? Human consciousness stays in the present, obviously. Our romanticizing about the death state – all wrong, by the look of it.' Again de Kruiff sighed. 'Cleves isn't going to be much impressed.'

'The project will go on. Even with a reduced budget.'

The cyclotrons had depowered; the future-ship swung round on the turntable. A hundred kilometres away, Zamyotov was operating the control to recall them.

As the ship rolled forward, Thiessen looked at de Kruiff and suddenly had an insight. He knew that de Kruiff's family had been mysteriously posted out east; now he felt he knew why. De Kruiff had arranged it for some selfish purpose of his own. He wanted them out of the way.

Something bad was going to happen to him. It was fate. Thiessen's intuition told him so.

He fell into a reverie. Thoughts of Peter came to him, however much he tried to push them away. A dreadful domestic scene was scheduled for this evening. It was inevitable, and he was powerless to prevent it. His feelings were too strong.

He had a sense of compression, of constriction. Perhaps it was the presence of so much electrical charge from the proton accelerators that was oppressing him, he thought, or perhaps it was the quark flux in some manner, but his foreboding was overwhelming. He had a premonition of some tragedy which he would do anything to avoid, but which he himself was going to cause. If only he could think what it was –.

The project will go on, he thought fiercely. We'll find a way. We'll get this ship working, with conscious passengers.

A vagrant memory came to him, a ride down a river somewhere, perhaps, but then it was gone. The accelerating vehicle flung the two men on, each to his private eternity of hell.

THE TRAVELLER

by
Colin Greenland

Colin Greenland's first book was *The Entropy Exhibition: Michael Moorcock and the British 'New Wave' in Science Fiction* (1983). The book was slightly longer than the title. He is the author of three novels: *Daybreak on a Different Mountain*, *The Hour of the Thin Ox* and *Other Voices*. He lives in England and writes in Colorado, although not simultaneously.

That winter the wind from the mountains was fierce, prowling and shaking all around the house like a great wolf. It scattered the icicles from the trees in the park and licked the thick snow that crested the walls into strange peaks and curlicues. From the window seat in the drawing room I watched it at play: desolate entertainment indeed, but I could not always be reading. When I was alone, and not reading, I preferred to stare from the window than face into the centre of the room like any civilized and sociable person, for the drawing room reminded me of my father.

Father had departed some months previously on another of his journeys. Indeed, he was rarely at home any more; and when he was, preferred the solitude of the study and the laboratory to the company of mother and myself. Yet even in his absence the drawing room seemed imbued with an aura of him. His pipes lay on their rack above the fireplace. Albums of his travels, bound in dark leather, filled two shelves either side, and two glass-fronted cabinets of queer mementos flanked the window where I sat. Neither mother nor I ever sat in his chair.

When the sun shone I would go riding in the park, sometimes as far as the lake, but never off the estate. I would see people, very often, running away or trying to hide among the trees; or little children in rough clothes, staring at me as I rode by. They had stolen in from the village or the farms, in search of shelter, or expecting to find something, I know not what, on my father's land that they could not find at home. Perhaps they had no homes. Georgei would have driven them off, had I told him. I would never tell him. When my father was absent Georgei was never so assiduous about the estate, especially in winter. Georgei was not so young as he had been.

In the long nights I could hear mother coughing in her bedchamber. I believe now that her cough relented somewhat while father was not there to trouble her, but she was never altogether at peace with it. As the time drew near for his return, however, she grew morose and restless. I would see her from the window riding off through the snow with Sasha panting at her heels, as if she were hunting something; but she came back each day empty-handed. By some common, un-spoken consent we did not mention father, nor go down into the cellar.

The day father was due home she could settle to nothing. She strode in and out of the room needlessly rearranging things and continually glancing at the clock.

'Put on your black velvet, Isa,' she said, exactly as if I were still a little girl. 'And for goodness sake tidy your hair.' Then, when I returned downstairs in the dress she had recom-mended, she found fault with it at once. 'One would think you were attending his funeral,' she said. 'Well, it must suffice. It is the hour.'

From the bureau in father's study she took a ring of keys. The ring was small, the keys only two: a large one of black iron and one of brass no bigger than my little finger. She shook them briskly, without looking at them, and went before me down the cellar stairs.

With the longer key she unlocked the door of the laboratory. Within, all was stillness and gloom. The air was stale from long enclosure. I went to climb on the workbench and open the little window high in the wall, but mother stopped me. 'There's no time for that.'

Georgei had covered the cabinet and all the equipment in dustsheets as soon as father had departed in September. To-gether mother and I pulled off the dustsheets. Roughly I folded them as mother began to cough. 'Quickly, Isa, quickly,' she said, and tugged the great switch that governed the elec-trical machinery.

Revealed, the cabinet resembled more than anything else a single wardrobe, quite plain but for the small window of black

74

glass set in its door. Already a faint crackling could be heard from inside. When I looked, I saw a tiny tongue of lightning flicker behind the glass.

Mother pulled a chair from the workbench, gave it a perfunctory dusting with her hand, and set it to face the cabinet. The inside of the glass was radiant. I do not know how it should be expressed. It was as if it were frosted with light.

From the shelf above the bench mother brought down the tray that held the decanter and placed it beside her as she took her seat. She righted the little tumbler, poured brandy into it, and drank it at a draught, not looking at me. All her attention was concentrated upon the window of the cabinet, where the glow now sparkled and prickled. I stood behind her chair. Inside the cabinet I could see something thickening, a form taking shape where there had been none before. I tucked my hair behind my ears and stood up straight, resting my hand lightly on my mother's shoulder, the very picture of the dutiful daughter. Except at times like this, I was not accustomed to touch my mother.

My father was now complete. The fuzz of light went out abruptly and the glass misted over before his face. He was breathing.

My mother rose, took up the little brass key, and unlocked the cabinet. A strange smell flitted through the room, like soap and salt and violets, all at once. Inside the cabinet my father stood in a trance. His eyes were tightly closed, his hands folded on the scuffed and ancient satchel slung about his neck.

His garb was strange. He had on the rubber cap with wires attached that was necessary for travelling, but otherwise above the waist he was clad only in a rudimentary undergarment of some kind, a brief black bodice that left his arms quite bare. There was a lurid design worked on the front of it, altogether barbarous, of a human skull set about with flames and chains. Also he had on a pair of coarse trousers of indigo blue, but greatly faded. Strangest of all, however, was his face. His face was bare. He had lost his great beard and moustaches.

Mother took his hand. He shivered; he trembled. He opened his eyes. He looked straight at me. He opened his mouth, but said nothing. He dribbled.

'Isa,' said mother, indicating the tray, though she looked neither at it nor at me, but only at father. I took the upturned tumbler, filled it swiftly with brandy, and gave it to her. She held it to his lips and tilted it.

His eyes rolled as he swallowed. He snorted in a great breath through his nostrils, and sighed gustily. 'Magdalena,' he said. His voice sounded stifled, as if by some constriction or obstruction of the throat. He stepped stiffly out of the cabinet into mother's arms, where he lolled, smacking his lips as the brandy took effect. 'Isa,' he said then, gazing into vacancy over my head. He spoke a phrase in a language I did not know, and stumbling out of my mother's embrace, came lurching towards me. 'Isa!' he cried again, and hugged me, crushing me to him, bruising me with his satchel. The chemical odour I had smelled when mother opened the cabinet seemed to emanate from his body, like an embrocation.

I found the intensity of his greeting embarrassing, and then alarming; but I bore it. To my shocked imagination, my father was like a wild animal, intending to devour me. I told myself it was pleasure at seeing me once more.

He was raving. 'There are women everywhere!' he announced. 'More than you could possibly imagine!' He released me to gesture wildly, waving both arms above his head. I cannot now remember what else he said. While attempting both to calm him and to avoid accidental injury, mother and I paid no attention to his words. He was often thus incoherent on his return.

Soon enough he had put on his brown silk dressing gown and was striding up and down with his glass of brandy in his hand.

'One surprise after another,' he said. He paused in his striding to open his satchel, and began to dig around in it.

'I beg you, dearest, do not tire yourself,' pleaded my mother. Father dismissed her anxieties with a brisk shake of the head.

He did not look at her, but only disturbed the contents of the satchel.

I wondered where he had been, and for how long. The question is not as eccentric as it sounds. Sometimes when he came home he would seem older than I expected, as if he had been away longer than we were aware. By his own account, he often had; though the more he told us, the wilder and more elaborate his tales grew.

He would speak at first of a realm where horses were unknown, and every man travelled by means of a balloon of gas which he wore in a canister at his back and inflated at need by tugging a cord. By the end of the week, the tale would be exaggerated beyond all proportion. 'Great cruciform ships of steel roam through the skies, swept back and forth across the face of the globe by artificial winds!'

Though mother would never admit such a thing to me, I knew that she deliberately made herself forget everything he told her of his travels, so as not to catch him out inadvertently in an inconsistency, for nothing angered him more than to be contradicted when he was in the wrong. I had adopted the same policy of incurious acceptance; though I would wonder, in bed that night, what he had meant by his exclamation about women.

My father was not a large man. Nevertheless, observing him that cold and uncomfortable afternoon, I thought that if he seemed no older on this occasion of his return, he was yet diminished somehow; and I thought by his shaving. We were clearly not to mention it. It was as if a portion of his power had resided in his beard, like the wizard's in the fairy-tale.

Perhaps it was I who had grown older.

'I'm ready for a bath,' he said. 'Accompany me. Both of you.'

His very eyes commanded us.

Georgei, like a good servant, had anticipated his master's wish. Smoke had been rising from the bath-house chimney for an hour. While mother and I assisted one another to unlace our stays, father stripped off his dressing gown and his peculiar costume. I saw that his depilation extended no further than his chin.

In the bath-house he would not rest, but strode about in the steam, slapping his shoulders. His eyes never left us. Mother and I sat mutely on the bench until I could stand this scrutiny no longer. I begged leave and went in to break the ice in the cold bath. Father scorned it. He ran from the door, calling mother to follow. I glimpsed them from the window. He was tumbling her naked in the snow. I heard her laughing and coughing pitifully, while father shouted my name. I ignored him and plunged at once into the icy water.

Having washed and dried myself quickly, I was dressed before my parents came back indoors. I took the opportunity of examining the strange clothes my father had been wearing, which lay discarded in the corner of the dressing room.

The blue trousers were made of stout cotton stuff, such as a labouring man might wear. That they were so faded seemed to bespeak years of rough use and laundering; but the cloth was as new, and stiff with starch. The bodice was a brief, primitive kind of garment that might, but for its size, have been made for the merest child, for it was nothing but two rectangular pieces of smooth black cloth sewn together, all of a piece with two short flat tubes protruding at its upper corners by way of sleeves, and a hole worked for the neck. For all its crude form and hideous embellishment, I thought it would be a light and comfortable garment to wear in warmer climes; yet dare not take it up and try how it might fit me.

After bathing we sat together on the couch in front of the drawing room fire, drinking tea and eating currant bread. The wind had got up again, and was flinging snow at the windows. It only emphasized our comfort, and made us cherish the warmth. My father spoke further, more coherently if no more lucidly, of his discoveries. 'It is not as I had expected. They do not think of the machine as a saviour. They look upon it as a mistress, to be wooed, to be accommodated. And there are those who disregard her, who enjoy her largesse while insisting that the duty of mankind, the purpose of society, lies elsewhere . . .'

He opened his trophy satchel and spread the contents in his lap. Mother made a show of polite attention which masked, I knew, sincere disapproval. For years she had been witness to the arrival of such things in her house: curios, fetishes, inscrutable to her and so neither pleasant nor useful, but rather disquieting. My interest, however, was genuine; for now I was relaxed, comfortable in clean, dry clothes and properly warmed inside and out. At such times the fancy is apt to extend itself most pleasantly. Father's stories might be fact or fiction, but his souvenirs were real enough, I felt: not comprehensible, perhaps, but separate in their existence from whatever interpretation he might put upon them. They spoke to me with silent tongues of worlds where everything was not shrouded in snow and disdain.

Father was nodding, with mother's arm about him. His eyes were all but closed. I leaned over to examine this latest trove. He permitted me to touch some of it, which I did with a ginger curiosity.

There was a kind of wallet, square and flat, made of a remarkable substance he had shown us before, like glass but quite unbreakable. It was cunningly hinged, and contained in one side a little book of coloured paper, and in the other a silver mirror in the shape of a circle, with a circular hole at the centre. The mirror was small enough to encompass with the fingers of one hand. Father encouraged me to detach it from the case. It was as light as a seashell, and had writing printed on it. Some of the letters were unfamiliar.

There was another silvery item, a wafer of soft metallic foil as thin and pliable as paper, but studded with a double row of discs. To my fingers it seemed that things like tiny buttons were enclosed within the metal. Father's explanations became exiguous and vague. 'They have banished all disease,' he said, distantly, and yawned.

Also there were pictures, more of the highly detailed miniatures on glossy card he had brought back on other occasions. These, reluctantly, mother joined me in examining, while father lapsed into slumber with his head on her shoulder.

Foolishly I wondered whether everything in this strange new world was polished and shiny. The pictures seemed to suggest it was so. Everything they showed – the sleek carriages, the glass palaces and aerial pagodas, the subterranean orchards and the men who tended them, clad in their electrical armour – all these marvels were depicted with astonishing precision and fidelity. Yet fidelity to what? For such things never were on sea or land; nor beneath, I felt sure. Other pictures, showing scenes of violent death and smouldering ruin, mother slipped under the pile with a wince, and I made no further attempt to inspect them.

When the pictures were done, mother rang for Georgei to help her put father to bed. I went to my room and attempted to read; but the poet's words resisted me, and swam like senseless notes before my eyes. My mind was too full of father's tales to absorb any other matter. I seemed to see men and women with silver hair, their clothes embroidered with scenes from atrocities, beckoning me into glass chambers to the wild music of invisible orchestras.

I hoped my father would sleep out the rest of the day; but in vain. At six o'clock I was dressing for dinner when, without so much as a preliminary knock, the door flew open and father came striding in. He was still in his gown. I was sitting at the dressing table in my chemise and petticoats, combing my hair. He halted behind my stool, looking at me in the glass. His eyes were full of a fierce humour; his right hand was behind his back. The eternal fear I had so easily forgotten in the warm, peaceful afternoon rose up again and seized me by the throat.

'What is it, father?' I asked, as calmly as I was able.

'They think they know it all,' he said, intently, but indirectly, as if continuing a conversation we had that minute broken off. 'They think they see everything. They *think* the men underestimate them. Well, so they do. So they do, Isa.'

He smiled. There was no humour in it.

'Indeed?' I asked. I was capable of no more.

'It takes another kind of man,' said father, 'a very special kind, to understand them.'

He lay his left hand on my shoulder.

'I understand them, Isa,' he assured me. 'I do.'

He squeezed my shoulder.

'I see them, and I understand them, and I see that they are no different, Isa! No different from you.'

He took the comb from my hand and tossed it onto the dressing table. Then he took a fistful of my hair. 'Without all this,' he said, tugging it. 'But otherwise – no different.'

I cried out, calling for my mother, but she did not come. I suppose she was not in hearing, or was in some way incapacitated. In the glass I saw father bring out from behind his back a great pair of scissors; and despite my pitiful complaints, he chopped away at my hair until it was nothing but ragged ends all over.

Perhaps I should have turned on him then, but instead I retreated into silent tears. In truth I could have clawed his face for my curls dropping like shorn fleece into my lap and onto the floor; but I knew better than to provoke him further. His wild mood was upon him, as so often when he returned from a visit to those other worlds that were the subject and whole source of his passion.

'Now you look like one of them!' He stood behind me smiling and staring at me in the looking-glass. Through my tears I thought I resembled no one at all, unless it were some poor mad lunatic of the village; and I wondered who they were, burning in his memory, that he must perforce disfigure and abuse me so. Were they the ones who had shaved off his beard?

My mother stifled an exclamation when I appeared at table; but she asked no question, nor voiced any protest on my behalf, despite my wretchedness. With her own hair he had not tampered; perhaps she feared to cause him to think of it.

Throughout dinner father drank heavily and spoke in awesome hints of the conduct of war. He spoke not of the glories of the cavalry, nor yet of the courage of the foot-soldier. 'Two men,' he said, again and again, 'two men shut up in a small room underground, watching over the sleep of great engines of destruction. Who are they? Nobody! And on the other side, what? Two more! The same men, it might be. The very same.' His mood had become sombre again, as if he were appalled at the spectral visions he conjured up for himself. He looked unwell.

His meal unfinished, he pushed away his plate and rose awkwardly from the table. I stared at my food. I had eaten nothing. Father leaned towards me for an instant as if to berate me; then veered aside and seized my mother by the wrist. By mainforce he drew her thus pinioned to her feet and pulled her after him upstairs. In bed that night I buried my head beneath my pillow, but in my mind I could still hear my mother's cries and entreaties.

Next day, as usual after a day of such exertions, father remained in bed, resting. Mother did not wish to see him. I took up his morning draught on a tray. He lay in his nightshirt against a mound of pillows, breathing noisily through his mouth. His eyes were sunken in sockets black with fatigue. As I set the tray carefully upon his knees and directed his hands to the beaker, I saw that his beard was growing through anew, like a dark shadow smeared across his pale jaw.

His skin seemed clammy, his muscles tense. An unpleasing smell rose from him. It occurred to me that, far from being an idyll in a paradise free of all disease, his adventure had exposed him to some pestilence unknown to us, some more cunning and indifferent plague. He seemed hardly to know me. He drank his medicine with tremor in his lip.

He gave a profound shudder then and at once relaxed. In the grip of his beloved morphia he began to tic and twitch, as if his body were acrawl with energy.

He was making a tiny noise. I put my ear closer to his lips. He was singing. 'No loss, no problem,' he sang, over and over again. 'No worries, no error, no sweat.'

He looked suspiciously at me. In shame for the ugliness he had inflicted upon me, I was wearing a headscarf, like a peasant woman. Perhaps it confused him. Before I could move away he had taken hold of my arm again.

'If you knew where I came from – and where I have been –' he said, hoarsely; 'if you knew to what sights I have been privy in certain rooms, shall we say certain upper rooms, in the city . . . ?' He nodded, stiffly. 'Then, madam, you would not use me so lightly. You would accord me more respect.'

I laid my hand on his. 'Hush, father,' I bade him. 'It is I, Isa.'

'Isa?' He furrowed his brow. 'There is not enough light in here. I thought you were your mother.'

I knew it had not been to mother that he had been speaking, not even in his distraction.

'Shall I open the curtains, father?' I offered, as much to get away from the bed as to secure him such comfort as cold grey daylight might afford.

'Do.'

But while I stood at the window, attending to his wish, he heaved himself out of bed and approached me from behind with a springing step that quite belied his appearance of exhaustion. It seems to me now that he was always coming upon me from behind. He caught me under the arms and kissed my neck. I drew my head sharply from him.

'Isa,' he said. 'My daughter. How fortunate you are not to take after your mother. I can see in you the form of the woman you will be.'

He pressed himself against me, loathsomely. I resisted him. He seemed to have no strength. He released me and fell back against the bed.

'You will be as good as any son, won't you, Isa?' he said mockingly, but with something of his former debility. 'As good as any son.'

For a moment I thought I was free. I thought his relapse was complete. I was wrong. 'Except one thing!' he cried, and once again he came lurching at me.

My nerve broke. I twisted violently from him and fled the room, sweeping the door to behind me. But father had already grasped the edge of the door and was forcing himself through even as I dragged at the handle. He grasped at me. I flinched, let go of the handle and ran along the passage with him at my back.

I reached the door of my own room and there turned to defy him on the threshold. 'How dare you?' I cried. I tore off the scarf from my head and threw it at his feet. 'How *dare* you?'

'I dare,' he said, with a grimace. His eyes seemed to start from their dark hollows. He reached for me.

I whirled into the room and snatched up the first thing I seized upon, the stool from the dressing table. I backed away from him, swinging my stool as he came at me, holding it by two legs and trying to hit him with the seat. I should have clutched the seat to me instead, and thrust at him with the legs. I knew nothing of fighting.

Father seized the stool and wrested it from me. He flung it away and came on, his arms spread wide. Now the dressing table was at my back. I could retreat no further.

I put back my arm and felt steel beneath my hand. It was the scissors, the scissors with which he had cut my hair. I caught them up and brandished them at him, jabbing the air.

He seized my wrist, wrenching at me. I dropped the scissors. They fell to the floor between us, open. Father bent for them, and I heaved clumsily at him with my shoulder and caught him on the nose. His head jerked back; he staggered and lost his footing, collapsing and scrabbling for the scissors as he fell. I crouched to snatch them up. He grabbed at me and pulled me down after him; but I had the scissors in my left hand. In desperation I thrust them at him. One blade pierced his nightshirt and struck home in his stomach. It was a horrid, yielding sensation, like stabbing meat with a skewer.

At once, there was blood, spreading across the cloth of his shirt and welling through onto my hand. He clasped his hand to the place, knocking my own hand and tearing the wound. He cried out.

I rose in a strange state of fright. I recall crouching over him: it can have been an instant only, but it seemed longer, far longer. I was thinking I should help him, but I could not bear to touch him.

I ran to fetch my mother; but as soon as I was out of the room, leaving him behind there struggling on the floor, I suffered a change – I know not what to call it, a change of heart, a change of mind. In that pause I seemed to see my mother hurrying to my room and, at first sight of him, drawing away, shouting for Georgei. And Georgei would come, stumping up the stairs, and see to father as best he could, somehow staunching that horrid flow, bandaging it, and returning father to bed. And what then? Would the madness not redouble then? Would the tyrant defied not be twice the tyrant?

And what if he did not recover? What if he died? Would my mother then protect me? Or would she deliver me up to the law? Would she even hesitate?

All these questions occurred to me that instant, in the passage outside my room; and I did not know the answer to any of them. They have occurred to me again, since, frequently, severally and together; and still I do not know.

What I did know, there and then, was that it was in my power to escape them all. I ran downstairs, tearing at the buttons of my dress. From the closet by the garden door I dragged the old boots I wore for skating; and from the dressing room father's outlandish clothes that lay where he had discarded them. In the laboratory it was the work of a moment to throw the heavy switch and release the electrical power. While it spread, humming and buzzing, into the machinery, I pulled on the clothes and the rubber cap of wires, and laced my boots; and then, as the strange cold light began to glow behind the little black window, turned the key in the lock and stepped into the cabinet.

Upstairs, my mother began to scream.

CINEMA ALTÉRÉ

by
Andrew Stephenson

Andrew Stephenson was born in Maracaibo, Venezuela, but his name didn't fool anyone there. He refuses to reveal his present whereabouts, except to say that he lurks somewhere in the UK countryside, supervised by one cat. His first short story was published in *Analog* in 1971, and he is the author of two novels: *Nightwatch* (1977) and *The Wall of Years* (1979). His third novel is due any decade now.

Roll titles.

High summer, high noon, high temperature.

The overheated city teems with lunchbreak life: along congested streets the war of foot and wheel is fought with sullen resolution, each faction gaining ground by turns, as traffic lights wink through idiot rounds of stop and go.

Seen from this Olympian perspective, the pulsing corpuscular flow mimics that of living blood. Thus the great square, where arterial ways converge to mix their contents, surely is the pump and heart of this metropolis.

Pan across the square. Ordinary folk throng shop-lined outer pavements. Most prefer not to linger out of doors; but a few sit on benches beneath shady trees, nibbling sandwiches, tolerating the heat for the sake of daylight and open air. Overhead, on branch and cornice, starlings and pigeons hold mute parliaments, too torpid to beg for crumbs. Higher still, lofty façades glitter in the sun.

Fed and drained by side streets, a sluggish triple stream of motorized traffic processes around the square. Isolated within this cordon of metal and fumes is a tranquil scrap of green.

These are the ornamental gardens. At their hub, like a pivot for the entire city, the statue of a bygone king gazes blindly out from a high pedestal fringed by pink roses that slowly wilt in the heat.

Hold on gardens. Zoom in slowly on a bench, near the road, occupied by a well-dressed, balding, somewhat overweight man. He seems strangely alone amid so much human activity. Close-up: sagging face, eyes masked by lowered lids, big nose squashed down above pouting lips twisted into a semblance of distaste.

Distaste for what? There is no clue.

He might be dozing. But no, his mouth twitches. One eye opens, studies the large digital clock on the entablature above the portico of the Central Library, opposite. Black on white, the numerals show 11 : 55.

The other eye opens. Casually he turns in his seat, towards the statue behind him, as though to contemplate the stone monarch. No, not the statue. Rather, the intersection beyond, where the lights have just changed to green.

The unmarked black tanker truck eases into the square and commences the long circuit around to where the man sits. He turns away, trying to ignore it.

Sam Sensharra does not relish what will happen so soon.

He is finding it hard to wait for voluntary death, hoping this will be one of those times that never were, reflecting on how there must always be the consciousness of watching eyes and the dread of that ultimate finality that would ensue, should the scheme misfire.

He distracts himself by plucking a rose and sniffing at it.

On the table between the three men, sheets of plans and schedules rustled as Samuel Sensharra rearranged them. Several rooms away a clock chimed, tinkling sweetly in the quiet studio offices. A door slammed.

'This business stinks,' Sensharra conceded, 'but I try to be artistic, to give it meaning.'

Cody Lewis and Piotr de Veet made no comment. Lewis did not care to argue further. De Veet had known Sensharra too long to bother disagreeing. Both waited while he stared unseeing at the top sheet, a blown-up photomap of the new location. Abruptly he shoved it aside, disordering the pile once more.

'But who understands?' he demanded. 'Do the guys who grab at my work – the fat cat network bosses and the fat slob viewers – do they even make the effort? I try to shock, to teach them. They watch unmoved; and there they do me a wrongness, because I say gratuitous violence isn't art. It's obscenity.'

De Veet shook his head. 'What matter, Sam?' he said. 'We get top rating. We get paid. We get to eat.'

Sensharra stared at him. 'Pete, you been listening to me? It matters because nobody thinks it matters. Today's screen violence is a circus of pictures and noises. And that's what's screwed up with the world: at heart, nobody gives a damn. They sit at home in comfy armchairs and watch puppets on TV doing their hurting for them. That's what I've fought all my life, ever since it was still a thrill to see a guy shot in the movies and the real thing was unthinkable. God's truth, Pete, when those shmucks turn on one of my movies, I'd like for them to feel a real gut-searching panic. To *identify*.

'Still, you're right. We don't get to choose, do we? The Joe Show sponsors want their pound of flesh raw, blood and all. But mark me, Pete: this time, when I collar the man in the street and I yell in his face, *Joe Public, this is your life; and smile 'cause you're on camera, boy!*, by God I want him to *believe* it! When the viewers realize this is the Big Scene, where the world shatters and the blood runs in rivers, I want strong men to faint dead away, on account of how it *hits* them. You hear me?'

'For sure, Sam, I hear you.'

Out in the frosty parking lot a diesel engine coughed and grumbled. Sensharra inspected his watch. 'That's our cue. Cody, any late doubts? The location's right, no question?'

Cody Lewis, two metres of suntanned muscle garbed in khaki trousers and bush jacket, nodded slowly, then settled his stetson more firmly on his head. He met Sensharra's earnest stare with his own steady gaze, before the other looked away to de Veet.

'Pete, those cameras spotted where I wanted them?'

'Eight, near enough. The other two . . .' De Veet sucked his yellowed teeth. 'They got to be mobile. Headband jobs. So N'gabe goes with me, instead of with Cody. Sorry, Sam, I know you say to keep the kid out of it, but . . .' His wrinkled face creased along its worry lines like an old shoe retreading familiar steps. His shoulders seemed more stooped than usual.

'It happens.' Sensharra passed a hand through the remnants of his hair, and sighed. 'Time he learned the dirty side of our business. Okay, but double-check his gear. We can't afford to lose any footage on this scene. The budget won't allow for a retake, and God alone knows what the Civil Liberties Board would say to a reapplication. So let's go.'

*

The tanker dominates the traffic lane nearest the gardens. So close to the edge of the road is it, its tyres skim the kerb. It reeks of oil and diesel. And of something else.

Beyond the tinted glass of its cab is the rigid face of Wolfgang Brock, the stunt man, inching his charge towards its ordained position. Brock glances in Sensharra's direction. His lips are barely parted by a cigarette hanging loosely, unlit and dry, between them. The knuckles of his hands show white with the strength of their grip on the wheel.

Brock is the top suicide in the business. Sensharra reassures himself with this thought as he savours the rose. He regrets that he will not live to see the man's full performance at first hand. Also he wishes Brock had removed that cigarette: details matter.

He wonders whether his own simulated *sang froid* should be hailed as a masterpiece, under the circumstances.

The Library clock shows 11 : 58.

In the shadows of a deserted and inconspicuous alley a blue haze bloomed. Swelling rapidly to a diffuse cloud, it abruptly collapsed and darkened, coalescing into an apparently normal trader's van: dirty, green, undistinguished. On the van's flanks peeling signs in white paint claimed, *Deliveries Made, Anywhere, Anytime* – a feeble joke?

After a few moments, Sensharra and de Veet emerged from the front. Then the back doors creaked open and a youth joined them. The latter was rubbing his forehead to dispel the nausea that accompanied time travel. Sensharra looked at him.

'You okay, Woru?' he asked.

Worunga N'gabe nodded, but shivered despite the heat. His voice was unsteady.

'Uh, I guess. Is this the first or second time through?'

De Veet, tinkering with his headband camera, eyes masked by dark glasses which were really viewfinders, allowed his mouth to smile. 'Always the second time, unless . . .' The smile faded.

Sensharra frowned at him. 'Cut that, Pete. No call to rattle the kid. Save the ad-libs for when we're checking the rushes. Woru, don't you fret. Cody'll come through.'

Locking the van, together they moved towards the mouth of the alley. In the bright sunshine ahead dense traffic crept by: cars, buses, people afoot and cycling, all unaware of the deadly threat the three men posed. Sensharra studied his watch, said to de Veet, 'What time have you got? Local, that is.'

Both de Veet and N'gabe looked at their wrists. De Veet hesitated, preparing to say something, thought better of it, answered flatly, 'Ten before twelve.'

N'gabe's breathing deepened. De Veet's momentary mis-interpretation of Sensharra's question had not escaped him. They might have all too little time.

At the main road, Sensharra halted and covertly peered along it. 'Stand by,' he said. 'Brock's coming.'

It had been agreed at the studios that it would be left to the stunt man to make contact. So the three stayed put, acting like innocent tourists. When the black tanker finally came level it braked noisily; only then did they pretend to notice it.

Brock jumped down from the cab.

'Hey, I got a load for the library,' he shouted. 'You folks direct me?' He joined them. A nearby policeman scowled, first at Brock, then at the tanker which was now impeding the traffic. He advanced on the group, reaching for his notepad. In a hurried undertone, Brock demanded:

'Okay, what do I do?'

'You there!' yelled the policeman.

Brock looked around.

'Be moving it in a moment,' he called. Slightly appeased, the policeman nodded and retired to the shade of a shop front, where he made notes.

Sensharra gesticulated, in the manner of one directing a stranger, but kept his voice low, watching the policeman all the while. 'Take this road. Go to the square at the end. Circle halfway around, staying close to the middle. You'll see me. Get as near as you can. When I nod, do it.'

Brock drew a cigarette from a squashed pack and stuck it between his lips. 'Suits me,' he said, his words slurred by the cigarette. 'Do I survive?' The cigarette bobbed as he spoke.

'No chance.'

'Good. Better get on with it then.' He pulled a lighter from his pocket and put the flame close to the cigarette. Before it caught, Sensharra said:

'I want this to be as good as the shopping mall you did for us. The critics liked you in that.'

Brock paused. 'How jolly for them,' he remarked. He put away his lighter, forgetting the cigarette was still unlit. 'Me, I never watch your flicks.' Returning to the tanker, he climbed in, smiling ingratiatingly at the policeman.

'So it's the first time,' N'gabe said. 'No sign of Cody.'

'Looks like it,' agreed de Veet.

Sensharra said nothing. Brock's remark had stung.

The tanker passed them slowly, belching sooty exhaust.

There is dust on the rose, Sensharra observes. But then, why should there not be? A busy public place like this, with so much traffic. A spell of dry weather. The dust will soon rise. Yet the scent remains sweet, evoking for him a lost time of innocence, when beauty was a pleasure, not an industry.

He has made many films, or – as he calls them, being a traditionalist – movies. Techniques have come and gone, to be exploited as fashion and expediency dictate. This is but one of many: the folding of a life upon itself, the pinching-off of a segment and its preservation in the timeless limbo of the camera stacks. This is simply one facet of his art, as he calls it.

The process inherently has obviated earlier subjective proofs. Now his eyes are being opened. He never suspected how intense, how mystical, could be these seconds before the rock plunges into his private pool of tranquillity. At last he can be satisfied that his other self, the one who survives, has not been wrong all along. He is pleased. The thrill of participation is truly overwhelming and increases by the second. Indeed, he is intrigued to discover that it verges on being erotic. No more the remote director, the lofty overseer, now he knows what it is to be the person on the other side of the little screen, the one who will perish alongside the cyphers with whom he chooses to share his dissolution. To be Joe Public.

Oh, Sam Sensharra loves his trade. He feels honoured to give himself to it, literally. He imagines he has principles.

He makes a point of appearing in the Big Scene in all his productions. Thus he preserves his objectivity, his humility and his self respect. Or so he tells those in whom he confides. 'Otherwise,' he often adds, seriously, 'I might forget I'm just a human movie-maker with a duty to my characters, and start imagining myself as God.' Here he laughs. 'I mean, hell, only gods direct real lives without suffering the consequences.'

This, then, is his excuse, which he believes.

The three had reached the outer edge of the busy square and were preparing to go to their marks when an urgent shout made them pause. It was Lewis: he was running drunkenly, obviously still dizzy from his jump through time.

'Thank you, oh Lord,' whispered N'gabe, eying the heavens. By their expressions, the others shared his relief.

They stopped to let Lewis catch up and gathered round him while he recovered some of his composure. A small audience of curious onlookers gradually drifted away.

'Problems with the equipment,' he panted, before gulping several deep breaths. 'I set the coordinates right, but it put me down here late.'

'Good that you come no later,' commented de Veet. 'I think then we all have been in trouble. For always. You also.'

Lewis rounded on him. 'Look, I said what happened. So keep the lecture. Just because you were panicking like some old –'

'We were starting to worry,' Sensharra interjected mildly. Abruptly his manner changed. 'My God: the tanker! If Brock decides to let rip without the signal we'll have a real disaster. Woru, stop him – *run!*'

And N'gabe ran. Already the tanker waited at the lights, on the point of entering the square, too far away to see what Brock was making of their meeting, or whether he had even spotted them in the crowd. N'gabe raced towards it, dodging most obstructions with reckless swerves, bowling over anyone who got in his way. Just as the light changed to green, he leapt forward and managed to bang a fist against the driver's door.

By the Library clock, the time was 11 : 55.

Watching the tanker creep closer, Sensharra tries to stay calm. He fails. One minute ago he used the remote control in his pocket to start all the cameras, so this has to be the first time through.

Big and messy, that's the bomb inside the tanker. Three hundred kilos of explosive act as trigger and dispersal agent. The remainder of the load is naphthenate palmitate. Napalm. About one hundred thousand litres of it.

The Special Effects Department have promised Sensharra excellent results. They anticipate thorough coverage of the square and of the seven major roads radiating from it. The napalm includes a new fluidizer, to make it flow faster and further, leaving its combustion properties unaffected. Adhesion is not of paramount importance in this application. The script merely specifies 'a terrorist outrage', and Sensharra is talented enough to compensate for any lack of descriptive detail. He sees no reason to doubt the Department's estimates. He also trusts Lewis, who claims to have found the most inflammable city centre available under the terms of the relevant laws.

The clock stands at 11 : 59.

Somewhere recent – even Sensharra does not know where or when – Lewis will have been waiting in a time-travelling van, alone . . .

Cut to interior of van. An oblong box pierced by a row of slots looms over a workbench in front of Lewis. On the bench is a picture stack viewer. He presses a switch on the box. The slots flare blue, one by one; suddenly each encloses a camera. Methodically, he reviews what images every camera contains. If none holds what is wanted, he has the strictest orders: to take the van back to the studios and conduct the rest of his life as though he never heard of Sam Sensharra or the current project.

But always the cameras seem to have recorded the required scenes. That is the wonder of the process, which some take as conclusive proof that the Creator has a sense of humour.

Sam Sensharra loses no sleep over the question. It works for him.

He tries to pick out the eight fixed cameras in various positions around the square. There are five which include him in their field of view. He knows this and where they are situated but cannot see them. Instead his imagination lets him hear their scan circuits whistling, shuttling images into solid-state stacks as the countdown proceeds.

The clock trembles on the edge of noon. The tanker is very close.

Brock spun the wheel to full lock and gunned the engine. Turning ponderously into the alley, where two vans now waited, the tanker squeezed between opposing pavements with no room to spare. The rear wheels mounted the kerb then dropped onto the tarmac. Engine rumbling, the truck moved up to the nearer van and stopped. Brock killed the power. The fog of exhaust fumes began to dissipate. Sensharra and the others watched him dismount.

'What a bitch,' Brock breathed. 'Hell, I done some stunts, but naping a rush-hour crowd beats all. What kind of flick is this, Sam? Sado-porn?'

'You know better than to ask,' said Sensharra. 'Just take your money.'

Lewis proffered a plastic card. Brock accepted it and ran his pocket reader across it.

'What's the bonus for?' he asked.

Lewis answered, non-committally: 'Results.'

Brock raised an eyebrow and put the card in his breast pocket, sealing the flap carefully. He hooked a thumb at the tanker. 'And her?'

'I'll take it back,' said Lewis. 'You can go. We'll be in touch about the next job.'

'Which is . . . ? No, I don't suppose you'd care to predict.' The stunt man grimaced and stepped clear, adjusting the studs on his ornate belt. 'Close-mouthed bunch, aren't we?'

he remarked, dissolving into a blue mist that soon dispersed.

'We need to be,' murmured Sensharra, as though to himself. 'My public wouldn't understand.' To Lewis he said, 'What about those results you mentioned?'

'It's a ratings-buster.'

'So tell me.'

'Sam, I don't know where to start. Just one glance and I felt sick. Me, Iron-Guts Lewis, I almost puked. Such footage! The slow motion, for instance: there's a mother and her child –'

'Is that it? Only suffering?'

Lewis dropped his eyes. 'What else did you expect?'

'I'd hoped for something to give it a purpose. Heroism. Dignity, perhaps. Proof that people can be human, even today.'

'There was an old blind guy knocked his dog unconscious with his white cane.'

'That'll have to do, I guess. And the spectacle?'

Lewis perked up, eager to gloss over his embarrassment. 'Fantastic. Best disaster footage we've staged since we switched to paradox production. It goes on from where *Quo Vadis* left off. You never saw a city burn like this: two square klicks ablaze, with a smoky column of roaring flame as the firestorm catches hold; half a million casualties at least; flames washing across the streets; melted fat running in the gutters; buses like islands in the fires, their paint bubbling –'

'That's *enough!*' Sensharra had paled: whether in shock, or in fury, it was hard to know; but one hand trembled, as though on the point of striking Lewis. 'While your wages come from me, Cody, there's one thing you don't forget, ever: those were real people we killed.' Suddenly the trembling hand relaxed, waving Lewis away; and tiredly Sensharra said, 'Take the tanker back.'

Without a further word, Lewis hauled himself into the cab. The tanker shimmered and vanished, to reappear five months later in the snow and ice of the studio parking lot.

'Pete,' said Sensharra, 'you take Lewis' van. Woru and I will travel in the other.'

But even after de Veet had gone, N'gabe stayed where he

was, head tilted slightly backwards, surveying the narrow confines of the alley. His face showed puzzlement and disbelief. 'Mister Sensharra,' he asked in a small voice, 'did I really die here?'

Sensharra came and stood next to him, and he too regarded the crumbling eaves of the dilapidated buildings, and the pale strip of sky beyond. 'We all did,' he replied at last.

'Don't seem possible. How'd we make a film when nothing happened?'

'It did happen.' Sensharra laid a reassuring hand on N'gabe's shoulder. 'And we made a movie of it. Or we would have, except Cody stopped us, because the camera stacks he received held the right images.'

'But if he stopped us, where'd the images come from?'

'They were there to start with.'

N'gabe squinted dubiously at the pudgy hand resting on his shoulder. 'That sounds crazy.'

'Not at all. The logic is perfect. Suppose the factory makes a stack, a chunk of crystal doped with bits of this and that, a random mix. Nobody plays it, so it could hold anything. Anything, not just white noise. Among the anythings that stack might hold are pictures. So we push it through the process and get a sequence of movie footage. The universe doesn't care. That footage is one of the possible random mixes. Paradox production makes sure that mix suits our own purposes; the events the movie shows never actually took place, that's all.'

'Then why do I feel so dirty?' asked N'gabe, bitterly. He shook off the reassuring hand and faced the other man. 'Why, Mister Sensharra? What did you almost make me do?'

'I wish I knew,' said Sensharra. 'I really do.'

Shortly thereafter, in their turn, van and men faded into the future; and moments later the clocks of the city began to chime the noonday hour.

The tanker's engine is clearly audible above the general traffic noise. To Sensharra its growl is the only sound in the whole world. The front wheels are drawing level. Brock awaits the signal, one hand down out of sight, resting on the trigger.

Sensharra crumbles the rose between his blunt fingers. Petals flutter to the ground, a shower of purest pink against dusty grey. He offers a short prayer to his private gods before raising his eyes and gazing around the square at where he knows the cameras are.

Look at me, he thinks. Look at us. See how we die. Wallowing in comfort, in safety, will you contemptible swine understand what chances at heroism I am granting these little people here? Will you learn by their example? If not, try at least to enjoy the spectacle: some of you have earned that right; some of you are here with me. Find yourselves – if you think to look.

Standing, he meets Brock's staring, frightened eyes.

Angle: medium long shot, on Sensharra's back, such that the Central Library clock is visible, defocused, beyond him. Hold to establish, then smoothly refocus on clock. Numerals change: 11 : 59 becomes 12 : 00.

Fade down street sounds into silence. Cut to front view of Sensharra, and fade in first chimes of city clocks: cascades of metal-throated belfry song, joyful carillon and sonorous tocsin, all the famous tunes beloved of rhyme and legend –.

Sensharra nods.

Cut clocks. Freeze action. Catch the mask of ecstasy upon his face; trap the shame of it, forever. Swell Sensharra to full screen, revealing loathsome rapture. Then zoom out, skyward, framing bench and gardens, the square and its traffic stilled an instant before extinction, buildings a heartbeat from destruction, the radiating streets, the crowds, the surrounding blocks and their networks of human life, and – in the mind alone – on out to the limits of sympathy for prey and predator alike.

THE PLEASURE GIVER
TAKEN

by
Storm Constantine

Storm Constantine doesn't want it known that she lives in ********, makes her living as a *********, and collects rare and exotic *************** as a hobby. She is the author of the Wraeththu trilogy: *The Enchantments of Flesh and Spirit*, *The Bewitchments of Love and Hate* and *The Fulfilments of Fate and Desire*. Her next novel will be *The Monstrous Regiment*. This is her first short fiction, and she plans to write more Tavrian Guilder stories.

I

I am not by nature vindictive, neither am I particularly vengeful. If the slight is slight I am prepared to overlook it. Not for me the grinding anguish of damp, dark nights nursing an over-ripe grievance. I have seen the unnecessary consequences of such behaviour and decided long ago that the boredom of it is superseded only by its utter pointlessness. Me, I can turn my back and walk away. Anytime. Well, nearly anytime. Naturally, the exception proves the rule, otherwise there wouldn't be a story to tell and far be it from me to tire you with a fruitless paean to my self-restraint.

At the time I had just successfully walked away with pride intact from the kind of insult that normally severs all philanthropic feeling between mind and soul forever. I walked away laughing. I didn't want to live with the woman, I'd made that clear from the start; but they never quite believe you even when you spell it out in words of single syllables. When you try to exercise your prerogative of escaping their nerveless clutches, they have the affrontery to complain, and then, if they feel the occasion merits it, they try to destroy you. I didn't want to get involved in that kind of mess, so Lenora Sabling had been left screaming at her mirror, claw marks visible only on my credit statements. I knew her tactics would never work. The plans lacked decisiveness, and the killer instinct was completely absent. She was a fool; I could have taught her so much.

Whenever I was a woman, I never disgraced myself by such histrionic displays. I can't understand why other people can't live up to my standards or why they have to deliberately misconstrue my intentions. I'm not dishonest nor hampered by outmoded concepts of morality; a combination of traits that once very nearly broke my heart. I try not to think about it nowadays. Lenora, as a contrast, feasted on my income rather than my affections. She began to bore me with tedious possessive inclinations that were dangerously near to getting out of hand. It wasn't just a self-preservation measure to leave the planet; I had work elsewhere. Goodbye Lenora. It was nice knowing you.

Asher Tantine is a small, solitary world, circling its angry sun devoid of companions. I'd been offered the position there some months earlier but, even though there'd been veiled hints of enormous payment, the vagueness of the commission had put me off following it up. Because of the incident with Lenora, which had effectively rendered me fundless, I decided to accept the job and trust that the lack of detail didn't conceal something unpleasant. I am a professional and my talents are nested in an interstellar reputation of excellence. There used to be a time when any job that came my way was leapt upon with dog-like enthusiasm and a desperate desire to please. Now, I'm older, more experienced and can usually afford to be choosy. Discerning clients make offers designed not to offend my dignity and thus, I choose them. And what is my profession? Well, that is the beginning and end of most of my problems. It is why I've learned to be strong and unassailable. I am a Pleasure Giver. Pleasure in all its forms, however dark, is available from my fingers, eyes and body. I began my life as a white-skinned male but, over the years, have found that several adjustments to my pigmentation and physical form improved the appearance not only of myself but also my bank balance. I was apprenticed to a veritable master of the craft, Eeging Lampeter, who is sadly now unavailable for commission. He trained me well. For many years I couldn't afford sophisticated equipment to aid me in my work and relied wholly upon what the gods had given me, plus whatever hardware can be obtained from an average kitchen. Sexual gratification is not the only form of pleasure in this universe. It is one of them, certainly, and one at which I am exceptionally gifted, but there are many others, some explicable only in the language of their planet of origin. Suffice to say, I know my stuff.

On arrival at one of the two spaceports on Asher Tantine I was feeling alert, invigorated and looking forward to serious employment. The evening air was very sweet on that world, almost like a thick liqueur in the lungs. The sun was sinking behind the grotesque, skeletal forms of slumbering space-yachts, cargo vessels and those sleek, nippy cruisers that burn out after only a couple of years. This spoke of affluence. The population may have been small, but it was monied. There were a few weary moments at the customs kiosk, during which I had to endure comments from the officials that weren't very clever and didn't inspire hilarity within me at all. Naturally, I have become inured to the effect my papers have on insects of such nature. It occurs with depressing regularity on each world I visit and has long since lost any entertainment value. 'Ah, a *Pleasure Giver!*' they say, winking roguishly.

'Yes,' I sigh. 'That is correct. Is everything in order?' Why such words should be viewed as a *double entendre* is a mystery to me. They are inevitably followed by sniggers and further winking. Only by refusing to become involved in any repartee do I escape without wasting my precious time. If it gives them pleasure to imply things about my private life, then they should be paying for it. Asher Tantine was no exception; the ritual was enacted and my silence guaranteed the return of my papers.

I left the spaceport and faced the town. Having already taken the precaution of forwarding my equipment and luggage to the Hotel Evening, I found I had a few minutes to survey my new terrain. It is considerably helpful to sniff around the environment before commencing work. All worlds are different and I've found it beneficial to observe local habits and customs so as not to appear completely alien to my employers. In this case, it was a Mrs Amberny; a quaint and old-fashioned way of addressing oneself. Titles had more or less become obsolete once gender changes became so prevalent. I've always been just plain Tavrian Guilder, whatever my sex. Mrs Amberny had sent orders that had been oblique in the extreme. It wasn't very often that I arrived for a job completely unprepared, but the veiled and cautious nature of all communication I'd had with Mrs Amberny meant that I had no idea what was expected of me. For the last job, it had been required that I take a skin pigment of viridian hue, which had also affected my eyes and hair. I saw no reason to change that; there'd been no special requirements from Mrs Amberny on this score. Only once have I refused a request of this nature and that was when some exceedingly fat person had asked me to double my body weight. I had starved for nearly a week after turning the job down, but I didn't regret one agonizing moment of it. I have my principles and though some might criticize me for being vain, I am not ashamed to admit I take great pride in my appearance. I may have mutilated other people's bodies in my time, but it causes me untold grief if I as much as break a fingernail. Now I have a perennially youthful appearance, a body as svelte and slim as a whisker and luxurious waist-caressing hair – currently the same colour as tarnished copper but with a better shine.

Violet Way, which I understood to be the largest town on this sparsely-populated world, was an urban complex of modest size, whose industries were primarily tourism, because the planet is beautiful and unspoiled, and crystal-growing, because the planet sprouts the things like weeds. Kids in the street can scoop up handfuls of pyratitanite or shellamine; on Asher Tantine such gems are two-a-penny. Not so upon other worlds of course, where a single splinter of pyratitanite will sell for more than a fleet of night-cruisers with luxury trim. What a happy circumstance it would be if the traveller could pop such street-littering treasures into his pocket before taking his leave of the place. Unfortunately, this is impossible and we can thank the same technology that prolongs my youth for that.

No one gets a toe out of Asher Tantine's atmosphere in possession of a single stone. They have ways of detecting them, and heavy corporations from larger worlds who have a commercial interest in Asher Tantine supply effective weaponry to act as a deterrent. I must admit it's discreet. I never saw a single sign of surveillance the whole time I was in Violet Way.

Walking through the brightly lit streets, past noisy casinos thronged with glittering catamites and women of the blight, I found my thoughts straying to the subject of Lenora Sabling. It had been a mistake to let her get involved with me. Why I should still be thinking about her now was an enigma. Only on reflection did I realize it was a portent. She was a hairdresser; that alone should have warned me. I disliked her personality at once, but if she kept her mouth shut she looked mysterious and vampiric. She complemented my appearance like my hair, my jewellery, my brindled hounds. Out of those items all I'd got away from her with was my hair. As far as I knew she was still in triumphant possession of the jewellery and hounds. Ah well, no use sighing. I'd earn more than enough from the Amberny woman to replace my lost belongings.

I checked into the Hotel Evening, a delightful palace of subdued lighting and crystal encrustations that looked like plants. The receptionist stared at me rather rudely. Obviously, Asher Tantine was quite a provincial place on the planetary scale. I doubt whether many Pleasure Givers give the Hotel Evening their custom. I dialled Mrs Amberny directly I was installed in my suite. The screen displayed, as usual, an inoffensive graphic design instead of the face of who I was speaking to. Mrs Amberny was very cagey. I recognized her breathy yet clipped tones. 'Tavrian Guilder,' she said. 'How relieved I am to hear your voice. You sound so close.'

'I am, Mrs Amberny. I'm at the Hotel Evening,' I replied.

'Good, *good!*' She laughed, which sounded like an exhalation of tension. What did this woman want of me? I was quite intrigued. 'Come to my house tomorrow before lunch,' she said. 'The Hotel should be able to provide you with transport.'

'I'll be there, Mrs Amberny.' I paused a moment to indicate that what followed was slightly distasteful to me. 'Perhaps we could broach the subject of remuneration at this point?'

Mrs Amberny laughed nervously. 'No need for concern, Mr Guilder. You will be recompensed beyond your expectations if your work proves . . . satisfactory. Perhaps we can discuss this further once I've briefed you on what will be involved.'

'Very well, Mrs Amberny. I look forward to doing business with you.'

'Yes.' She laughed again. 'Goodbye.' The screen fuzzed and whined. I broke the connection.

In sunlight, the following day, I discovered that the streets of Violet Way are not quite so glitzy as they appear at night. Crystal trees lining the pavements looked dusty and chipped and I could see that all the buildings were crusted with a grey scale of encroaching unpolished grisacite. I sat in an open-topped hovercar and the inhabitants of the town stared at my unusual colouring. Perhaps they thought I was a new strain of crystal. Anything is possible nowadays.

My driver took me to the outskirts of the town where large residences squatted amid brittle, crystal-scoured trees of gem-like hues. Beyond these manses, I could make out the shimmer of fertile crystal-fields crawling up the sides of gentle hills; above them a cloudless sky of lilac blue. The landscape of this world was beautiful, even if somehow sharp and un-welcoming. That day the air seemed full of salts and minerals that left a metallic taste on the back of the tongue; a contrast to last night's balm. I presumed it not to be toxic.

Just as I could see the gates of Mrs Amberny's house, Violet Way Villa, the road became blocked by a group of people holding banners, milling their way towards the town centre. I leaned forward to speak to the driver. 'What is this nuisance? I'm expected at Mrs Amberny's before lunch.'

'I apologize, Mr Guilder,' the driver replied. 'It's the church, you see.'

'Church? What do you mean church?' I was irritated and decided not to hide it.

'The New Church of Infant Jesus.'

'Oh, for God's sake! What are they doing?'

'Singing, Mr Guilder. They like to sing about sin.'

'As do we all, driver. Is there no way we can get the car through them?'

'Not without injuring them, sir. I advise against that because the Church of the Infant Jesus has considerable voice on Violet Way Council and it might be looked on as an offence if we mow them down.'

'Perhaps it might be quicker to take a detour.'

'As you wish, sir.' The car purred and rose and swung around. I caught a last glimpse of ecstatic, smiling faces in full tongue. It was not a sight conducive to a healthy appetite. There was a banner that proclaimed, 'Denounce the spawn of Satan in our midst'. Perhaps it was a welcoming committee for me.

So, by necessity, I arrived at the back gate to the Amberny estate. This caused confusion with the servants who had all been looking out of the front. The car swept grandly up the rear drive. A fussing gang of white-gloved retainers swooped on me as I alighted from the vehicle and ushered me towards window-doors that led into a sun-lounge at the rear of the house. My driver was shooed away. The gardens were splendid. Long lawns of furry verdaline threads were groomed by huge, white birds wearing collars. Fountains tinkled and plants grew in strained formation over trellises. A woman came hurrying out onto the terrace holding a tall glass clinking with ice. She was tall and skinny, wearing a spare but concealing lilac gown. 'I'm Mrs Amberny,' she said, but I'd guessed that already.

'Tavrian Guilder at your service,' I said and extended my hand. She looked at it quizzically before taking it in her own, which was cold and damp from holding the glass. She was a mature and elegant creature, with coils of upswept red hair and exquisite make-up, but was clearly a stranger to the processes of holding age at bay.

'Won't you come into the house,' she said, directing the way with a graceful hand. I walked beside her. She took a deep breath. 'Forgive me, Mr Guilder, but you aren't quite as . . . well, you don't look as *masculine* as I thought you would.'

'Forgive *me*, Mrs Amberny, but I don't remember you stating any preference as to my appearance.'

She shrugged. 'No matter. You are male, aren't you?'

'In a universe of shifting ambience, I am as male as I can be, Mrs Amberny. What exactly do you require of me?' We were now in the lounge.

'Do take a seat,' she said. 'Have you eaten? No? Splendid. Lunch will be served shortly. I hope you like Asher Tantine cuisine.' I made some polite remark and sat down on a low couch, brushing aside the fronds of a prodigious fern that stood on a table next to it. Mrs Amberny took a stance against a high, white fireplace, where no fire burned. She leaned on the mantelpiece and lit a cigarette; an old-fashioned addiction. At her gesture, a servant glided to my side and mumbled a list of drinks available for my consumption. I expressed my preference and he slipped away.

'What do I require of you?' Mrs Amberny took a long draw of her cigarette; squinting into the smoke, she exhaled on the next breath. She spoke without taking another. 'It is difficult for me, Mr Guilder, because of certain . . . circumstances. Of course, I appreciate that in your profession you must come across many unusual requests.'

I nodded with a smile. 'If you are afraid of embarrassing me, don't be.'

She smiled back. 'That isn't what I'm afraid of, Mr Guilder. What I want you to do is, well, I regret that it is against the law in Violet Way.'

'Really. How intriguing. What is it?'

She sighed and folded her arms. The servant returned with

my drink on a tray. Mrs Amberny kept one eyebrow raised until he had left the room.

'What is it? Well, first I had better explain some of the background to the legal situation. You are aware of our *Church of the Infant Jesus*?' There are few people who have the knack of speaking in italics. Mrs Amberny was one of those privileged with the talent.

'Yes. Some of its devotees were singing in the street outside. We had to take a detour.'

Mrs Amberny nodded. 'Mmm. Quite. Their founder, Matthew Breed, came to Violet Way about a year and a half ago. He came here to Spread the Word.' She raised her arms and rolled her eyes. 'A cursed day, one might say.' Then she paused suddenly, her arms drooping. 'I hope I'm not offending you, Mr Guilder. Do you have any religious beliefs?'

'That depends on whether it's necessary for the job or not.'

She smiled. 'Then I'll continue over lunch. This way please.' A servant had come to hover in the doorway and preceded us into another room. It was entirely white, the dining table an astounding piece of furniture cut from a single gigantic crystal. The only colour was provided by the steaming tureens of vegetables and meat standing in the middle of the table. We sat down and the servant began to spoon helpings of the fragrant food onto our plates. Mrs Amberny smiled appreciatively as I complimented her on the meal. In truth, I found it rather bitter. Mrs Amberny took a glass of wine and twirled the stem in her hands. 'As you no doubt realize, Asher Tantine is not a heavily populated little world and Violet Way is not a large town. We need tourists to survive.'

'I would have thought the crystal farms brought in more than enough revenue,' I said, taking a large mouthful of wine to help cope with the food.

'Of course they do, but they virtually run themselves. There is no need for manual labour and the farm owners jealously guard their land. I should know, I'm one of them. Thus we have a population of people whose families have lived here for hundreds of years with very little to do. Tourism is their livelihood. We sell them crystal stock at a cheap rate (inferior quality, naturally) and they produce curios for off-worlders to purchase. On top of that, we have the hotels, the wilderness package firms, the casinos, and a host of other trades that support the industry.'

'I don't understand what you're getting at, Mrs Amberny. Where do I come in?'

She tapped the wineglass with long, lacquered nails. As yet, she'd made no move to begin eating. 'I told you this request might be unusual. You'll have to bear with me, Mr Guilder.'

I made a contrite gesture. 'I apologize for the interruption.'

'Matthew Breed is a dangerous man,' she said acidly, and lit another cigarette before taking a small forkful of food. Perhaps nicotine improved the taste. 'He comes here with his talk of sin and salvation, his resurrected religion and his unbelievable, unshakeable charisma. He *talks* to our young folk, he infects them and fills their heads with his sanctimonious claptrap! He reviles the evils of drinking, gambling, whoring and dancing. He rants and they listen. It's astounding. At first, he had a following that consisted only of all our subnormal degenerates. They hadn't a hope in the world till he took an interest in them. Now he commands hundreds of our people. An army! Terrifying! The man is an absolute pest! A threat to the livelihood of Violet Way. Of course, as an elder of the town I've had parents coming to me begging for help, but what can I do? The wretched man nicey-niced his way into the town council. At least a third of the councillors are enchanted by him! Now there's talk of setting up religious retreats on Asher Tantine, of closing the casinos and clubs.'

'But Mrs Amberny,' I just had to interrupt, 'why haven't you had him seen to? It's not a Pleasure Giver you need, it's a Life Taker.'

Mrs Amberny made an irritated gesture. 'You don't understand, Mr Guilder. He has too many followers for that. If we had him *removed* tomorrow, it would only increase the zeal and determination of his devotees. Then you'd be talking about civil strife rather than a potential threat of inconvenience.'

'I still don't understand what you expect me to do. Seduce him?'

Mrs Amberny gave a bitter laugh. 'Don't be ridiculous, Mr Guilder. I doubt that even you, with all your reputed talents, could lower the trousers of Matthew Breed. He is above reproach. Don't think we haven't looked into the possibility of trying to discredit him. We have. But there's nothing. He's left a trail of happy Christians right across the galaxy. That may be fine on other worlds, but Asher Tantine is just not big enough to take it. Violet Way certainly isn't. Mr Guilder, it is said that every known form of depravity is an accomplishment with you . . .'

'I'm flattered, Mrs Amberny.'

'You must help us. There is only one way. I could think of no one other than a Pleasure Giver who is sufficiently discreet to perform this service.'

'Which is?'

She squashed out the cigarette on a side-plate, her eyes taking on an eerie, girlish glitter. 'Witchcraft,' she said.

'Witchcraft,' I repeated, to play for time.

'Yes. We must fight fire with fire, or in this case, cult with occult.'

I was sufficiently perturbed to throw down my fork. 'Mrs Amberny, I'm not a witch. And if anyone has said I am it is doubtless because of some petty offence . . .'

'Be quiet, Mr Guilder. I know what you are. In this universe the only person who can be trusted to utter silence is a Pleasure Giver; their income, their life depends on their discretion. As you yourself said, the only other alternative is some sordid kind of hired killer and you've heard my views on that.'

'Perhaps a real witch may be discreet, Mrs Amberny.'

She shrugged. 'Perhaps so, but I was advised against it. Discretion cannot be guaranteed in any profession but yours I trust no one. If Breed found out about what I'm planning, he'd ruin me. I'd be thrown off the council. Frenzied acolytes of the Baby Jesus would tear my crystal fields to shreds with their bare hands. Only witchcraft can remove his allure, and of course, the first policy he instituted on the council was to outlaw all alternative religions. You must do it, Mr Guilder, even if you know nothing about the occult at all.'

'I wouldn't go so far as to say that, Mrs Amberny,' I said, making further investigation of the meal, even though the plate did not appear to be getting any emptier. 'I know a little obviously for, as you said, my work takes me upon unusual paths, but I don't know enough to bewitch someone – if that is what you're implying you want.' My mouth was apparently getting used to the unusual flavours. I discovered that eating was becoming less of a trial. Mrs Amberny still had not taken more than a mouthful.

'Mr Guilder,' she took another breath, 'your name came to me from a *very* reliable source. I can't say more than that. I know of your reputation; no other Pleasure Giver's can rival it. I trust your ingenuity and wit. After lunch, I would like you to return to your hotel to ponder upon the problem. I will see you again tomorrow.'

I rubbed my face with a cautious hand. 'This may seem indelicate, Mrs Amberny, but you did say we could discuss it. How much can I expect to earn if I complete this task?'

She smiled widely. 'How much? Oh, you saw the cruisers at the spaceport no doubt? Well, you could buy all of those and a freighter to transport them on. Is that enough?'

'I'm already working on a solution to your problem, Mrs Amberny.'

'Good boy.'

'One more thing, and it's merely curiosity, why were you so concerned that I should be male?'

'I would have thought that was obvious. You say you know a little about the occult, well, I am female and need to work magic with a male. You will be my High Priest, Mr Guilder, and you will teach me what I need to know.'

I thanked the Infant Baby Jesus I'd shelved the idea of having an additional female orifice implanted before coming here. I raised my glass. 'To our success,' I said and drank. Mrs Amberny smiled.

*

Riding back to the Hotel Evening in Mrs Amberny's own silver hovercar, complete with female chauffeur who had eyes with slit pupils like a cat, I was already considering a certain course of action that could be of immense assistance. Several times my well-trained brain tried to skirt the idea; the sensation of wincing was quite alien to me, but there seemed no alternative. I was under no illusions as to the state of Mrs Amberny's mental health – her solution to the problem was wild and emotional and highly impractical when looked at with an objective eye. However, it was what she wanted and I was in no position to question it. Neither did I want to because it gave me a reason to make a particular holoscreen call that I'd needed an excuse to make for years. This was what was causing the wincing. I was shamefully aware of how my spirits had leapt when she'd mentioned the fateful word: witchcraft. How absurd it sounded in this age of space cruisers and gender implants and black hole bistros. Witchcraft. A dark word that draws one inexorably into the dim, haunted past of our race, to a time when people lay in the mud of Mother Earth and worshipped the sun and the moon. Did anybody nowadays adhere to that ancient religion and wield the ways of the elements? Yes, they did. I'm sure of it because there is a name in my address file beside which I have inscribed the legend, 'Sneaky, snaky WITCH'. It was a bitter time when I wrote that, the extent of the bitterness illustrated by the fact that I've never scrubbed it out. What Mrs Amberny didn't realize was that witches were extremely reluctant to actually harm people, despite popular myth, and especially so in the case of the one of my acquaintance. There was no one else I knew who could help me with this job, and I did need assistance, because my knowledge in this field was slim to say the least. On the one hand I shied from getting involved with this person again, on the other hand, no matter how hard I tried to deny it, I was overjoyed.

I suppose there are two popular images of witches. The first is the raddled hag armed with various parts of batrachian anatomy, and the second is the lissom seductress against whom all men are witless. Pharoah Hallender was neither of these. Half of all available witches are male. Pharoah was born male. The last time we'd met he hadn't changed sex at all, but that had been some time ago. Knowing him as I did, however, he probably had some deep-seated principle about interfering with one's external expression of polarity. I expected him still to be a 'he', although I knew for a fact that his principles didn't extend to refusing rejuvenation. We'd been friends for a while, on a far world that in my memory is a paradise of summer evenings and slow-moving water and shady trees. I can still see his house, dim lights through a veil of fern trees and I can smell the heady incense that smouldered in a dish of ashes on the porch. Our friendship ended with a mis-understanding on his part that left me powerless against a barrier of protection he cast about his house to keep me away. No amount of pleading, contrition, gifts, rage or avowals of love would affect his decision never to speak to me again. It was a long time ago, and I never let anyone get to me like that again, as Lenora Sabling would no doubt have been able to tell you. I only hoped that enough time had passed for his anger to have cooled. He may even be speaking to his sister again by now. They were both beautiful. Was it my fault I couldn't make up my mind?

I paced my bedroom for half an hour back at the Hotel Evening. I kept looking through the door to the other room, eying the holoscreen with aversion and longing. Eventually, I found myself quite suddenly sitting in front of it and speaking his code to the long-distance operator. It must be an old system they have on Asher Tantine. There was a discernible delay before my call clicked through. And then with a shiver and a brief, whining purr, the screen gave me a picture and the face of Pharoah Hallender was before me, enchanting as a dream, exactly the same as the last time I'd laid eyes on it. He wasn't looking into the screen but was leaning down to fiddle with something on the floor, holding a towel unsuccessfully to a tumbling mop of wet, black hair. I could see the room behind him. That, unlike him, had changed. The shawls on the wall looked more expensive than I remembered. Clearly, fortune-telling was an expanding business. 'Yes, who is this?' he said, now peering into the screen. Perhaps they had bad reception at his end.

'An old friend,' I said confidently.

He looked blank. 'Who is this?'

'Tavrian Guilder.' I tried to control a desperate note in my voice.

'*Tavrian Guilder?*' He stared at the screen suspiciously. '*The* Tavrian Guilder?'

'Of course.'

He looked bewildered and my heart gave a helpless leap. 'What do you want?'

'I wondered whether you'd give me some assistance on a contract I have.'

'Are you still a Pleasure Giver?' he sneered.

'Yes. Are you interested? It's just your kind of job.'

'Tavrian, it is painful to remind you that we haven't spoken for years, even more painful to remind you why. I suppose there is a kind of charm in you calling me up like this with such an insulting suggestion. It's almost childlike. I really don't think anything that comes within the line of your profession could ever be termed "just my kind of job".'

'You don't know what it is yet.'

'This is true. Neither do I expect to in the near future.'

'Your words are bleak, but I am encouraged by the fact that you haven't broken the transmission.'

'You have green skin, Tavrian.'

'I know. This woman wants to work some spell or another. I can't talk about it now, but it's beyond my abilities. I thought . . .'

'Tavrian, you have green hair.'

'I know. Are you listening? There's a lot of money to be earned here.'

An interstellar sigh travelled all the way from his world to Asher Tantine.

'All right; tell me.'

'I can't really. It's not a rat promise, Pharoah, I need you. It's genuine, it's lucrative.'

'And where is it?'

'Asher Tantine.'

'Asher who? Is that near Gulfride?'

'Sort of. More near Ilthante.'

Pharoah closed his eyes and shook his head. 'Are you asking me to come there, Tavrian?' he asked in a low, dangerous kind of voice that I knew of old. My finger was poised over the recall button.

'It will be worth it.'

'Do you know how much it will cost me? Is the job that lucrative? Can it possibly be worth it?'

'Yes.'

He sighed. 'Give me directions.' There was a fatalistic note in this. I experienced a thrill of victory. Patience had won. I always knew I'd get the better of him. I wanted to leap up and dance around the room. I'd won – after all this time. He couldn't resist me. He was coming. My elation was bordering on hysteria. Send me packing would you, you little witch? Ha, I'll show you!

'How is the charming Raifina?' I inquired, after delivering the information on where I was. Pharoah did not flicker.

'Fine. Goodbye, Tavrian.'

2

Even on the fastest transport available, Pharoah would not reach Asher Tantine for three weeks or so. Mankind may have conquered the concept of space and its traversal, but was still struggling with the concepts of timetables and connections. I used this time to cast a wary eye over the antics and cavortings of the New Church of Infant Jesus. I went to listen to Matthew Breed speak, but could only stomach it once. There was a newly built church in the middle of town, its walls crystal-scum-free and adorned with framed representations of the man himself. He was a very prominent figure in the town and death was clearly not a spectre he left the light on for. Any enterprising Life Taker could have disposed of him neatly a hundred times a day, so lax was the security around him. His appearance was much as you'd expect; clean cut, shaved raw, eager. His eyes, as is the custom with his type, were exceedingly pale. All men of God tend to look at the world through oysters, I've found. Matthew Breed was, of course, a very rich man.

Mrs Amberny began to twitch when I told her about Pharoah Hallender. The woman was paranoid to the point of delusion. I heaped assurances upon her as to Pharoah's irreproachable discretion. She was only half convinced. More than the downfall of Matthew Breed, she looked forward to being able to wield some kind of power herself. The slap in the face, the appeasing knife thrust, the silver bullet, were denied her because Matthew Breed was too popular to be harmed. In the place of such delights, she longed to gather dark power to her breast and throw it in his direction. Not murder but the curse of ill-luck. Matthew Breed must lose his allure, his sincerity must become questioned by even the most stupid of his followers.

Pharoah Hallender arrived on the evening flight and I went to the Violet Way spaceport to meet him. The customs officials were almost as delighted by his papers bearing the occupation 'Occultist' as they had been with mine. Standing beyond the doors, I could see Pharoah smiling and joking with them as is his way. His tolerance of other humans was one of the few things I disliked about him. When I saw one of the officials extend his hand for Pharoah to read the palm, I decided I must interrupt. Mrs Amberny was meeting us for dinner at a fashionable restaurant in town and I did not want to be late.

'Pharoah,' I said, 'it's me, Tavrian. We have a dinner appointment.' I indicated the door. The customs official looked downhearted. Pharoah followed me out into the sharp fragrance of an Asher Tantine evening. Hire cars hovered hopefully around the entrance to the spaceport. I hailed one and we climbed inside. Pharoah is the kind of person with whom people are irresistibly tempted to fall desperately in love. Not just because of his beauty, which is unique in itself, but because he brims with innocent wonder and vivacity, that is healing and infectious at the same time. I was not surprised when he told me of his success as an Occultist. Even if his predictions were completely made up, which they weren't, people would pay vast amounts of cash just to be soothed by him and listened to. I sat leaning against the door of the car, discreetly appraising him. He was looking out of the window taking in the harsh, splendid sights of Asher Tantine. I still couldn't believe he'd agreed to come. 'I'm pleased to see you, Pharoah,' I said.

He turned and smiled wanly at me. 'Weird kind of place this, isn't it?' he said.

Mrs Amberny fell under the Hallender spell as soon as he swanned into her line of sight, which I considered to be quite an achievement on Pharoah's part. She was quite a hard nut. The restaurant was furnished in dark, midnight blue and startling white. Crystal chandeliers shone dimly from tented fabric. Mrs Amberny was sitting smoking at a table set on a dais at the back of the room, in front of windows through which the night-life of the town could be seen emerging for another evening's rampage. The white cloth of her table was littered with ash; her glass of wine stood half empty. I admired her svelte body in its white gown; she was really quite a stunning creature. Pharoah and I took our places beside her and she summoned a waiter. By now I was thoroughly acquainted with the local cuisine and ordered our meals with calm expertise. Then I had to sit and listen to Mrs Amberny pouring out her heart to Pharoah. She heaped scorn upon the New Church, at which Pharoah twitched uncomfortably. I did not dare look up to witness his response.

'Forgive me, Mrs Amberny,' he said, his voice full of gentle censure, 'but although I can understand your grievance, it would not be appropriate to cast a malison over this Mr Breed. Everyone has a right to their own beliefs, even if they do happen to conflict with your own.'

'You are correct,' Mrs Amberny said, at which I just had to look up. 'And if it was just a case of that, I'd do nothing. But as I explained to your colleague, Matthew Breed will destroy the livelihood of this town, indeed this planet, if he's allowed to continue in his fanaticism. I cannot believe that religious retreats can earn half as much as a single, decent nightclub.'

'Clearly, you are unfamiliar with the Church's reputation in this galaxy,' Pharoah said drily. 'I really don't think you have anything to worry about if it's only the financial aspect that concerns you.'

Mrs Amberny shook her head. 'It's not just that,' she said. 'How can it be right for this parasite to come here and inflict his ways upon our society? It smells of conquest to me. It is empire-building, and I, for one, will fight most vehemently against subjection.'

Pharoah considered her words. 'There is a happy solution to every problem in this universe, Mrs Amberny. I shall just have to find the one for yours.'

After the meal, we rode back to the hotel in silence. The journey took longer than expected because of another detour we had to make around a group of yelling Breed converts. I didn't mind. I was just happy to sit there. Only a few weeks before I would never have dreamed it possible that I'd be in the presence of Pharoah Hallender again, never mind working with him. Another, more rational, part of my brain was flashing warning signals that I was entering a dark and dangerous place, which I ignored. The moment was too sweet. Back at the Hotel Evening, I asked Pharoah to come for a drink in my suite. He said no, he was tired. Then I suggested that he come for a drink and then sleep. His face assumed a hard expression.

'Tavrian Guilder, if you as much as *think* about getting within touching distance of me, I will remove your throat with a blunt instrument. Is that clear? I came here to work. Although I've forgiven you for the past, which is purely the fault of genetic abnormalities on your part, I have not forgotten. You are a trail of slime across the gateway to hell, Tavrian, you are hollow as a rotten mag-fruit. You are as sincere as a starving man who says he is a vegetarian. In short, I despise you.'

'I suppose sex is out of the question then?'

He didn't answer.

The next evening, a car arrived to take us to Mrs Amberny's estate. Pharoah had been locked in his room at the hotel all day, emerging at sundown looking tired. By the time we reached Violet Way Villa he was full of energy again. I guessed he'd found a solution to Mrs Amberny's problem though he was reluctant to tell me what it was. In olden times, a witch would stand and summon up the elements with the power of her own voice; not so in our wondrous golden age of technological miracles. Pharoah had a set of resonating machines, which were housed in four hand-sized silver boxes, enscribed for effect with runic symbols. When activated, these machines produced sounds that conjured up the elemental forces necessary for any occult work within seconds. It took years of training for a human being to achieve such an effect.

Mrs Amberny had cleared a room for us. It overlooked the lawns and was floored in spotless, white marbeline. Pharoah paced the room, sniffing, and then positioned his machines around the edge. Next, he placed long, white candles at each compass point and lit them from a glowing taper. Mrs Amberny turned down the lights and the room became a temple, dim-lit, mysterious, the air hushed.

'Will this . . . *spell* take effect straight away?' Mrs Amberny asked anxiously, in a low voice. 'How many times will we have to do this?'

'It will only have to be done once,' Pharoah replied, setting up his portable altar and draping it with a rich, dark cloth.

'Just once?'

'Trust me, Mrs Amberny. I assure you I know what I'm doing.' He laid out his magical tools on the altar and produced some self-igniting incense from a packet of silver foil. 'I prefer to work naked, Mrs Amberny, though you and Tavrian may wear robes if you prefer. You'll find some in that bag over there. One of them is bound to fit you.'

Mrs Amberny's eyes went quite round as Pharoah wriggled without affectation from his clothes, to reveal a body that looked scrubbed and clean and which I knew would taste of salt. I led our hostess over to the bag. She looked at me once and her eyes said, 'Such hair, such a face, such perfect flesh.' Poor woman.

'Remember, you wanted magic,' I said.

She smiled vaguely and took the robe I put into her hands.

The sun had disappeared beneath the horizon of Asher Tantine. In the white room of Violet Way Villa, we stood within the circle of silver boxes and candle-light, Mrs Amberny and myself clad in sombre black, Pharoah white and naked as a laser. He turned on the machines and went to sing to each in turn. In the east, he sang of air, in the south, he sang of fire, in the west, water and in the north, earth.

'Hear me, oh shining beings of the air . . .'

The machines sang back to him and began to emit a glowing blue-white radiance. Above each box hung a spectral five-pointed star sketched in beams of light, each the size of a man. They were connected by a trembling, glowing cord which formed the circle itself. The candle flames flickered and danced and a faint but rushing breeze brushed Mrs Amberny's red hair back from her face. She stared straight ahead, mouth open. Pharoah never needs a High Priestess because of the incredible control he has over his own polarities. When he needs to be female, he thinks 'female' and he is; it's as simple as that. However, as a concession to Mrs Amberny, and because she was paying us, once he'd cast the circle, he beckoned her to his side. She gingerly stepped forward, timorous as a woman half her age. Already, she was in love with him. He must find his attractiveness quite an inconvenience at times. Beautiful poetry fell from his lips, which Mrs Amberny repeated breathlessly at his side. I closed my eyes and allowed myself the luxury of letting their words drift over me, drinking them in, helping to make them real. I doubted whether Mrs Amberny could understand what we were asking for exactly, because I certainly didn't. The invocation had a weird effect though; I felt quite light-headed. I also experienced a peculiar tickle in the back of my head, the sort that cannot be scratched. Pharoah's voice rose in timbre, Mrs Amberny's leaping gamely behind. Their words described the mystery of the universal fabric. For a while, I stood entranced, only half conscious.

A half-heard sound summoned me to open my eyes. The room seemed different, the atmosphere almost strained. Pharoah threw back his head, and at that very moment the door to the room opened and slammed against the wall with a resounding crack. Mrs Amberny squeaked, distracted from the invocation. Pharoah ignored it. I looked at the door. What I saw there removed the middle section of my courage with one easy slice. How . . . ?

That she'd possessed the ingenuity to follow my trail was astounding enough, but *why* in this universe, did she want to? Surely no one could bear such a grudge that it was worth the time and expense of interstellar travel. There in the doorway stood Lenora Sabling, looking as devilish and powerful as if Pharoah had conjured her up himself. A brief panic turned my veins to wood. Had he? No, surely not. She was looking right at me, black eyes round and wild, black hair sticking up in a crazy halo, red lips smiling. In her hands she held a shiny black object which was pointed right at me. The customs officials may not have recognized it as a weapon, but I did. It was from my collection of antique firearms; another thing I lost in my flight from the sordid relationship.

'Lenora!' I said in surprise. She did not appear to hear me or even notice me at that point, but walked forward a few paces, eying the glowing blue circle nervously. Pharoah had come out of his trance and was looking at her with interest. He did not appear to view this event as unexpected. Mrs Amberny had one hand to her throat, no doubt thinking that this was part of the spell. Lenora turned around sluggishly and saw me. She lifted the gun and I instinctively put up my hands to shoulder height.

'Tavrian Guilder,' she said, 'I'm going to kill you.'

'Don't be hysterical, Lenora,' I said, trying to be reasonable.

'Just a minute, young lady,' Mrs Amberny butted in. 'You can't kill him. He hasn't finished his job yet.'

'Be quiet!' Lenora ordered. She looked drunk. Never in her life had she enjoyed such power, I'm sure. 'Don't look so scared, old woman. It's not your blood I want, it's his! Now Tavrian, perhaps you think this is a selfish gesture on my part. It isn't. You are paid to give pleasure; that's fine. The only problem is, you're so mean, you can only give it when you are paid. Perhaps your work sickens you. Perhaps you find relaxation by giving pain; I don't know. All I know is that you wrecked my life, destroyed my self-respect and shattered my heart.'

'Ah, you'll overlook ruining your best carpet then.'

She wailed in an undignified manner and waved the gun dangerously. 'All right, all right,' I said, hands aloft once more. 'Let me remind you, my dear, you have my hounds, my jewellery, my collections, my cars. Sell them. Then you'll be able to buy a new self-image and a new carpet.'

Now she made an angry, spitting noise. 'Vermin! Get on your knees. Go on: down! I want to see you grovel before you die. No one will ever be destroyed by you again. This is the end, Tavrian. Let your life, such as it is, flash before your eyes. See all those broken lives that have your name burned into their flesh.'

Naturally I would not kneel to her. Who did she think she was? Bullet wounds could be quite nasty, or so I believed. I made a mental calculation about the repairs I could afford, and how much damage I'd receive before death was inevitable. From the way her hands were shaking, I even doubted whether she could score a direct hit. I stepped forward slowly, intending to take the gun from her.

'No!' Pharoah leapt upwards. 'Don't break the circle!' he cried and went to throw himself against me. I can only presume Lenora panicked. There was a shot and then, in an arc of blood, Pharoah Hallender's body flew backwards from my arms, hit the south pentacle and was swallowed in the blue light, disappearing with a short hiss and a curl of pale smoke. I stared aghast at the South. Of Pharoah, all that remained was a streak of dark red upon the floor. Mrs Amberny had gone utterly stiff with shock and said nothing. Lenora was looking round the room as if unsure of how she had got there or what she had done. She had also begun to cry. As I thought: she had no killer instinct. Heedless of whether I was breaking the circle or not, I charged through the ring of light and knocked the gun from her hands. She looked up at me, imploring, helpless.

'Tavrian, Tavrian,' she murmured. It was a nice touch that she died with my name on her lips. I broke her neck.

Mrs Amberny stood, drooping, within the circle. The ring of light spluttered and faded in places, pulses of power running through it. Mrs Amberny was a ghost in its centre. She seemed dazed. Now that the blood-lust had been spent, I was reluctant to cross the glowing threshhold again. I stared at the South, at the stripe of dark upon the marbeline floor. He was gone. He was really gone. For a while I sat on the floor, truly stunned. I'd been given a chance to make amends; Pharoah had come to Asher Tantine at my summons. Now he was dead, and at the hands of another of my self-pitying ex-lovers. What a shitter. Why had I been cruel to Lenora and made her hate me so much? Why indeed had I ever seduced Pharoah's sister Raifina all those years ago? Must I forever blight my own future with vomit-pools of my past?

Lenora was just a dark huddle on the floor behind me. The

gun lay a few feet away, shining blue with reflected light. Mrs Amberny didn't move. The machines hummed and spat. Then a breath of night-air came into the room and a tall, dark figure was drifting past me, bowed and stumbling as if walking in its sleep. It paused, wagging its head from side to side and then passed through the blue light; the current surged and rippled as if it was water. Mrs Amberny raised her head. I scrambled to my feet. Matthew Breed was standing within the circle, facing her. In the vague light, I could see he appeared disorientated, frightened, confused. His clothing was dusty and runkled, his hair in disarray.

'Mr ... Mr *Breed*,' Mrs Amberny said. 'What are you doing here?' In an instant she had recovered all of her poise. Her voice came right from the back of her nose. Matthew Breed shook his head.

'I don't know. At least ...' He looked around the room, seeing nothing. 'Mrs Amberny, I've been meaning to speak to you for some time. At least, I *think* I have. I'm a lonely man, Mrs Amberny. I admire strength in a woman ...' He spoke as if reciting a set of well-rehearsed lines. Mrs Amberny was aghast.

I just began to laugh. Pharoah had found a solution all right and it would harm no one. Admittedly, it was rather more manipulative than he usually felt happy with, but it had worked. Now Matthew Breed was desperately, irretrievably, helplessly captivated by the allure of Mrs Amberny. He loved her, would do anything for her, would worship at her feet until the day he died. The Church of Infant Jesus would mean nothing to him unless the woman he loved was by his side. Naturally, the woman he loved could then more or less dictate what form that church would take. Even in my shocked state, I couldn't help thinking of holy whores, gospel nightclubs and religious holiday gambling events. Ingenious. Even though my face was wet with tears, I couldn't help but laugh. Ingenious!

Order returned to Violet Way Villa. Mrs Amberny discarded

Pharoah's robe and smoothed her creaseless dress. She called for her man-servant and murmured something into his ear, briefly waving a hand in the direction of Lenora Sabling's remains. The man-servant did not even change his expression of bland servility. He nodded and left the room, perhaps to find a spade. With a commanding hand, Mrs Amberny led the confused Matthew Breed into another room. By the time he came to his senses he would have forgotten what he'd seen; the body, the blue light, the blood upon the floor.

I stood for a moment, staring at the fading circuit. A ball of vague light glowed above each of the four boxes as the resonance died. I would not touch the blood upon the floor. As I turned to leave the room, something tapped my shoulder. I looked back. Behind me were clustered a group of shining beings, tall and spectral, glowing with brilliant, shifting colours and emitting strange, half-familiar odours.

'What about us?' one of them said.

'Excuse me? Who are you?' I backed carefully towards the door.

'You summoned us. Now we must be dismissed.'

'And how do I do that exactly?'

The elementals shrugged *en masse*. 'We don't know; that's your job. But we can't leave until we're dismissed.' I could tell they didn't want to stay, but how do you dismiss an elemental? The only person who knew had disappeared in a vapour of his own ichor through the south quarter. Sighing, I pushed through the eerie throng and began turning off the machines. I didn't know whether that would work, but even as I watched the creatures vanished with a slow, vibrating hiss. I went into the next room.

Mrs Amberny didn't want to discuss what had happened. She wrote me a banker's order, gave me instructions on how to cash it at her bank in Violet Way, and then handed me four bags of crystals. 'Thank you for your help, Mr Guilder,' she said, tight-lipped. I wanted to smack her face. Pharoah had died because of her. It made me sick.

'What are these?' I asked her, looking into the bags.

'A fitting payment,' she said drily. 'They are elemental stones, pyratitanite, aqualine, egrecite, cave-diamond. They're worth a fortune. Your business seems risky, Mr Guilder. If I were you, I'd use the revenue from these stones to retire. Here is the declaration certificate; you'll need it to get them off Asher Tantine. It was . . . interesting doing business with you, Mr Guilder.'

Thus, I was dismissed.

I went back to the Hotel Evening and ordered a bottle of liquor to drink in my room. Lying in darkness, I thought about what had happened, glancing occasionally at the four bags of crystals sitting on the bedside table. Pharoah Hallender was dead because of me; that fact was inescapable. There was no way I could blame Mrs Amberny really. Now I would have to contact Raifina and tell her. She would be distraught, alone, in need of comfort. A slow grin curled across my face.

I leaned over to turn on the light and a cold hand gripped my wrist. From nowhere a sylph had materialized by my side. This was a creature of the air, tall and gaunt and robed in grey-blue. Its touch was icy, a breathless wind raised its long, tawny hair from its back. 'You did not dismiss us, Tavrian Guilder,' it said menacingly. 'We are still here and we want to go home. You must dismiss us.'

'How?' I cried. 'The witch who summoned you is dead! It's nothing to do with me! Pester Mrs Amberny instead.'

The sylph looked at my bedside table. 'You have the crystals,' it said.

'Yes.'

It folded its arms. 'They have the power to return us to our lovely realms. Give them to me and we may leave.'

'And if I don't?'

'We shall be with you always and we shall be *very* unhappy. Have you ever been in the company of an elemental who's very unhappy?'

'No, I can't say I have.'

'Not many people can. They don't last long enough to tell anybody about it.'

'Take the crystals,' I said and held out the bag of egrecite, the air stones. With a puffing sound, both elemental and bag were gone. I lay back on the bed and sighed, wiping a mist of perspiration from my brow. Had the others returned to their realms as well, or was I going to have to give away all my crystals before I was safe? This job had gone thoroughly sour on me. Mrs Amberny's suggestion seemed attractive. Retirement, if only as a temporary condition. But without the crystals, I wouldn't have enough to finance such a plan. Saving had never been one of my strong points. Easy come, easy go. I felt as if I wanted to turn my back on the whole human race. None of them was fit to receive pleasure, no matter how much they paid for it. I wanted out.

About an hour later, an undine pooled itself into existence on my bedroom floor. This was a water elemental, naked and beautiful and quite without qualms about taking my crystals. The aqualine had to go. Tomorrow I would leave this world, crystals or no crystals.

By dawn I thought I was safe but was accosted by a gnome in the hotel corridor, a dark, brown-robed entity of Earth who smelled of rich, carrion fed soil and who rudely demanded my cave-diamonds even as a hovercar waited outside to take me to the spaceport.

Carrying only a bag of pyratitanite, I boarded the cruiser that would take me to Ganymede East. I knew it to be a quiet, tranquil place. I needed time for reflection; anywhere else would just be too damned fast.

3

Asher Tantine receded beneath me. I watched it from a window in the cruiser's cocktail lounge; a small, revolving jewel, mother gem, fertile in her own bristly, spiky way. In my pocket the bag of pyratitanite remained intact. I sat down on a sofa and picked up a newspaper, another anachronism of the quaint world I was leaving. The journal informed me that already Mrs Amberny and Matthew Breed had announced their nuptuals. Some people, at least, were happy. I put the paper down on a nearby table. Although no longer as rich as I could have been, the pyratitanite would secure me a modest future. If I was careful, and invested it wisely, there would be no need for me to work again. On top of that, I had Mrs Amberny's money. As soon as I reached civilization I would have it changed into standard credits. It could grow, as long as I wasn't stupid with it. I didn't want to lower my standard of living, which was disproportionately high, but neither had I the stomach for work at the moment. Perhaps this would change. Perhaps not. After a while, I decided to go to my cabin and contact Raifina Hallender.

The cabin was in darkness. I fumbled for the light, passing my hand back and forth over the heat sensitive panel that should have turned it on as I entered. Nothing happened. Grumbling, I backed out with the intention of finding a steward to complain to.

'Wait,' a voice hissed. This voice smelled of sulphur and ashes. The door slammed shut behind me and I pressed my back against it. 'You did not dismiss us, Mr Guilder.'

'Oh no, not again,' I whimpered. A salamander is not a cute little lizard as you might expect. It is an eight-foot flaming warrior who takes no shit from anybody. Now there was one in my cabin holding out its hand. Goodbye retirement. 'The crystals . . .' I began.

'However,' the salamander interrupted, 'because of the arrival of a certain Pharoah Hallender in our laps, it was not necessary in our case anyway.'

I breathed a sigh of relief and then said, 'Why are you here?' The salamander folded its arms, drops of liquid flame from its hair causing unusual holes in the fire-resistant bedspread.

'Well, we thought you ought to be offered a choice. After

all, Pharoah Hallender is known to us. We have worked with him many times. My brothers thought you might want to give us the crystals instead.' It extended a glowing hand and illuminated the bed. Now I could see that within it lay the body of Pharoah Hallender, his breast rising and falling gently, his black mane covering the pillows, his shoulders, the sheets. His colour was healthy; there seemed no sign of injury. 'You can keep him or the crystals,' the salamander said. 'It's really up to you. Mrs Amberny gave you the stones. Pharoah cannot give them to us.'

'And what will happen to him if I keep the crystals?' I asked.

The salamander shrugged. 'It is doubtful whether he'd survive long in the realm of fire, at least not in this form.'

I walked over to the bed and looked down. 'Take your time,' the salamander said sarcastically. Beautiful Pharoah. Forever a boy, full of love and life and laughter. He also hated me. I was everything he despised and loathed, and it took an awful lot for him to despise and loathe anything, however foul it was. I realized that once the salamander had gone, it would be quite possible that Pharoah Hallender would still hate me just as much. On the other hand, if I let the fire elementals keep him, I could retire and remove him from my system altogether by forgetting about him. If only I could know now what he'd be like when he woke up.

The salamander cleared its throat. 'The crystals or the witch, Mr Guilder?'

Too bad. I turned my back and said, 'Take him.'

Or at least I thought I did. It was like someone else was in my body saying, 'Take the crystals. And go.' The salamander whipped the bag from my hand with an air of glee. Pharoah stirred and writhed upon the bed. Had I really said that? No, of course I hadn't.

'You have just ruined me,' I said.

He sat up and brushed the hair from his eyes. 'Where are we?'

'Aboard a cruiser on its way to Ganymede East.'

'The spell worked?'

'Yes, with your own inimical mark upon it.'

'A sticky moment. I was nearly lost.'

I threw up my hands in disgust. 'Pharoah, I have just saved your life! All I've earned from this venture is enough to keep me well-fed for three weeks!'

'On the contrary. You have also learned a very important lesson. But it wasn't you who saved my life, Tavrian. If I hadn't been so resourceful, at this very moment you would be speaking to my sister Raifina and doubtlessly arranging to meet her somewhere.'

'Don't you trust me?' I asked acidly, aware that an unfamiliar tinge of real anger was colouring my voice.

He rolled his eyes. 'As I said; childlike.' He hopped from the bed. 'I'll have to use some of your clothes for the time being, Tavrian.'

I sat down on a chair, dejected, as he rummaged through my bags. A thought was hammering through my brain; I'd disobeyed my own, first commandment. Walk away, always walk away. For Pharoah, I'd turned back. What lesson had I learned from this, other than to trust my own instincts? I should have told Mrs Amberny I didn't want the job, couldn't do the job. But no. I just had to use it as a means to lay eyes on the incomparable Pharoah Hallender once more, thinking I could turn the tables. Now I was a wreck, defenceless, bleeding, directionless. 'Why aren't you dead?' I asked, dully.

He carried on rummaging. 'What? Oh, I always take precautions. Only a fool wouldn't and I'm certainly not that.'

'So it's back to where we were, is it, when you first arrived on Asher Tantine?'

Pharoah turned and smiled at me sweetly. 'Not exactly,' he said. 'I never bear a grudge. You obviously like me, Tavrian, so I'm prepared to let bygones be bygones.' I stood up and held out my arms in premature relief. He raised a cautionary finger. 'However, I feel it's only fair to warn you that should you attempt any course of action that may cause me harm or grief, I shall have to put your new psychological implant into play.'

'What do you mean?'

He came and kissed me briefly on the lips. 'Tavrian, two spells were worked in Mrs Amberny's house. The bewitchment of Matthew Breed was child's play, and took me barely a minute. The potential for his affair with Mrs Amberny was there already; I soon worked that out. So, it required hardly any effort at all to remove the obstacles, namely the more unsavoury aspects of his moral character. The other work took more time, but I am happy to say that it too was successful. Tavrian, I can govern your words. I can make you say anything I want to. I can govern your actions too. As you can no doubt predict, this could cause you considerable embarrassment should I wish to exercise it.'

'You monster,' I croaked. 'I'll fight you! I . . .'

Pharoah shook his head and smiled. 'No, no, no, Tavrian, you can't. If you need an illustration of the effectiveness of this technique, cast your mind back to how Lenora Sabling answered my call.'

'What?' My croak had degenerated into an undignified squeak.

Pharoah shrugged carelessly. 'Naturally, I had you investigated, Tavrian. Did you really think I'd come to Asher Tantine unarmed?'

'I could have been killed!'

Another shrug. 'I doubt it. Did you see the way her hands were shaking? Anyway, I wouldn't have let her. That wasn't part of my plan. Foolish of you to try and break out of the circle. Foolish of me not to have protected myself more thoroughly; an oversight. Still, the salamanders burned me into health again. It's fortunate that I have such an excellent relationship with them. Perhaps the injury was karmic punishment for my display of pride, but I'm afraid I couldn't resist it. I have no excuse. You've tasted the extent of my power, Tavrian. It has grown considerably since we last met. I haven't been idle these past few years. You humiliated me in the past, before my family and friends. It's bad for you to get away with things like that and I looked upon it as my duty to make sure you don't in the future. You thought you were so clever, calling me to help you, didn't you? I expect you thought it an easy way to squirm yourself back into my bed.' He laughed delicately, which stung as much as a slap across the face. 'But it was I who wove the web and drew you to its centre. You came like a child; a role that suits you, incidentally. Your brutishness does have a strange, infantile quality.'

I could not speak. The inhuman enormity of his plan appalled me. He touched my cheek. 'Don't look so downhearted, Tavrian. Some of your qualities disgust me but you are still beautiful, witty and proficient in the arts of pleasure. I loved you once; perhaps I can learn to do so again. We shall have a long and happy life together now. You earn a fortune as a Pleasure Giver, don't you? All you needed was a manager to stop you wasting your commissions. Coupled with the fact that I've removed the claws that used to lead you astray, I think you're now the ideal mate.'

My body had become icy cold.

'Poor Lenora,' Pharoah said, shaking his head. 'I hope she can organize the threads of her life again. I wanted to see to her before we left but . . . well. You didn't hurt her did you? How is she?'

'Oh, she's all right,' I managed to say. He didn't know everything and things were bad enough for me as it was.

'What she said was right, you know,' Pharoah said. 'You did destroy people with your heartlessness, but it certainly won't happen again. Now, I'm hungry. Is there a good restaurant on this boat?'

I'm not naturally a vindictive person . . .

WHITE NOISE

by
Garry Kilworth

Garry Kilworth won the first Gollancz/*Sunday Times* SF competition in 1974 and has since published over fifty stories. He is arguably Britain's best British short SF author. (He's five foot tall, and he'll argue with anyone.) His dozen books include *In Solitary* (science fiction), *The Street* (horror), *Witch-water Country* (general fiction) and *The Songbirds of Pain* (short stories). He describes his latest novel, *Hunters Moon*, as 'anthropomorphic fantasy' – but it's really about foxes.

*My grandfather, bedridden at the age of eighty, was once an
American football fanatic. They used to show the game on British
TV every Sunday evening and this hour was the centre of his
whole week. He knew nothing about the game, but was fascinated
by it. To him it was a strange cultural activity which outsiders
were permitted to witness but from whom insight was withheld. It
might have been an Aztec ceremony or a Maori dance. Then one
day some commentator decided to explain the rules of the game to
new viewers. Thereafter, he lost interest completely. It was the
mystery behind the ritual that had fascinated him, and after the
revelation all the magic evaporated. He found something else that
he didn't know about, and watched that instead.*

I was sitting at a street table under the awning of an Arab
coffee stall. Ben, my chief engineer, was drinking *mazqul*, a
coffee too bitter for my palate. Having been raised in Italy, he
was used to thick brown sludge. I drank orange juice.

It was evening and the sound of the muezzins calling the
faithful to prayer could be heard floating over the rooftops. I
suspected that like some English churches, with their tape
recordings of bells, the voices came from hi-fi speakers situated
at the top of minarets. Despite the fact that I was (and still
am) the Regional Telecommunications Manager in an in-
dependent Arab state, I dislike this dehumanizing approach.

Ben was talking about two of our technicians who had
recently been sent to check on an installation on the shores of
the Red Sea.

'They didn't go in,' he said. 'They were scared.'

My company's head office is in London, where they recruit
telecommunications personnel for overseas appointments.
Ben, now thirty, had joined us as a nineteen-year-old and his

English was impeccable. His full name was Peter Benoni and like myself he was a telecommunications man through and through. If you get into telecomms early enough, it becomes a religion. Ben was the same. We cut our teeth on morse keys, accepted the coming of teleprinters with eagerness, hailed the introduction of satellite communications and were patiently awaiting worldwide networks of fibre optic cables. One of its attractions was that it was continually changing, progressing, and its mysteries deepened rather than were resolved.

Ben seemed angry for some reason, as if the fact that the technicians had failed to do their work was a slight on him, personally. He had recently been through a terrible ordeal and I knew I had to be patient with his apparent moodiness.

'Scared?' I said. I couldn't think why the two Arabs should be frightened to enter a cable station. There was nothing in these unmanned buildings except terminals, where the undersea cable was converted to overhead cross-country lines.

'Yes, afraid.'

'What of?' I was thinking of terrorists – republicans opposed to the royalist government – but Ben's reply surprised me.

'They say it's haunted, the cable station.'

'I don't understand.'

A pi-dog slunk under the table looking for scraps. Ben moved it on gently with his foot. The creatures were covered in tics and fleas.

'Not much to understand. They're a superstitious lot.' He flicked a dead fly from the tabletop. There was contempt in his voice. 'They're terrified of ghosts. What can you expect?'

'I expect them to do their jobs. *Haunted?* The cable station? What about that old fort where they spend the night? Surely there are more ghosts in places like that than a newly-built cable station?'

Ben shrugged. We talked a little more, but the darkness had closed in around us and I wanted to be back in my rooms. I agreed with Ben that the best idea was to visit the station ourselves. At least we would get some first-hand knowledge of the situation and as manager I was expected to cover my region, checking on all installations at least once a year. Now was a good enough time as any to inspect Wadi Haalla.

Back in my quarters I began packing a few items for the trip the next day. Now that it was dark and the town was silent except for the dogs, sounds began to travel farther. I could hear Ben behind the thin walls, in his own apartment. He paced up and down for about thirty minutes, his flip-flops slapping on the tiled floors. Then he began his nightly prayers. I sat on the edge of my bed, the droning more irritating to me than the whine of a mosquito. Finally I put my hands over my ears. I had nothing but contempt for Ben's devotions. I had long since discovered that there was no God.

We set off the next morning. Apart from provisions we carried rifles in the Land Rover, since terrorist activity was reaching alarming levels. Ben had recently been kidnapped by some republican extremists and though he escaped he had to walk three days in the desert to get back to civilization. Characteristically, he maintained that it was his faith that had kept him alive. Once, when I asked him what that meant, he went into a tiresome lecture. The crux of his argument appeared to be the need for belief without conclusive proof.

'The existence of absolute proof negates the need for *faith*,' he said, 'and without faith we would be nothing more than automatons.'

The tyres of the vehicle hummed on the hot asphalt until we had gone about fifty miles, when we left the tarmac and followed a dirt track between two mountain ranges. Ben was silent most of the way. Sullen and uncommunicative, he left me to stare at the gravel wastes as we bumped and bounced along. I tried to fight the despair that hunted me down at moments like this, but it was a persistent predator, intent on devouring me.

We camped for the night at the foot of some rocks that rose like lava tongues out of the dust. I sucked on a bottle of scotch that I'd packed the night before, and sensed Ben's disapproval. He busied himself around the campsite while I got quietly drunk.

I lay back in the stillness of the desert, staring up at the stars. I thought about Sally. Sally had died in an aircraft accident, on her way out to join me. It had taken her a long time to decide, but once her mind had been made up, she wrote to me that she was on her way. Ironically, I knew that she was already dead by the time I received the letter. They said that there was a bomb on the plane, but no one knew for sure. What I never understood was, why Sally? I know, I know, *why anyone*, but Sally – Sally bubbled with enthusiasm for life. Why not some bastard the world would be better without? Why not some suicide, bent on going anyway? I know these things are not meant to make sense, but they damn well *should* do. I felt sure, absolutely sure, that if there had been a God he would never have wiped out Sally. She had done nothing but sung His praises all her life, and actively worked on His behalf. Why would He kill one of His most ardent supporters or even allow her to die? No, it *didn't* make sense, and therefore there was no God. Ben was wasting his breath on worshipping a void. The whole thing was a blank, a mistake. There was nothing to look forward to after death. And that was the worst thing – the very worst thing about it.

I finished the bottle, throwing it out amongst the rocks and enjoying the sound of breaking glass. I still found it hard to get to sleep. Even a day in the desert gives one a kind of circular mental perspective. The tedium of mile on mile of gravel and rock *must* make some impression on the mind. I used to think, before I came to know the desert, that such a place would leave one's head uncluttered and receptive. In fact, the real experience is quite the opposite. You tend to lock into a set of thoughts that go round and round, like those of an insomniac, and if you do not take care you begin to translate particular obsessions into visual images. Mirages. Each time I go back in I am surprised by the swiftness with which an empty desolate landscape can work on an active mind. After a walk in the desert one might see an ordinary bush burning and believe it to be something miraculous.

At noon two days later, we reached our destination. Ben and I had not been speaking to each other over the last few rugged miles. Some trivial argument had left us both feeling aggrieved: a common enough problem out in the wilderness. Once we got back to town we would forget it quickly enough.

The cable station was perched on a knoll above its surroundings. Between the sea and this hill, and stretching for several miles on either side, were the coastal marshes. It was a typical river delta, which would be completely flooded in the rainy season, but at the moment the wadi was only ankle deep in brackish water, maintaining the life of the reed beds around the station.

In the noon-day sun the rushes looked crisp and brown, rippling gently in the hot onshore breezes from the Red Sea.

The place was alive with insects, which danced in clouds above the tips of the reeds: a quiet, eerie landscape which had not changed in thousands of years. There was an alarming sense of a brooding past which hung over the region. It whispered of papyrus and reed boats, of infants abandoned in watertight cradles amongst the rushes. It murmured of fishers and hunters, and primitive tribal religions. And over the whole of the rock and dust hinterland, a throbbing heat, a moody sense of injustice over some imagined neglect.

The station on the top of the hill was the only object, natural or artificial, that anchored us in the modern world. It was the junction for the undersea telephone cable from Cairo. It was a simple square structure, built to house line checking equipment and terminals. On its land side, the incoming cable became overhead wires looped across the desert rockland on poles, and up, over the mountains, to the exchange in the nearest town.

We were making our way up the slope to the station, when Ben suddenly stopped and turned to stare out over the shimmering marshland.

'What's the matter?' I asked.

He waved a hand at me. 'Listen!'

I listened but could hear only the station. Someone had left a speaker plugged into a line and white noise was hissing out.

'No wonder the technicians were scared,' said Ben, after a few moments.

'What? I can't hear anything.'

'That's just it – we should be hearing wildlife. These marshes are crammed with creatures – birds, frogs, cicadas. They're normally singing their heads off.'

He was right. I hadn't noticed how quiet it was. Ben started off down the slope, and I followed him. If something was nagging at him, we would have to get it sorted out before going up to the station. I really could not understand what all the fuss was about. So the marshes were quiet? So what?

We went into the boggy ground and Ben searched amongst the tall grasses. I was hot. Sweat had soaked the back of my shirt. My hat was uncomfortable and my scalp prickled with the heat. I just wanted to get the job done and find a cool place to rest. Pretty soon he picked something up and held it out to me. A small green frog rested on his palm.

'Well?' I snapped.

'They're here,' he said, his dark brown eyes looking puzzled, 'but they're not making any sounds. That isn't natural, you have to admit.'

The creature's small black eyes seemed fixed on some distant horizon that was hidden from us. There was something about its position which for a moment suggested genuflection. I started to laugh. The situation was becoming ludicrous and our imaginations were running away with us. There was something quite sinister in the air, but I couldn't pin it down, and laughing helped to dispel it.

Ben's eyes were on my face at that point, but then he turned his head, very slowly, until his gaze was high above my left shoulder, and distant. He was staring at the cable station.

'It's listening to *that*,' he said.

I began to get annoyed.

'The white noise? Oh, come on. What are you, a zoologist now? How can you tell what it's listening to, if anything at all. This is crazy, Ben.'

I should have taken the initiative at that point. I should have left him there and marched up to the shack, disconnected the speaker, and begun the checks. If I had done that, I'm sure he would have shaken out of the mood he had suddenly fallen into. The practicalities of the work would have taken over, and he would have slipped into his routine. However, I did not do this. I simply waited, my impatience increasing with every moment, for Ben to put down the frog and get to work himself.

Finally he replaced the creature in the reeds and made his way up the slope to the station. I followed behind. There wasn't a lot of point in remonstrating with him. I'm not one of these autocratic managers anyway. I prefer reaching decisions democratically.

We unlocked the door to the building and entered the confined space. Musty, stale air hit us. The station was like an oven inside.

Sure enough, someone had left a speaker plugged into the line. There were microphone implants in the cable repeater units all along the sea bed. What we were hearing over the speaker was the noise of the ocean floor. The mikes helped us identify any interference with the cable, by sharks, or fishing nets, any external agent.

Ben disconnected the speaker and plugged a set of headphones into the same channel. Then he sat on a dusty stool and began listening intently to the white noise, the backwash of sounds from the sea bed. I stood and watched him for a while, but there was little I could do while he was sitting at the console, so I left him to it. I went outside to get some air. There were checks I had to make, too, but I wanted Ben to finish his work first, and leave me alone in the station.

I crossed the marshland, wary of snakes, to reach the beach. There, the thick black cable emerged from the ocean. Out on the Red Sea a dhow was treading slowly westwards, following an ancient road to Africa. I studied the point where the cable came out of the water like a satanic python slithering up the beach. Snakes. Satan. All my images were biblical. I couldn't even string a set of thoughts together without a religious intrusion, damn it. God and all his trappings had been invented by some sadist to torment people like me.

I must have fallen asleep, and some time later, perhaps an hour, a shadow fell over me. I woke, startled. Ben was standing there. He had a rifle in the crook of his arm and his eyes had taken on that intense look which meant he was disturbed about something.

'What's the matter?' I asked.

'Come and listen,' he answered.

I followed him to the station, wondering why he had gone back to the Land Rover for the gun. Was he expecting trouble? I asked him, but got no reply. Once in the station, he motioned for me to put on the headphones. I did so and my head was immediately swamped with white noise. There was a faint rumbling thunder, like surf crashing over groynes. A kind of hollow booming. Breakers along the beach? What did it mean? I took off the headphones and looked up at Ben, inquisitively.

'Do you hear it?' he said.

'Do I hear what?'

'The *noise*. The noise of the battle. It's coming directly from the sea bed. Cold current tapes – remember the article from Comms Monthly? I cut it out and left it on your desk.'

I was wilting in the oppressive heat. The situation seemed to be a little unstable. I said, 'Have you done the checks?' and he looked at me as if he were exasperated.

'The article,' he insisted. 'About the American submarine. Last year they were doing an oceanic survey and they picked up the noise of sea fights on the mikes they placed on the sea bed. I talked to you about it at the time.'

I recalled the article now. 'Yes, I do remember. They came to the conclusion that cold currents retained sound impressions . . .'

'That's it. Cold, dense water is less likely to disperse, or be infiltrated by warm streams. The circular currents weave their way intact around the ocean floor like blind worms.'

'And they retain sound patterns . . .'

'Like magnetic tape. When the scientists from that survey analysed the recordings they discovered they were listening to sea battles from the First World War.'

'So they say – it must have been guesswork. Anyway, you think that's what we've got here? Sounds of battle? What, from the Six Day War? Or Yom Kippur?'

Ben shook his head vigorously. 'No, not that. Not so recent. Some of the cold currents in these regions have been around for thousands of years.'

'And?'

'So what we're receiving from our mikes is an *ancient* fight – a retreat across the Red Sea. Listen again.'

He looked very wild and I obediently put on the headphones. I wanted to say something banal, about getting the job done, doing the checks, finishing up, and *then* perhaps discussing weird phenomena, but the atmosphere was tense. I felt myself being mentally pressured into humouring his mood. My idea at that time was to listen, to agree with him that he could be right, then suggest we do the work before the day ran out on us.

So, I listened.

'Close your eyes – concentrate,' said Ben.

I did as he asked. The problem with putting on a set of headphones is that you effectively lock out the rest of the world. You enter another world completely and you find that all your attention is directed towards the sounds in your head. After a while I *could* hear faint shouts and yells, under the rush and hiss of the white noise. Perhaps, perhaps the rumbling of wheels, the rattle of metal . . .? I tried rejecting these ideas and replacing them with the thought of trawler nets snagging the cable, or predatory fish worrying the repeaters. It didn't work. These were different sounds. I had heard that sort of interference and it was nothing like the noise coming from the headphones now. These were *new* sounds, the like of which I had not heard before. I began to get excited. Surely Ben was right! I could hear it. However, I know that if you listen to something hard enough, with preconceived notions, suggestion fills any hollows. I tried to clear my head, listen objectively. Still, I could hear the shouts, the clashing of – what? – bronze swords on shields? Surely those sharp cracks were whips? I looked up at Ben. His eyes were shining strangely. I took off the headphones.

'We have to tape this,' I said. 'Have it analysed.'

'I don't think that's a good idea.' He glanced at the console and then at me again. 'I don't think that's a good idea at all.'

I was surprised. Ben was one of those men who are passion-ately in favour of finding new uses for telecomms equipment. He loved to experiment with such things. What the hell was he playing at now?

'What's wrong with it?' I asked, calmly.

'We might hear something that would destroy us.'

His eyes had taken on a heavy hooded appearance and he began to fiddle with the rifle's safety catch. I did not have a clue what he was talking about, but his whole attitude made my skin prickle with apprehension.

He nodded at the headphones, which were still gushing out their sounds of battle. 'What we have here,' he said, slowly, 'is the flight from Egypt – Moses and his people.'

'Moses,' I repeated.

'That's right.' He paced up to the small window at the end and stared out at the sea. I was sweating heavily and I could feel the wetness trickling down my neck. Ben still seemed calm enough, holding the rifle loosely in the crook of his arm. I noticed that the safety catch was now off. My heart was racing but my brain felt leaden.

'You see,' he said, 'although there was a path across the Red Sea – the parting of the waters – there must have been water all around them, towering above them. A tunnel of water, recording the events that took place on the ocean bed. The crossing of the Red Sea. The flight from Egypt. You know where we are. It happened *here*.'

I heard screams coming from the speakers. The sounds of water rushing into a gap. Horses whinnying in fear. Harsh calls from the mouths of men who were used to being masters. Again, the cracking of whips, the slapping of leather harnesses. The rumble of chariot wheels. Surely I was just fitting images to random noises? *Fata Morgana*. Sound mirages.

'Impressionable,' I heard myself muttering. 'The desert softens our brains and suggestions leave imprints. We are seduced by each other's imaginations. We must be careful of our theories, we . . . our perceptions are warped out here. Too eager. That frog, for example . . .'

'The frogs and crickets? They know. They're waiting to hear.'

'Hear what?'

He turned to face me. He seemed completely in control of himself. 'The voice of God,' he said, simply.

I rocked back a little on my seat. Although he had spoken the words soberly, quietly, I felt as if he had shouted at me in rage. I was disorientated for a moment and had to pull my thoughts together, to regain my equilibrium.

'The voice of God,' I repeated, slowly.

'God spoke to Moses, and if we're right, that what we're listening to on that speaker is the flight from Egypt, then it will not be long before we hear the voice of God.'

Suddenly he strode across the room, reached over me, and pulled out the plug, so that we were in silence.

'What? – what the hell are you doing?' I cried.

He stared hard at me. 'We mustn't hear it,' he said. 'This is not meant for our ears. If we were to hear God speak, we would *know*. We would know for sure. If would make a worthless thing of faith.'

'You're crazy.'

'Perhaps, but I don't want to take the chance. Maybe God didn't speak to Moses while he was making the crossing. Maybe I'm all wrong about the whole thing. But I can't risk it.'

I knew his ideas on the evils of *proof absolute*, how such a thing would destroy the soul, the need for a spirit within a mortal. But what about *my* needs? Didn't I get a choice? I knew what I wanted, too. I had seen a way out of the grief that had been troubling me for so long. There was a way the nightmares could end, a way the cycle of obsessive thoughts could be broken. As far as I was concerned Ben could go to heaven or hell, so long as it could be proved that such places existed outside the human imagination.

I reached for the plug.

'Go and stuff – your ears. I want to know if I'm going to see Sally again – I want . . .' I felt a blow behind the left ear and I staggered, half falling, half crawling, to the open doorway.

'You bastard –' I began, but he pushed me through the

doorway, into the dust outside. I stumbled away, thinking he was crazy enough at that moment to shoot me in the back. My guts were churning with fear. I heard him firing the rifle in the station. I guessed he was destroying the console so that I would not be able to go back and record the sounds. By the time I had it repaired, the cold current would be gone. I reached the bottom of the hill and fell on my side, panting.

The next moment there was a tremendous explosion which rocked the whole delta. A hot wind blasted my cheek and I was showered with grit and small stones. When I was brave enough to look back, I could see that the station had been gutted. Although the walls were still standing, the window had been blown out and the roof had gone. Fire engulfed the interior.

'Ben, you bastard,' I screamed with rage. 'I wanted to hear. I wanted to hear His voice.'

Eventually I was able to approach the fire. There was an acrid smell coming from the charred ruins. Black smoke still billowed from the smouldering brickwork. I could not see any body, but then I couldn't get close enough to look inside the walls. It crossed my mind that Ben might have fired the station on purpose, from outside, and run away into the hills. Then again, he might have decided that the beginning of the end of faith was so near that he wanted to become a martyr to its cause.

The station would have to be rebuilt and by that time the cold current would have moved on. Perhaps it wouldn't pass this way again for another ten, fifty, even a hundred years or more? The old feeling of despair was on me again. Ben must have hit one of three drums of emergency fuel we kept stored under the back bench, for visiting vehicles.

Ben was one of those men like my grandfather. He needed a mystery. It might have been hi-tech electronics, or the wonders of the atom, or even American football – but it wasn't any of those. It was religion.

With the black smoke of the funeral pyre of *proof* obscuring the blue sky, I climbed back into the Land Rover and started the engine. Out in the marshes a change had taken place. The frogs were singing once again.

GARDENIAS

by
Ian McDonald

Ian McDonald was born in Manchester, but left there for the peace and quiet of Belfast. His stories have appeared in *Isaac Asimov's Sf Magazine* and *Other Edens 2*. In 1985 he was nominated for the John W. Campbell Award for best new science fiction author. His first novel was *Desolation Road*, published in the USA in 1988 simultaneously with *Empire Dreams*, his first collection; and his second novel, *Out on Blue Six*, has recently been published – also in the USA.

There is death in the Barry-O tonight but still they come down from the neon and lasershine of Hy Brazyl, the five of them. They have given themselves names, as the ones who come down will, names like Zed and Lolo and Cassaday and the Shrike and Yani. Noble they are, comely, their fathers are Company men, bound by blood and contract, their mothers are Company women; they are born to live lives of lofty altitude among the crystal pinnacles of Hy Brazyl. So: why have they exchanged their Projects and *corporadas* for the tar-paper and plastic *favelas* of the Barry-O, where the faces have no contracts and no consequence and the rain washes the names from the streets?

Because they are searching: dark she, bright she, silent she, sullen he, laughing he; they are searching for a place they have never seen, yet they know it as well as they know the luminous spires of their *corporadas*. Better, for ever since they first heard of it as a dark whisper in the arcades and bodegas where the young ones go, it has burned like a star in their imaginations. Their flashlight beams lance out through the needles of the rain that are always always always driving down hard, hard on the Barry-O, driving photophobic creatures wrapped in plastic polywrappers to shelter behind the piled garbage sacks. There is disease down here. There is quick, flashing death along the edge of a Barry-O blade beaten from old beercans, folded and forged and re-folded and re-forged. The people of the Barry-O remain eyes in their favela windows and leave the night and the rain to the garbagesellers and the razorboys and the brilliant creatures of the Company. Their flashlight beams go before them as they come splashing through ankle-deep rainwater streaming down the hills of the Barry-O. And there, shouldering out of the shadowlands, is the place their imaginations have burned for. In the days when the streets remembered vehicles, it was a multi-storey car-park; twenty-two levels of rentable space. Now, streaked and stained by acid rain, its former identity is submerged under the jungle of power conduits and ducts and cables and home-brew chicken-wire power-beam dishes. The web of cables spasmodically drips fat blue sparks onto the paving slabs.

For a moment they hesitate, these children of light. For a moment some might turn back. But one steps forward through the cascade of blue arclight: the dark girl, the one who calls herself Zed, and the power she draws out of the night and the warm rain calls the others after her; bright she, silent she, sullen he, laughing he. The lower levels are piled to the ceiling with black plastic refuse sacks. Weaving flashlight beams disclose furtive movements of blacque on blacque, lines of wet sylver drawn along blade-edges. Whatever it is that rests in this place of heart's desire, it has its guardians. Death beats its wings in the abandoned car-park, and then with a rush, it is gone.

'I don't know about this . . .' The breathermask mutes his words, his identity; only the eyes of the boy who calls himself Yani can be seen and they are not laughing now. Lose a little of that Project arrogance, that Hy Brazyl braggadocio, child.

The endless rain has leached little calcite stalactites out of the ceiling joints: the lights transform the beads of water at their tips into pearls. The dark girl, the one who calls herself Zed, rips off her breathermask. It clatters across the drip-stained concrete. She breathes in the rot and the stink and the pus.

'Then go back.' She goes to the boy, strokes his hair with the back of her fingers. 'Go on. It's all right. There's no shame in it. It's just not for you. We won't blame you.' His fingers strike to seize her stroking, stroking hand. Anger, humiliation, flare up in his eyes above the mask. Zed smiles.

'I'm coming with you. See . . .' He rips off his own breather-mask, throws it away from him. He fills his lungs with the garbage stink of the Barry-O.

'I'm glad.'

And the bright she and the silent she and the sullen he throw away their breathermasks and breathe in the stink and the sourness and they all smile, all friends all pilgrims all Company men together. They press onward and at the touch of their light all the collected shadows flee and fade: level after level after level of ringing, dripping darkness lit by fitful blue flashes; the powergrid is restless. Anticipating. Zed stops, hands held up, hush, be still. Her eyes, her nostrils are wide, sensing for a something, a hint, a memory of gardenias.

'Auraelian?'

The name chases around the squat, square concrete pillars.

'Auraelian!'

She holds high a small plastic cylinder. She shakes it and the floating things within catch the blue arclight. 'Brought you something, Auraelian! A balm for your mortifying flesh, old stumbling, crumbling man, a cessation of corruption! Good stuff, Auraelian, Company stuff, you hear me, Auraelian?'

A sigh in the darkness. Amplified by the ancient acoustics of the car-park. Flashlight beams fan into a wheel of light: nothing. Only a sigh.

'Not more of you. Oh well. Bolder than most, I suppose, but no less stupid. Or vain. Very well, give me the stuff.'

Zed's hand closes on the plastic vial of synthetic death hormone suppressant with a snap of rat-jaws. 'Give us purity.'

'Purity,' mumble-mutter bright she silent she sullen he laughing he. Like a prayer.

'Purity. Purity purity purity. Of course.' The powergrid shivers and cracks and Auraelian is there, out of nowhere, out of anywhere. He is tall, tall and stately as any son of the *corporadas*. He wears a white linen suit and panama hat and shoes. In his buttonhole is a black silk carnation, his hands rest lightly on the gilded knob of a malacca cane. He has beautiful hands. Zed has never seen such beautiful hands as the hands of Auraelian. The odour of gardenias overpowers even the Barry-O stink. 'Purity. Impetuous youths.' He smiles. Imagine an angel long-since fallen through the fingers of God remembering its former estate. Imagine how it would smile. 'Come then.'

Question: what is it Auraelian sells one half so precious as the goods he buys?

This.

A heptagonal metal frame. Tall as a Company man. Dripping with conduits and cables and clumsily grafted compumodules. Suggestion of a gateway. Suggestion of a mirror. In a sense, both. One entire level of Auraelian's little kingdom has been set aside to serve it. As the click, tap, click, tap of cane on concrete guides his pilgrims, the cables shudder with power and for the briefest quantum of comprehension, the heptagon fills with a plane of blue light.

Zed touches the smooth metal frame, strokes the humming cables, peers into the spasming blue light as if to see if there is a beyond, what that beyond might be.

'Nothing,' says Auraelian. 'That's the reason for it, isn't it? Nothing, and everything. Tell me, am I a religion yet? I ought to be.'

Impatient, spirit-hungry, Zed is already removing her clothes. Fine *corporada* silks and leathers lie like empty skins on the rust-coloured concrete. Auraelian runs a tiny iguana-tongue over his lips. It is not Zed he hungers for. It is the vial in her hand.

'I presume that having heard of my mattercaster, you must at least possess some rudimentary understanding of the DaCosta Postulate of Universal Position by which it operates; namely, that at a certain mathematical level, the probability of an object's existence is equal for any and every point in the universe . . .'

'Auraelian . . .' Zed slips the rings from her fingers, the brass and bone *zuvembe* bangles from her wrists. She shakes her hair free from its leather thonging. 'No theory, old man. No postulates. Just do it. Do it now.' She presses her soft meat against the hard metal frame. Blue in the infinity light. Perfect child of the Company. Auraelian shakes his head, dry, mock sorrow. He clicks his fingers twice, opens his beautiful hand. The vial of glittering things arcs through the air. Black market immortality. Auraelian takes it with a darting trap-snap of fingers and it is safe in the heart-pocket of his linen waistcoat. His hands, his beautiful, *beautiful* hands, move over the ugly, incongruous compumodules.

And the concrete hull of the long-dead car-park hums to a rising swell of power. The hum becomes a migraine drone; for an instant the floors, ceilings, pillars shudder and shammer as the powergrid finds and loses their resonant frequencies. The metal heptagon is a solid plane of blue light.

'Heesus,' someone whispers.

The girl who calls herself Zed tosses back her black hair and walks into the teleport field.

She cannot even scream.

She dies, annihilated, shattered scattered splattered to the furthest curve of the isotropic universe, spread throughout time from eternity to eternity. She is nothing. She is everything, made one with the universe in a moment of omnipresent nirvana that lasts for ever and ever and ever and ever and ever and ever and ever and still not one instant has ticked away on the clocks of infinity.

It is Heaven.

It is Hell.

And in that same instant as she is shattered and scattered and splattered, she is gathered out of infinity and recreated. She lives again.

She steps from the teleport field. She shines. Hands, face, body. All human dross burned away in that instant of union with the universe. She is pure. She is enlightened. She is holy. Her friends are afraid: what is this? Not Zed. Cannot be their Zed. But she stands among them, inviting them to touch her shining body, and they reach out their hands to touch, they peer through her brilliance. They see. Then they too strip off their fine fine Company clothes and step naked into the matter-caster to be annihilated, shattered scattered splattered across the universe, to die, and live again, pure, sanctified creatures in the warm dripping of an abandoned car-park down in the Barry-O: bright she silent she sullen he . . . laughing he?

Laughing he? The boy who calls himself Yani hides from the laughing, brilliant creatures which seconds before had been his friends. He hides in the shadows they cast. He does not laugh. He was afraid. He was afraid to annihilate himself in the mattercaster field and he slips away from the company of the saints down through the ringing, dripping levels haunted by the scent of gardenias and the glitter of blades, out into the warm rain and the streaming streets, back up the alleys and stairways to the glowing towers of Hy Brazyl, the laughing boy who will not laugh again.

And what had been five is now four.

Now they have new names for themselves. New names for new places, new names shaped like the glass scimitars of the *corporadas* or the luminous vaults of their arcades and gallerias and loggias and cloudwalking plazas. They call themselves the Lords Cardinal.

Whispers in intimate conversation booths in neon and tube chrome cafés. Slash of red paint spray-bombed across a corridor wall down in the residential levels. Dataweb code pencil-scribbled on a public booth. Slip of paper slid down plunging necklines into stocking tops between flybuttons into waistbands *zuvembe* ear-bangles next-to-heart pockets: *The Lords Cardinal.* Most have no eyes to see, no ears to hear, they pass by as the September clouds pass and part about the aerocurves of the arcologies. They say, *Qué?* What kinda gar*bage* (to rhyme with ga*rage*, as in repository for old automobiles, as in Auraelian's twenty-two level domain) this? And they say, *Qué, neh!* no time for this gar*bage*, gotta work gotta play gotta live gotta love gotta life to live at lofty altitude, you only walk this way the once, *compadre*, so let's drink let's shoot let's make let's fake let's dance; we're Company men!

But for a few the whisper cannot be forgotten. The red slogans drip down the imagination and say, *Walk the way that is not the way. The way that a few have walked before you, down from your* corporadas, *out of the lights into the darkness beneath the clouds that is better than any light.* And they look at their sweeping swooping towers and they say, Heesus, is that all there is? Working for the playing for the screwing for the chewing for the making for the faking for the living for the dying for the glorious the generous the wonderful the Company? And they say, I'll walk that way that is not the way, I'll pull that code, I'll call up that address, I'll walk that narrow and winding way that leads to the darkness that is better than any light.

And they find, out there, the Lords Cardinal. Reclining among floform cushions on live-fur floors. Contemplative lotuses at coffee on glass galleries, the clouds a sheer two kilometres below. Warriors of the mist down in the perpetual gloom of the industrial cores. And this is the gospel they preach.

Everything is nothing.

Nothing is everything.

Possess all the wealth of the soaring curves of Hy Brazyl and you are poorer than the poorest *noncontractado* down in the Barry-O. Become nothing, and you will receive everything. Nirvana. Nihilism. The blessedness of annihilation. Of having been nothing, and then, being again. Of the purification that comes when the slag of merely being human is burned away by that moment of nothing-and-everythingness. And of that inner strength (call it courage, call it faith, call it foolhardiness) in the one step that takes you through the teleport field, into death, and out again. It is a dark and desperate gospel they preach, but there is something about these Lords Cardinal that draws those who seek, some force, some magnetism, some light. They would call it holiness if they knew what the word meant. All they know is that it is a purity of life that is missing from their own lives.

'Become nothing and you will become everything,' says the one who calls herself Zed. She looks into the eyes of her disciples sprawled about on her floforms in the conversation pit of her executive level apartment. In some she sees doubt. In some she sees fear. In some she sees an emptiness like the emptiness that was once within her. In some she sees her hunger. In some, the flame of desire. 'Sanctify yourselves. Die, and live again.'

God save us from those who would take our every utterance as gospel.

She came before dawn, the silent one, Cassaday, the one of the four who seemed least comfortable with her new creation; calling and calling and calling at the door.

'Zed . . .'

'Quiet. Please.'

Oh-five-twenty and the dawn is welling up over the edge of the cloudlayer. A wedge of light slowly climbs the curving faces of the *corporadas*; red light, dawn light, spills through the window, washes over the girl standing by the glass, across the live-fur floor and the scattered floforms, into the conversation pit. It seeks out Cassaday, the silent one, in her corner by the door.

'Zed . . .' Something has forced her out of her silence, something terrible and fearful.

A hand raised, a command for silence. Zed's brow is furrowed, intense concentration, the pretence of contemplation. Hands outstretched. The light fills up the world like the cracked crazy yolk of an egg broken into a jar of isinglass. The lower limb of the sun clears the cloudbase.

Oh-five-twenty-one.

Thanks to the Company, Hy Brazyl enjoys the most spectacular sunrisings and settings this side of Jupiter. Atmospheric pollution, apparently.

'I always think it's wrong to keep the sunrise to yourself. You should share it with a soul-brother, a soul-sister, don't you agree? Coffee?'

'Zed?'

But she has moved hurriedly to the pot and the bowls and the ritual.

'Cass, you're one of my oldest, dearest friends. I feel I can tell you the things which are important to me. So I feel I can tell you this: I'm afraid. Afraid that I'm losing it. Can you understand what I'm saying? Here, inside. It's just not the same any more. I feel like there is dirt in my veins. I feel like there is shit in my mouth. I feel like the fire inside is just . . . embers.'

Zed keeps little metal bells in her kettle. When the water boils, the bells sing and ring and chirrup.

'It's them. The others. There're too many of them. They need too much. They drain me, just by being with me, they drain me. They dirty me, can you understand that?'

'Zed, I've killed someone.'

'It's like, because I am so pure, even the slightest contact with anyone less pure than I am taints me. Dirt shows on white more than black. I feel covered in fingerprints. And each time they come to me with their stupid questions, their "Teach mes" and "lead mes" and "guide mes" and their "how can I how do I what do you mean Zeds?" the fire goes out of me. I can't move. It's a crust on my skin. Shrike and Lolo feel the same. We're losing it. We're being swallowed by the dust.'

'Are you listening? Are you listening?' Cassaday's voice rises to a scream. She who had never screamed before. Before Zed. Before Purity. Before holiness. 'Simón Herera Reis jumped from the four hundred and twelfth level sun terrace! Heesus!' Coffee falls in a small, precise arc from the spout of the pot into porcelain bowls. 'He was in my circle, he hadn't been coming to meetings for very long. He was having trouble with his parents, with his girlfriend, with his educator; they didn't like him being involved in the circle. Indoctrination, they called it. I was trying to get him straightened out. Last night he called; public dataweb, about two. He'd had some big thing with his folks. Kept on saying everything had come apart, everything was just piling up around him, up and up and up and he couldn't see any way out from under it all. Heez, Zed, it was oh-two, I was pretty well shot, so I gave him the first bit of advice came into my head; standard stuff, you know the sort of thing: try to become nothing to this situation and everything will pass right through you and you will emerge on the far side of it victorious. That sort of thing. Then. God. Oh God.' She cannot contain the tears any more. Zed watches her cry with dispassionate curiosity, as she might an interesting geological sample. She sips her coffee, watches. 'Then I heard he'd jumped. Off the four hundred and twelfth level. One of his friends told me. He'd tried to talk him down but he just kept saying over and over, "This is the way out, die and become nothing and I will be everything." And it's my fault. I am responsible. I am as responsible for Simón's death as if I pushed him off that sun terrace myself. I killed him. I am guilty. And I don't know if I can cope with that. I don't know.' Through the dawn windows she sees Simón Herera Reis falling like a human star toward the moonsilvered cloudbase, sees him smash himself to nothing on the grim angularities of the industrial cores below. 'I don't know. I just feel that maybe everything would be better if I were to follow him. You understand?' She sniffs. Black eye make-up has trickled down her cheeks.

Zed looks up from her coffee, smiles suddenly.

'But don't you see, this is exactly the problem! You feel responsible because you have let yourself become tainted by the values of other, impure, people. It's not your fault; how can it be your fault? You only think it's your fault because your holiness, your purity, has become clouded by other people. What we need is a re-dedication. A re-purification. Another pass through the infinity mirror to be purged of all the dirt and darkness. I've contacted the others, they all feel the same, they all agree that it's the only way to restore the light we shared. Down to the Barry-O again. Walk through the fire again. Be reborn, again.'

'Are you serious? Are you quite serious? A boy is dead and all you can talk about is your precious purity and holiness?'

'Of course I am serious. What has happened is, of course, quite tragic, which is all the more reason for us to repurify ourselves to ensure it never happens again. Will you come?'

'No! No!' She stands up. She is the silent one no longer. 'No, I am not coming. I have had it. I want nothing more to do with this, with you, with any of you. Don't call me, don't visit, just leave me alone, I don't want to see any of you ever again. That's it.' Hands scissor. 'I'm out.'

Oh-five-thirty. Door slams. Half-empty coffee bowl on the

live-fur floor. The sun stands high above the horizon, another beautiful day, like every day lived at the lofty altitude of the *corporadas*, and what has been four is now three.

'Longer?'

'Longer.'

Only the three of them this time. Auraelian contemplates one of his dry, dark little jokes, dismisses the notion. They have no sense of humour. And they are not fearful, excited, guilty kids. They position themselves comfortably, powerfully across his concrete, each one the precise centre of his or her space, commanding that space with the easy panther poise of the Company born. Darklight image-amplifying shades fix him at the centre of their foci. Lean. Hungry. Do not joke with these people. His razor-boys are all paid up and jacked up and only a button away but Auraelian feels vaguely threatened. Thin black iguana-tongue flicks over his lips.

'Longer. So. There are, you must understand, certain difficulties in that. The process is designed to be virtually instantaneous, no more than a couple of picoseconds in duration. It would require resetting the temporal randomizers to function in macrotime and, quite honestly, I could not absolutely guarantee one hundred per cent reintegration.'

'Meaning?'

'Possible physical or mental malformation, in all likelihood fatal. Possibly the body might fully reintegrate but without life. Possibly, total randomization.'

'Total randomization?' That lean hunger in their voices makes them all sound the same.

'I take it you have enough intelligence to work out what that means for yourselves.' Iguana-tongue flicks in, out. My, but it is hot down in the Barry-O tonight.

'But it is possible.' That one is their leader, that girl; she is the darkest and hungriest of the three.

'Certainly.'

Temptation shimmers in her hand. Shake the vial, set the life-swarm swirling.

'Good stuff, Auraelian. New stuff. Tell him, Shrike.'

'Cut with APFE growth factor. New, new, Auraelian. We're not just talking life extension here, we're talking rejuvenation. Fountain of youth, old man. Took a big risk smuggling this stuff out of my work. Make it worth my while.'

A waft, a gag of gardenias; the scent Auraelian uses to conceal the smell of hundred-and-fifty-year-old flesh. The flesh which cries and wails for what the dark girl is holding between her fingers. Growth factors. Not a mere postponement of death, a grasp at life again. Real life. Life is the drug and Auraelian is hooked.

'As long as you are aware of the risks.'

'I think you explained them quite adequately.'

'And that I cannot be held responsible for any . . . unforeseen circumstances?'

'Yes.'

'Then we have a deal.'

They grin at each other, these *corporada* children in their slick leathers and sleek black nylon. Fists clench in gestures of victory, solidarity. Thunder shakes the Barry-O, lightning caught in the metal monoliths of Hy Brazyl's industrial cores. Down where the automobiles used to growl and coil, black plastic things move, restless, thunder-shaken, catching the lightning on their thin blades.

Do not imagine they are the only ones. Do not imagine that no one else has ever made that pilgrimage down to the trampled mud streets of the shadowlands to seek out Auraelian with dashing, flashing beams. The Lords Cardinal have their disciples. As the Lords Cardinal were themselves, once, disciples at the feet of other masters. So do not imagine that they are the first. Auraelian's body has been defying mortification for half a century now; there are a lot of little plastic vials of synthetic death hormone suppressant in fifty years. Junior Company executives burning with junior executive ambition and anxiety; spiritual searchers who have tired of the starshine and the neon and seek a brighter enlightenment down where the streets have no names; inadequate souls needing to prove *something* (they can never quite say what) to themselves, to others, to the world; the hollow men seeking in emptiness a filling, in nothingness a universality of experience. Artists. Daredevils. Fools. Sensation seekers. The merely fashionable. All at one time or another in his century and a half have paid Auraelian to step through his teleporter. And not just in synthDHS. Other scrips, other species, other drugs. Auraelian did not get to be one hundred and fifty in the Barry-O without well-paid allies.

Never many. Auraelian does not advertise. Word-of-mouth is the best recommendation. A thing the angst-ridden junior advertising executives would do well to remember. But enough. It pays him enough. Enough to keep him alive and ticking for just about forever. Forever should be long enough for Auraelian to pay back the investment he has made in the mattercaster. It is not an investment that the Directors of the Projects would understand; pain and loss and disillusionment do not appear in credit and debit columns.

He had been an engineer in those early, heady days when the vision of corporate grandeur had sent the industrial cores into the clouds above what had once been Sao Paulo. She had been a mathematician, a DaCosta, a member of the founding families throwing their glass and steel towers into the stratosphere, as graceful and elegant as her equations. They had been friends, soul friends, a relationship deeper and more bonding than any formality could ever express. And out of the spirit between them had come the idea. An outrageous, enormous, incredible, intolerable, wonderful idea. The transmission of matter. Instantaneously. Across unlimited distance. Teleportation. They produced plans and schemes and pilot units and projections. And it worked beautifully. The abolition of distance. It would revolutionize trade. They took it to the Project Directors. And the Project Directors cut off its head. Its hands. Its feet. Because the soul friends had not realized what the abolition of distance would do to the laws of supply and demand and free market forces. Transport, transportation, areas of production and supply; the whole concept of markets and manufactories and thus, ultimately, the *corporadas* and the Company itself, were threatened. They would not invest in the razor which cut their own throats.

Dreams and soulfriends do not wither and blow away so easily. The *corporadas* forsook them; very well, they would forsake the *corporadas* and take their idea to those who would appreciate it, to the poor and dispossessed who huddled in their *favelas* at the feet of the shining spires. One day the dispossessed might bring those shining towers toppling down. For decades they dedicated every free *crusado*, every spare moment to the construction of a full-scale matter transmission system. Everything was sacrificed to the dream with the sole exception of their soul-friendship, for it was that which kept the dream burning. Then with the base station completed and awaiting testing, DaCosta caught a stupid little infection and died because they could not afford the price of black market antibiotics. Parched of the spirit between them, the dream shrivelled into disenchantment and cynicism and ultimately to a sordid little mill grinding out dollops of plastic immortality in the vain hope of some day, some way, outliving those arrogant skyscrapers. He had always been a coward, Auraelian of the beautiful hands.

And still they come. Very few return for a second walk through the fire. Only the exceptionally spiritual, the exceptionally greedy, return again and again and again. Only the spiritually greedy push and push and push at the limits of experience; two, five, ten seconds of annihilation, ramming body and spirit through the mattercaster until a twist of void is twined around every molecule of every cell of their bodies.

Spiritual pride is real.

Spiritual arrogance is real.

Spiritual greed, that drives the master to always walk before the disciple, is real. The fist of spiritual greed grips as tight as the fist that holds Auraelian to his little blue plastic vials, an addict to his drug.

*

It was inevitable that they become lovers; Zed, highborn daughter of the Founding Families, and the tall, solid, sullen boy from down in the industrial levels who calls himself the Shrike. The mattercaster had spread them so far, so thin, that there was no longer any possible point of contact between them and their disciples. Except revelation imparted. And thank-offerings received. The Shrike had given up his job in the pharmaceutical unit that had provided the Lords Cardinal with their drug-money: he could no longer bear the presence of the impure. Immaterial that they found his company equally intolerable. Inevitable, then, that in their isolation sullen he should be drawn to dark she.

So they lie together, wrapped around each other on the live-fur floor with the morning breaking over them. Dark she's hands explore sullen he's body; the strong curves of thighs and buttocks, the smooth syncline of the back, the rounded slopes of the shoulders, stroking stroking stroking, absently, thoughtlessly, as if he is stone, or plastic, or a small, pet animal. She watches the day rise over Hy Brazyl. And she does not know what she is seeing. The geometrically abstract plane of the cloudbase. The shattering, penetrating thrust of the towers. The globe, the atom of light at the edge of the world: colours red, purple, gold.

What are they? What is this? What does it mean?

Something? Anything?

Nothing?

A moment of panic as she realizes that it means nothing. It is not important. It has no meaning. It is nothing. Her panic leaves here as she realizes that it, too, is nothing.

This body draped across hers, this collection of curves and planes, softnesses and hardnesses; this body, this *Shrike*, means nothing.

Means nothing.

Is nothing.

Zed smiles. She is almost there.

And:

'What do you mean, we can't see each other again?'

She sighs, sweeps back her hair in exasperation, in

that way he finds so attractive.

'I knew you wouldn't, I knew you wouldn't understand. It's because this physical thing has no importance, can't you see that? Ultimately, it doesn't matter, and I think, I feel, that you're making it, making me, out to be the reason for everything, and it can't be, you know it can't be, it can't mean anything, ultimately.'

'Are you saying that I don't mean anything to you?'

'No! No! Try and understand. It's the physical thing: you're giving it too much importance, we are objects to each other, physical objects, and that's not what matters.'

'You are saying that I don't mean anything to you.'

'I'm saying that no thing, no physical thing, should mean anything to me. Does mean anything to me. Means anything to me. Everything is nothing, that's what we believe, isn't it? Well, now I *know* it. I feel it. Everything is nothing. And the nothing inside, the void, the spiritual reality, is everything.'

A pause.

A silence.

'You're not Zed.'

'Yes I am. I am Zed.'

'No you're not. Maybe you once were Zed, back then, you were the girl I just couldn't get enough of, the girl who fascinated me. I had to be near you, it was the most important thing in my life, being near you. And now I don't know what you have become. Do you know how long I admired you from afar? Do you know how long I've waited for this, what I went through just to be near you, all this spirituality shit? And now, I can't understand what you've become. Nothing human.'

'That's not Shrike talking. That's the old Shrike. But you're beyond all that, aren't you? That's what it's all about, becoming more than just the Shrike or Zed, becoming more than ourselves, more than human.'

'I would not say that. Not seeing what I've seen. I would say less than human.'

'If you're trying to bait me, it won't work. I'm beyond all that pettiness.'

'Beyond love too?'

'You just don't understand. I thought you did. I thought you were one of us.'

'Well maybe I just guess I wasn't.'

'I can't see you again. It's too important for you to hold me back. I won't see you again.'

'Zed! Zed! Zed . . .'

And what had been three is now two.

Ten seconds twenty seconds thirty seconds. Half a minute, one minute, one and a half minutes. Two minutes.

The clocks of faith bring them back to the Barry-O, dark she and bright she, again and again.

Four minutes.

Auraelian is not happy.

'The probability for a successful reintegration is not good.'

'How not good?' This place is theirs now as much as Auraelian's, its dripping concrete levels, its plastic-shrouded shadowpeople as much home as Hy Brazyl's immaculate *residenzas* peopled with the beautiful children of the Company.

'You want odds?' And Auraelian is no longer the hybrid angel–demon–treasurer of the Mysteries, he is just another worn component of the machine that shrives their souls. 'I would say only an eighty per cent chance of successful reintegration.'

Zed laughs. 'That is one hundred and fifty years speaking. I can smell your gardenias.'

'You only live once.'

'Not us. We have lived a dozen lives and more.'

But Lolo, the bright one, the small, bright glow of a girl, is not happy either. Four minutes . . . Zed is peeling off her tight leather and shiny black nylon, slipping the rings from her fingers, shaking her cloudburst of hair from its thonging. All part of the ritual now. She crouches like a runner under the gun before the glowing heptagon. She looks at it as she might a friend who has become an enemy, or an enemy a friend. She laughs, shakes her head, and launches herself through the teleport field.

Ten seconds. It is all a question of relativity, really. Subjectivity, objectivity. *Twenty seconds.* Time does not move for the teleported and the dead. Chronon and eon are the same to them. Four picos four micros four minutes four eternities, *thirty seconds*, you can't tell, *you're dead*, randomized to each and every part of the universe. *One minute.* Nor is there any purification; there is nothing present to purify. Yet, in a sense, when a man dies, his sins die with him and are not reborn with him. But his nature is not changed, for without his nature he is nothing, and so the darkness returns and he returns to the light of the mattercaster. *One minute thirty.* It is the recreation that purifies, that first glissando of glions through the cerebral cortex that says, that knows, *I have been dead and now I am alive again.* That is the purification. That is what the eye of faith sees. *Two minutes.* The clocks of faith mark four minutes as more holy than four micro-seconds and say, for four minutes (*three minutes*) you have been nothing, separate, beyond the timebound structure of the universe. And now, you are again.

That is what the clocks of faith mark. That is what the eye of faith sees.

Four minutes.

She plunges from the teleporter, tumbles across the damp scabbed concrete, smashes herself against a concrete pillar. She feels no pain. She is burning. She is on fire and by her own light she can see further than ever before, into the heart of everything. The sour concrete floor of the car-park is transparent as glass to her eye of faith. Lolo, the bright one, bends over her muttering words of concern and comfort which she cannot understand and the eye of faith strips away meat and bone to the centre of her life. Zed's sees her friend's light beside her own and it is like a candle flame beside a furnace. And she sees Auraelian's soul, like black, twisted wire.

'You've got to do it.'

Her mouth is full of stars and light.

'Zed, you all right? The way you came out of the field; you sure you're all right? Did you hurt yourself?'

What is she saying? What is she saying?

'No. No hurt. All right. Everything all right. You've got to do it. Lolo, you do it too. Go. Do it.'

'Heesus, I don't know, Zed, when you stepped through that machine, it was such a long time, I was scared, I didn't know if you were coming back! You know what Auraelian said . . .'

Auraelian stands amidst his machines. He does not hear, much less care, what they are babbling about. In the spaces of his imagination, he watches the towers falling.

'You've got to do it. It's the way forward. The quantum leap to new levels of spirituality; to know that you can overcome the fear and that nothing can ever scare you again.'

'I don't know Zed, the probabilities . . .'

'When you die, your fear dies with you and is not reborn. That was what was wrong with the earlier times we went through, it was not long enough for us to be afraid and take our fear through. But with the longer times, you bring your fear with you on that first step, and it is annihilated. Do it, Lolo. You've got to do it.'

'You think I should?'

'You've got to.'

And the bright girl, the one who calls herself Lolo, strips away all human affectations and becomes just herself, nineteen years old, fair, a little fat, a little scared in the blue light.

'Do it!' says Zed. The one thing her eye of faith cannot see is what lies beyond that plane of blue light. One step two step three step four. Lolo passes through the teleport field and is randomized. The clocks of faith are running. Ten seconds. Zed leaves her Company things where they lie, squats on the damp floor. It does not matter to her. Nothing matters to her. Twenty seconds. She watches the mattercaster but inwardly she is wholly absorbed in the contemplation of her own experience. Thirty seconds. Half a minute. Thunder crackles, lightning pricked out of the stratosphere by the needlepoints of the *corporadas* runs down through the industrial cores to earth

179

itself in the Barry-O. Nothing. Nothing at all. One minute. Her eye of faith penetrates the perpetual cloud-layers and the mighty *corporadas* are confections of glass filled with little squeaking crystal figurines, fearful manikins waiting for the hammer to finally fall. Nothing. All the power and arrogance of the Company and its Projects: nothing. One minute thirty.

'It's drawing a lot of power, running it this long,' advises Auraelian. Zed looks through him to his writhing reptile soul. Nothing.

'We pay you well for your inconvenience.' She resents having to speak. 'We've brought you good custom these past few months.'

Two minutes. At last she knows it. Not an intellectual headknowledge, she knows it in her spirit, *lifeknowledge*; she is it. Everything is just . . . nothing. Compared to her own experience. Nothing. Three minutes. There is no longer anything she cares for outside her own experience. Nothing matters except her own spirituality.

Four minutes . . .

Four minutes.

Four minutes.

Auraelian's little murmur of concern penetrates Zed's self-contemplation to alert that something is not right. Four minutes? Lolo . . .

She has not come back.

'Auraelian: Lolo, where is she?'

'Even for you, that is a singularly stupid question.'

Shadows in the universal brightness.

'Auraelian, do something. Bring her back. Now. You bring her back.'

His beautiful hands are dancing across the compumodules.

'Don't you think I am trying? Inverse phase, possibly . . .' The powergrid shudders with energy, shakes the building like a man a snake.

'Auraelian, what's happening?'

'Be quiet. Just be quiet.' The powergrid howls as Auraelian commands it to draw more energy from the broadcast power net. The heptagonal plane of angel-light swirls violet and indigo.

'Auraelian, you built this thing, you know what it can do.'

'And. I. Also. Know,' shouts Auraelian, punching command after command after command into his computers, 'What. It. Cannot. Do.'

A spit of electricity shorting out. From outside in the rain, blue and yellow flashes. The howl ebbs to a drone, a hum, a purr of power. The mattercaster field is uninterrupted blue.

'Burned out a powerdish,' says Auraelian. 'Lost it. I told you, I told you the probabilities. Impetuous youths. I wash my hands of you.' He lets his shadows reclaim him.

Zed remains in front of the teleporter, gazing into the one place her eye of faith cannot see. Nothing. Ultimately, it is nothing. Lolo is nothing now, and that is good. Zed need no longer care about anyone. She is free. And she is very glad.

After half an hour Auraelian returns to shut down the mattercaster. And what had been two is now one.

Lean days in the Barry-O. Ever since that girl vanished. Sorry. *Failed to reintegrate.* They just stopped coming. Schism, a falling away of the faithful, the old fat demon Apathy; Auraelian does not care, it is twenty years since he even stirred out of his little kingdom into the streets, why should he care what the children of privilege do miles above his head? All he misses is their income. Since they stopped splashing down the hillsides to find his brand of revelation, one hundred and fifty years of flesh have taken up their full weight again. He misses that new, good Company stuff, cut with growth factor or whatever they called it. The memory is going. He has to be careful with his rationing, one hundred and fifty years will not be easily cheated. Some memories he is glad to lose. That girl, the one who failed to reintegrate, now he cannot even recall her name, her face, her body. Barely enough synthDHS left after paying off his razorboy friends (and are they, will they, can they ever be *friends*, or just immaculately disguised parasites?) to keep himself ticking along. But for his faithful provider, these bad times would be the worst of times.

Faithful provider. She will see him through the hungry years until a new generation grows up there to disillusionment and indolence and has need of his services again. Until then, he will listen for her voice calling through the lower levels: 'A moment, a minute, a jot a joint a shot of your purity for a soul which dearly needs it.' Regular and faithful, she brings him her little dribs and drabs of blackmarket DHS. He does not ask how she comes by it, though he can guess how a *corporada* child fallen from grace with the sky earns a living down in the Barry-O. He does not doubt that some of those plastic vials contain his own junk, working its way back to him in a rondo of recirculation. For her, he coaxes life into the old, battered circuits; too long since he was last able to afford an overhaul, and she peels off her layers of street waterproofs to stand naked before him, blue plastic vial trembling in her hand.

Once she was beautiful. Life in the Barry-O has weighed and paid for her beauty and taken it away, by the gram, by the *crusado*. The framework remains, no one can take that away, the planes and curves and the angles, but the light which changes handsomeness into beauty is gone. Taken away in rainsoaked alleyways, in plastic and beercan hovels, among the steel and chrome of the industrial ziggurats by guilty Company brothers slumming it for the night, by the gram, by the *crusado*. She sells her handsomeness so that for a moment, a minute, an hour, an afternoon, she may be beautiful again. So that in the teleport she may die and forget the pounded mud streets and the stink of human sewage and the black weatherproof polywrappers and the hunger and the mould and the disease and the rain which washes the names and the dignity from the faces that pay for her; to be shattered and scattered and splattered to the end of the universe and to die for everything that is ugly and sour and used-up. And be reborn, new, pure, holy and bright and beautiful. For an afternoon, an hour, a minute, a moment.

'Auraelian! Auraelian! Old stumbling crumbling man, a

balm for your mortifying flesh, a cessation of corruption! Look, good stuff, Company stuff, you hear me, Auraelian?'

So, is it that time again? His memory, really, terrible. He can hardly even remember her name, that odd name, like a name someone makes up for themselves, not a real name at all. Sometimes he can remember her name. Mostly he thinks of her just as Faithful Provider. Something about her reminds him of himself, a nostalgia of heaven. He is certain that she is years younger than she looks. Auraelian has little to do these days, other than speculate on his Faithful Provider.

Already she is removing her clothes, layers of peeled-away plastic and paper. The rituals are important to them both.

'Brought you your stuff, Auraelian. Good stuff, Company stuff.' She tosses the plastic vial. His beautiful hands snap-trap his payment, then move to the compumodules. Hum of power, the old building shudders again, all for her, just for her. She tosses back her hair and just for an instant she is beautiful, she is fire and light and darkness and all those paradoxical things a woman can be. She steps into the mattercaster field, and is consumed and all that remains is the scent, the memory, of gardenias.

FEMINOPOLIS

by
Elizabeth Sourbut

Elizabeth Sourbut lives in York, and her story *The African Quota* was a runner-up in the second Gollancz/*Sunday Times* SF competition in 1986. This is her second published story, and thanks to a secret source of revenue she is currently writing full-time and working on her first novel.

Waiting for Areen was worse this time. Jirela felt the newly budding life within her belly and prayed softly to the Earth Mother. If Areen failed to conceive this month they would be too far out of synch, it would spoil the partnership of shared motherhood.

She jumped to her feet as the waiting room door opened and Areen was ushered in by the nurse. She looked pale, but smiled when she saw Jirela's worried face.

'Well, how did it go?'

Areen shrugged. 'It doused the itch. He was a bit over-eager, but then you found that out the other day, didn't you?' She grinned, and then relented. Her eyes met Jirela's almost shyly. 'I held concentration. It took, and it's going to be a girl.'

For a moment they stared at one another, slowly breaking out into silly, delighted smiles. Then they enfolded one another in a fierce hug. Jirela buried her face in the sweet scent of her lover's hair. 'Oh, my darling.'

After a few moments, the nurse gently disentangled them and led them through the foyer to the exit. 'Look after each other,' she said, 'and if there are any little problems, come back and see us.'

Jirela nodded, only half-aware of being spoken to, and they began slowly to descend the steps into the street. Areen was weaker than usual, her reaction to the monthly hormonal upset this time exacerbated by exhaustion. She leaned heavily on Jirela's arm, occasionally saying in wonderment: 'I'm pregnant. Goddess, we're pregnant. No more PCT for at least a year. Oh joy!'

Jirela held her close and said nothing. She could think of nothing to say that would do justice to her feelings. She felt as though she were skimming over the paved streets, floating along in the balmy summer air. The whole world must be working perfectly today.

'Look,' said Areen suddenly. 'What's going on in the park?'

'Hm?' Jirela looked up and saw a crowd of people milling about on the grass in Gaia Park. 'Strange,' she said. 'I haven't heard there was anything on. What's that thing they're looking at?'

'Let's go and see.'

'Don't you want to get home? You should lie down.'

'We need only stay a minute. It might be something fun. Come on.'

Jirela nodded, curious herself, and they strolled between two of the ancient trees which bordered the park, and onto the grass.

Nodding to their many acquaintances, they made their way between knots of chattering women until they came to the front of the crowd. Rising above them to the height of three people was a silvery egg-shaped structure. A number of women were inspecting it closely. It gave out a hollow sound when they knocked on the sides.

'What on Earth is it?' asked Areen.

'We don't know,' said a voice behind her. It was Honna, Jirela's simsister, looking rather worried. 'It's not a scheduled event. We think some out-of-towners must have brought it in, but the funny thing is, it wasn't here this morning.'

'No,' said Jirela, 'it wasn't. We went past on our way to the clinic, and it wasn't here then.'

'Oh, yes, of course,' Honna exclaimed, turning to Areen. 'How did it go? Did you . . . ?' Areen nodded, smiling. 'Wonderful!' Honna embraced her. 'I'm so pleased for you both. Look, I –'

A sudden mass exclamation silenced her. They turned back to the egg to see a part of the shell swinging down towards them. The women who had been inspecting it came hurrying back into the crowd.

The top of the door thumped onto the grass, forming a ramp to the ground, and three women appeared in the entrance. They were tall and flat chested, wearing unflattering grey coveralls. Their eyes swept over the crowd and they muttered amongst themselves. Then one stepped forward and raised her hands, palm upwards, in a stylized gesture of giving. She spoke, gibberish, in a deep ringing voice.

'Wow,' whispered Honna, 'if we gave her citizenship do you think she'd sing in the choir? What a bass!'

'Shh, watch the performance,' Areen hissed.

There was a longish pause. The tall woman muttered again to her comrades, who shrugged.

'Forgotten her lines,' someone giggled. 'What an anticlimax!'

The woman took a metal box from a pocket in her coveralls, and fiddled with it. Then she spoke again. The box squawked and spoke in a flat, uninflected voice. It said: 'Greetings! We come in peace. We have travelled across the timestream from another universe. We are explorers and scientists. We would be honoured to speak with your leaders.'

'Leaders!' said Areen. 'How quaint. The dialogue doesn't match up to the props, does it?'

'I think they expect some audience participation,' Jirela suggested as the strange actors still hesitated at the top of their ramp. 'Go on, Honna, you're on the Committee.'

'Oh, Goddess, I hate this sort of thing.' Honna stepped forward awkwardly, and raised her hands in a copy of the stranger's action. The audience cheered.

'Greetings!' she said clearly. 'Welcome to our city. I am what might be termed a leader here.'

Someone clapped. 'Go for it, Honna!' called a voice.

The box was relaying Honna's message. 'Oh, this is going to get boring,' Areen groaned. 'Do you think they'll keep it up for long, or will they pretend to have suddenly learned the language and start talking properly?'

'I don't know.' Jirela frowned at the three strangers. 'There's something odd about them. Gaia's womb, what's the matter now?'

The three actors had turned away from the audience again

and appeared to be arguing amongst themselves. People were growing restive. They began to drift away.

'Lovely egg,' said someone, 'but really!'

'I don't know how they have the nerve. No talent.'

'How did it get here anyway?'

'Honna,' called Jirela. 'We'd better be going. Areen's tired. Can you manage?'

'Oh, yes. We'll move them on. Shame to lose that voice, though.'

Areen laughed. 'You and your choir!' They turned away and headed back towards the street.

Louise looked up from her monitor screen as the three men climbed in through the airlock door. Wallace tossed his translator onto the mess table in disgust. 'What's wrong with that bloody thing?' he snapped.

'Probably loose wires, sir,' said Dunnett moodily. 'I'll fix it.'

'They didn't look very impressed,' said Louise, glancing again at the view of the park on her screen. 'And I don't think it was the translator.'

Wallace scowled. 'If you bloody scientists are so smart, you come up with something.'

'I've done my bit,' said Staines. He sprawled into a chair and rubbed his face. 'The biosphere definitely checks out Earth-norm, though almost certainly pre-industrial. We're a lot closer to home this time . . . Sir,' he added as an afterthought.

'Control learns quickly anyway,' said Marie. 'I was dreading another of those moonscapes.'

'Third time lucky,' chuckled Louise. 'Except that the locals want us to leave. I think this is a command decision, captain. What do you say we should do?'

'We don't know that woman was any kind of official,' Staines pointed out.

'Didn't look very official to me, sir,' said Dunnett. 'A bunch of women in summer frocks out for a picnic. And half of them were lesbians.'

'Yes, I noticed that,' said Louise softly.

Wallace ran a hand through his greying hair. 'We'll have to do some ground-work,' he said. 'The first thing must be to find the people in charge and announce our presence officially. We'll go in pairs.'

'Right,' said Staines. 'Marie can come with me, yes?' He and Wallace stared at one another for a long moment. Then the captain grunted.

'Dunnett, you come with me. Tarrant, stay here and look after the ship. I want everyone back in an hour. Is that clear?'

'Yes sir, captain.' Staines grinned and eased himself to his feet, stretching his powerful frame. 'Marie, grab a translator. Let's go.'

Louise watched the two pairs walking in opposite directions across the park. As soon as they were out of sight, she picked up another translator and stepped into the airlock. She had a few ideas of her own concerning this world.

Having seen Areen safely to sleep, Jirela found herself drawn back towards the strange object in the park. Something nagged at her about the three grey-clad women, and she wanted to see them at close quarters.

Two or three streets from the park, she noticed one of the ugly grey coveralls amongst the colourful dresses of the citizens. The woman wearing it was shorter and a lot more shapely than the other strangers, but was still clearly one of them. She was walking slowly, gazing about her as if everything was utterly alien. She stopped and stared as a couple strolled past, arm in arm, and when Jirela drew close she saw a look of wonder on the stranger's face.

'Hello,' she said, gently touching her arm.

The woman jumped and stepped back in alarm. She spoke, and the box at her side said flatly: 'Sorry. You startled me.'

'My apologies. My name's Jirela. Welcome to our city.'

The woman took a deep breath, and smiled. 'Thank you. 'I'm called Louise. Were you in the park earlier, when my colleagues spoke?'

Jirela nodded. She wondered how to be tactful whilst still eliciting information. 'That was the first performance of your play, I think?'

Louise stared. Then she burst out laughing. 'Yes, this was the first time we've done that particular routine. How did people take it?'

'Well ... Look, may I invite you to my home? We could talk in comfort there, and I've one or two things I'd like to ask you about.'

Louise nodded eagerly, almost too eagerly. Jirela felt a twinge of unease, but ignored it. This out-of-towner was fascinating.

As they walked up the street Jirela pointed out various sights, and talked of inconsequentialities. Passers-by stared curiously at Louise's clothes and close-cropped hair and Jirela wanted to be alone with her before asking anything important.

Areen was up when they arrived at the house. 'Jirela, where – oh,' she said, seeing the stranger.

'You should be asleep.'

'Oh, don't fuss. I'm fine.'

'You look tired.' She touched her lover's shoulder and they kissed tenderly. 'Louise, I'd like you to meet Areen, my partner.'

Louise was staring, dumbstruck. Jirela smiled. Areen had that effect on a lot of people. She stepped forward now and kissed their guest politely. 'Please, take a seat. Are you an actor too? I didn't see you earlier.'

They sat. 'I'm one of the ship's company, yes.'

'Funny sort of ship. How did you get it to the park?'

'That's rather a long story. But really, I'd like to apologize for my companions' performance. It wasn't very good, was it?'

'I've seen better. What was it all about?' Jirela inclined her head curiously. 'I have a feeling that we missed something significant.' She glanced at Areen for confirmation, but her lover wasn't listening. She was very pale, and looked suddenly ill. Jirela touched her shoulder sympathetically.

'You were right as usual, my dear,' Areen said. 'I should have stayed in bed.'

Jirela helped her out of the room and settled back under the covers. 'Now sleep,' she said. 'You'll feel fine tomorrow. I did.' She stroked Areen's face, wanting to stay, to hold her close.

'Go and look after our guest. I expect a full report.'

When she returned to the communal room, Louise was staring at the floor. She didn't look up. 'What's wrong with her?' she asked.

'She's pregnant. We both are.'

Louise looked up then, her eyes transfixing her startled host with some desperate emotion she couldn't understand. 'By each other?' she hissed.

Jirela laughed. 'Hardly.'

'Oh. So you do have men.'

'Of course. Don't you?'

'What do you mean? You've seen our men.'

Jirela frowned. 'I don't think so.'

'They were the ones who performed so badly earlier.'

Jirela understood. 'Ah. We seem to have a translation problem. By "men", I mean studs, the ones who father children.'

'Yes, ours do that too, amongst other things.'

Jirela tried another tack. 'The ones who I saw earlier were different from you, yes?' Louise nodded. 'But different also from your studs?'

Louise leaned forward. 'You fascinate me,' she said. 'Tell me more about these studs.'

The streets seemed designed for foot traffic. Staines strode along the middle of the broad, paved ways, Marie hurrying by his side to keep up. Sunlight cast dappled shadows on the strolling crowds as it glinted through the bright foliage of oak, ash, and beech trees. His quick eyes took in the cleanliness of the roads, the gleaming whiteness of the gaily frescoed buildings. Painted awnings shaded the entrances to any number of small shops and cafés. The goods on sale spread out into the roadway, though never encroaching beyond the lines of trees into the central avenues. Marie strayed from his side to look more closely at a display of brass pots and pans. He paused impatiently and the crowd parted to flow by on either side.

'The artwork is exquisite,' she said, soon rejoining him. 'It takes skill to produce some of those intricate designs.'

'Yes, yes, but they don't seem to be mechanically far advanced. No vehicles, no machinery on display in the shops.'

'True, but they can't be poor. Look at the range of goods, and the extravagant way the women are dressed. They're creating wealth somehow, and a lot of it.'

'We can explore that later. Right now we want the business district, not the shopping centre.'

'I suppose so,' she said wistfully. 'You know, Richard, I haven't seen a single man yet.'

'What? Oh, don't be silly. Look –'

'No, you look. I'm sure I haven't.'

They walked on in silence for a while. All the streets seemed to be much the same, lined with trees and a mixture of shops, homes, and cafés, and filled with bustling crowds of women. Look where he would, Staines couldn't see a single man.

'Well,' he said, chuckling, 'it looks as if the women do all the chores around here. No men wasting their time with the shopping.'

'Doubtless they're all in your business district,' replied Marie tartly.

'Quite possibly they are.' He looked around again, beginning to feel rather self-conscious. Many of the women were watching him curiously, and it occurred to him to wonder if, on this world, it was considered unmanly to be seen on the streets in daylight.

'I think we should go inside one of the buildings,' he said at last. 'We're not learning anything here.'

'I don't know. Shouldn't we report back to the captain first?'

Ignoring her, he pointed to a large detached building which was set a little way back from the road. 'Look, this is obviously a public building. We'll go in here.'

He led the way up a broad flight of steps and between a pair of huge oak doors into a busy foyer. Women hurried to and fro, and there was what looked like a reception desk towards the back of the room. Corridors led off to left and right and, apart from its relaxed atmosphere, the place reminded him of a hospital.

'Do you have an appointment?'

He looked round to see a rather elderly woman regarding him with a frown. 'Er, no,' he said. 'We were just looking.'

The translator startled her, but then her brow cleared. 'Ah, you must be the out-of-town actors. You are, of course, welcome to use our facilities if you have the need.'

'Thank you,' said Staines. He glanced at Marie and nodded slightly. Now they might learn something. 'Do you think you could show us around?'

'Of course. This way, please.' She led them across the foyer and along the right-hand corridor. 'Which of you require our services?' she asked. 'Or is it both . . . ?'

'What exactly is it you have on offer?'

'See for yourselves.'

She led them through a door back into the open air, and they found themselves standing on a narrow walkway which ran around an enclosed courtyard. Their guide gestured into the space below.

'Oh, my God.' Staines gaped in disbelieving horror.

'Wow,' said Marie. She clutched his arm. '*Wow!*'

The grassy space below had been divided into dozens of pens, and in each pen stood, sat, or lay a naked man. They looked like caged animals. From his vantage-point on the walkway, Staines could feel their pent-up energy coming at him in waves, and from her reaction it was pretty obvious that Marie could too. They were the most magnificent specimens of manhood Staines had ever seen. They ranged from sleek athletic types through to men whose stature left him in awe, but every one was a perfect physical specimen.

Several of the nearer men had seen him, and they raised beseeching eyes. Some held out their hands, and they began to shout. Those further away leapt to their feet, and soon all the men were crying out to him.

The horror welled up inside him as he saw the desperation

of these poor, caged humans. His breath came quicker and his heart thundered in his chest.

'I can see that you are both in need,' said their guide calmly. 'Make your choice, and I will take you to your chambers.'

'That one,' said Marie, pointing dazedly.

'What? What are you talking about?'

'Select a mate.'

'A *mate*?' The full import of what he was seeing struck home, tying up with other observations. 'You keep men prisoner, penned up, just to act as breeding stock?'

She looked at him blankly, as if his question were meaningless.

'Marie, come on, we have to report back. Marie!' He grabbed her arm as she continued to stare, mesmerized, into the courtyard.

'I think I'd better stay,' she said weakly.

'Marie, pull yourself together!' He dragged her away from the railing, back into the building. Halfway down the corridor, she shook him off.

'Shit!' she said. 'All right, I'm coming. Yes, it's horrible, but God – those bodies!'

He turned on her furiously, but she grinned and squeezed his arm. 'Women are human too, you know,' she said. 'But I'd rather have you. Come on!' They hurried into the street and back to the ship.

'The rest of the time they live semi-wild on reserves,' Jirela finished. 'It keeps them fit and healthy. Really we don't pay the subject a lot of attention. It's just a biological urge, and this seems the most efficient way of dealing with it whilst giving the males a decent life. Some people abstain, but I find it best to succumb and then forget all about it. That's all.'

Louise leant back on her couch and laughed helplessly. Jirela watched, puzzled and intrigued. She was really very attractive, although she appeared to have done her best to ruin her looks. Perhaps it was the fashion, back wherever it was that she came from.

'Why do you laugh?' she asked at last.

Louise tried to pull herself together. 'You make it all sound as tedious as menstruation,' she gasped. 'Something to be dealt with efficiently and then forgotten. I love it!'

'Well of course it coincides with menstruation,' said Jirela, even more puzzled. 'Where *are* you from?'

'I'm from Earth. From very close to here, in fact.' Louise calmed, although she continued to smile at her private joke. 'But I come from another universe.'

'That doesn't make sense. You can't have it both ways.'

'Yes I can. You see, there isn't one universe, but an infinite number, all coexisting in the same space. Whenever a decision is made, from the atomic level upwards, reality splits. Every possibility is catered for. Everything that can happen, does happen. Somewhere.'

'So what is the basic difference between your universe and mine?'

'In my world, men are sentient too,' said Louise sadly.

The three men emerged from the clinic and Staines silently led them to a bench. His companions sat down, while he paced up and down in front of them, chewing at a thumb-nail.

'It's horrible,' said Dunnett. 'I've never seen anything like it.'

Wallace looked more shaken than Staines had ever seen him. He stared at the ground. 'My orders say we are to observe, record, and report,' he said, almost to himself. 'I've got them in black and white.'

'We can't leave them,' said Staines. 'Did you ever see such a set of men? They'll go crazy locked up like that.'

'With a platoon of men like those . . .' said Wallace. He shook his head. 'But it's not our reality. We can't meddle.'

'We have to help them,' Staines insisted.

'I don't know. They're well cared for, as you say they're healthy. Obviously well exercised –'

Dunnett choked off a laugh. 'I'll say.' He gestured at the activity around the clinic, where women constantly came and went in ones and twos. 'The girls are making the most of it, I'll give 'em that, sir.'

Wallace ground his teeth. 'Breeding stock!' he exclaimed bitterly. 'I had a wife. When I'd given her three kids she threw me out. And I'm still paying maintenance. Making the most of it? Yes, they all do that.'

'And it's been going on here for – who knows how long,' said Staines. 'Look around. There's no sign of war or riot. This could have been going on for centuries.'

'It's for their own good, sir,' said Dunnett. 'The women as well as the men. I think we should do something. They'll thank us in the long run.'

'But we're here as observers!' cried Wallace. 'There's nothing in my orders about military coups.'

'I think we could be a little more subtle than that,' said Staines. 'What do you say, captain?'

Wallace looked up and shrugged helplessly. 'I don't see what we can do.'

'Well,' began Staines slowly. 'I have a plan . . .'

Louise awakened suddenly, aware of strange surroundings. She sat bolt upright and stared around, confused.

Someone laughed, and a voice spoke in a lilting, foreign tongue. She looked over her shoulder, and recognized Areen. Memory returned, and she grinned, and switched on the translator.

'Good morning. I was still in a dream. Are you better today?'

'Perfectly recovered, thank you. I get PCT very badly, and it takes a day or so to get over it.'

'PCT?'

'Pre coital tension. Don't you get it?'

'Something very similar.' Louise threw off her blanket and stretched luxuriously. Halfway through the action she remembered the rest of the previous day's experiences, and froze. 'Sorry,' she said, relaxing in embarrassment. 'I'm so used to sharing quarters with Marie Jarvis.'

'Your lover?' asked Areen, smiling.

'God no. She's into men.'

'Men?' Areen looked puzzled. Then her eyes widened. 'What, all the time? Ugh!'

Louise chuckled and reached for her coverall. 'Yes, all the time. It's quite common where I come from.'

'Wait. I'll get you a gown. That thing's so – well, unflattering.'

'Service uniform. I'm paid by the military and I have to wear their clothes.'

Areen brought a bright scarlet gown and helped her to dress. The cloth felt cool and pleasant to the touch. 'Is it wool?' she asked.

'Linen. I help with the harvest and the spinning in season. Here, it goes like this.'

As they finished arranging the gown, Jirela came into the room, accompanied by another woman. Louise recognized her as the one who had yesterday spoken to Wallace at the ship. She was short and broadly built with a square, humorous face. She turned clear brown eyes on Louise and looked her up and down.

'Honna, may I introduce our friend Louise,' said Jirela.

Louise smiled uncertainly, and held out her hand. Honna ignored it. She met her eyes squarely and Louise felt a sudden shock go through her. This woman was something special.

Suddenly Honna relaxed, stepped up to her and, placing a hand on either shoulder, kissed her. 'Welcome to our city,' she said. An extra pressure of her hands, a piercing look, and then she had stepped back. 'I gather from Jirela that your performance yesterday was not in the nature of a play at all.'

'No, we –'

'I'm relieved. Such a poor performance pains me. But tell me, the one who spoke, can she sing?'

Louise, poised to give her explanation, was brought up short. 'Sing?'

'I've seldom heard such a rich bass voice. I want her for the choir.'

'I'm afraid I haven't told Honna very much yet,' said Jirela apologetically. 'I didn't want to get it wrong, so I thought it might be better if you . . .'

Louise nodded. The last thing she wanted to talk to Honna about was men. But she had landed herself in this. She wondered how to begin.

'Jirela!' Someone came rushing breathlessly through the open door. 'Oh, Honna, there you are. Everyone's looking for you. One of the studs is loose. There's chaos in Market Square!'

'Goddess!' Honna leapt to her feet. 'Have the Keepers been sent for?'

'Of course, but they won't be here for a while. The shoppers are keeping him penned in, but he's not responding to calming tactics. Nobody fancies tackling him.'

'No, no, that's all right. I'll come at once.' Honna hurried out with the messenger.

'Oh dear,' said Areen. 'I hope he's caught before he hurts himself. They're so easily panicked.'

'Does this happen often?'

'No, they're very carefully looked after, but no system's foolproof. Honna can handle it though.'

'I'm sure Honna could handle anything,' Louise agreed.

Jirela smiled. 'I'll bring her back again later. Honna's on the Committee, so the two of you really ought to have a long chat.'

'Good. I'd enjoy that.'

Wallace and the two remaining crew members sat gloomily around the mess table. 'Tarrant had no business going off on her own at all,' he said. 'I told her to stay here, and now she's still not back. Anything could have happened.'

'She is the anthropologist,' said Marie, 'and this is the first time she's had anything to do. I expect she got engrossed. I'm sure she'll be safe enough. They are all women.'

'Lesbians,' said Dunnett sourly. 'I wouldn't feel safe alone out there.'

'Anyway, that's not the point,' said Wallace. 'She disobeyed a direct order, and while we're in the field you people are not civilians, you're under my command. Is that clear?'

'All right. I haven't done anything wrong, have I?'

'Just keep it that way.' He drew a deep breath. 'We need Tarrant here. Our resources are stretched to the limit. With Staines locked up in that human cattle-pen it only leaves three of us to create a diversion, steal the keys, and open the gates. If one of us gets caught, we're really in trouble.'

'I don't think Louise would want to help anyway,' said Marie bluntly.

'Why not?' snapped Dunnett. 'D'you think she has some kind of sympathy with this culture?'

'Oh, no, no. But, I mean, she probably wants to study it properly before we liberate it.'

'It's no good,' said Wallace firmly. 'We've got to find her. We need the manpower. We'll split up. Dunnett, you and I need to shave before we go out again. Jarvis, you can start at once.'

'But – alone?'

'Captain, she might get raped.'

'Jarvis, I would expect you to go out alone in a male culture, so what's the difference?'

'Even in this liberated age, there are still some fates worse than death,' Marie muttered, but she went.

As soon as she was safely out of sight, Wallace began rummaging in the back of the equipment locker. 'Right, that's got her out of the way. We'd better get going.'

'But I thought we needed everyone.'

'Not with these on our side.' He dug out a box and blew the dust off the lid. 'God, these things must have been lying around since we started training. No, this is best done as a purely military operation. She's better off out of it.'

Dunnett nodded. 'I'm sure you're right, sir. And I've never yet met a woman who could keep her head in an emergency.'

Wallace grunted noncommittally. 'Come on. Let's go.'

*

203

The streets seemed busier than before. Marie wandered rather helplessly, keeping close to the trunks of the trees, nervously eyeing the passers-by. Most of them returned her inspection, their eyes sweeping lasciviously along the lines of her breasts and thighs. Before she had gone a mile she felt like screaming every time someone new turned to look at her. She found herself rounding her shoulders and shambling gracelessly. Perhaps if she rolled her eyes and drooled it would stop them ogling.

'Oh, this is ridiculous,' she muttered at last. 'She could be anywhere.' Gathering up her courage, she approached an elderly couple and asked timidly if they had seen another woman dressed like her. They shook their heads and continued with their chat. Marie hurried on.

At the third attempt, a shopkeeper told her that yes, of course, her companion was a popular topic of conversation. She thought that Louise was staying with a woman called Jirela, but anyone would know.

Marie asked twice more and finally located Jirela's house, sandwiched between a café and a clothes shop in a quiet side street. The door was open, so, after a moment's hesitation, she went in.

Two women were fondling one another on the sofa. She was backing out again when she recognized the one in scarlet. 'Louise!' she shrieked.

Louise's head snapped round, and she leapt to her feet. 'Marie! What the hell are you doing here?'

'I – I – I –' said Marie.

Louise strode across the room, seized her by the elbow, and pulled her in through the door.

'Don't touch me!' Marie cried.

Louise released her with a look of disgust. 'Sit down and pull yourself together,' she snapped.

Marie sank into a chair. 'But, but, you were – she was – all that time in training I shared quarters with you!'

'Yes, and I never touched you once. Doesn't that show remarkable self-restraint?'

'You mean you *wanted* to?'

'No, as it happens, I didn't.'

'Oh.' Marie sank back in her chair. Louise was looking overheated and annoyed. The other woman, reclining on the sofa at a safe distance, seemed amused. Marie straightened her coverall, smoothed down her hair, and wondered what to say next. 'Louise ... the captain wants to see you back at the ship.'

'I assumed you hadn't come barging in here by accident. Look, I'm busy researching this most unusual culture. Can't it wait?'

'I take it the research can't?' Louise looked suddenly embarrassed, and Marie felt her confidence returning. She pressed home her advantage. 'No, it can't. And I have a feeling there are things you haven't been told about this "most unusual culture".'

'Such as what, for instance?'

'Such as the way they treat their men.'

'Oh, God.' Louise ran a hand through her already tousled hair. 'Just what do you think you've found out?'

'I've seen it. Grown men penned up like animals.'

'Marie, the men here are animals.'

'You would say that, wouldn't you? I suppose you think Richard's an animal, and the captain, don't you?'

'No, of course not. Even Richard has his good points. I meant it literally. On this world, men are non-sentient.'

Marie was thinking of Richard, now penned up like the rest, naked, helpless, relying on his native wit to win over the men to his purpose ...

'Non-sentient!' she yelled. 'What do you mean, non-sentient?'

'On this world only women developed intelligence, as a by-product of having to rear children, create a home, and avoid being beaten to death by their somewhat violent mates. Meanwhile, the imperatives of hunting, holding territory, and winning wives kept the men chained to the dark master of instinct. I suspect the dividing line between the two cultures is not as broad as you might think.'

'But Richard's in there,' said Marie in horror.

'What do you mean?'

'He's in there, in the pens. We were going to rescue the men from their slavery, set this culture back on the right path. We thought –'

'You idiots!' cried Louise furiously. 'Let him stay there. He deserves to be ripped to shreds.'

The other woman had been following the conversation via Louise's translator, which lay on the floor beside the sofa. Now she said: 'If he tries to approach any of the studs he probably will be. They have to be kept strictly apart, or they fight to the death.'

'Louise, some of those men are *huge*. Richard hasn't got a chance!'

'Oh shit. Honna, where was that captured male taken? We'd better rescue the bastard.'

The pen seemed smaller when viewed from the inside. Staines lay on his back digesting the fact that he had just been scientifically immobilized by a single woman. It hurt. Physically it hurt and his ego was bruised even more. Still, he was where he had planned to be, in with the men. He could smell good, honest male sweat, like the changing rooms after a hard workout at the gym.

He clambered to his feet and looked around him. The pen had a grassy floor and strong wooden walls. A thick wire mesh ran across the top, making it impossible to climb out that way. It was bare of everything except a pile of straw. Come to think of it, he could smell good, honest male urine too. Barbaric.

The front of his pen was a grid of solid iron bars. He took hold of them and shook. They didn't even rattle.

Across a wide pathway was another pen. The man inside wandered curiously to his door and stared at Staines. He was almost a giant in stature, his arms and chest ridged and corded with muscles. They rippled smoothly under his bronzed skin as he copied Richard's gesture, wrapping huge, blunt-fingered hands around the bars. They bent a little as he tugged.

'Hiya, mate,' said Staines cheerily. 'I'm glad you're on my side.'

The man grunted, a dour monosyllable.

'Don't worry, I'm getting you out of here.'

The man's lips parted in a fierce grin as Richard pointed along the passage. He shook his mane of black hair and tugged at the bars again.

Staines examined the door to his pen. It was fastened with a complex catch, but there seemed to be no lock. He stared, pressing his face against the metal grid. He reached a hand through one of the gaps, and touched the mechanism. Surely that couldn't be right. He fiddled with the fastenings. They were small, made for women's fingers. His hand sweated and slipped, but after an agonized couple of minutes he got it undone. The door swung open.

'Captivity's softened your brain,' he said sadly, shaking his head. 'You could have done that yourself years ago. Here, I'll show you.'

The giant watched silently as Staines unfastened the catch on his door. 'There you are, mate.' With a flourish, he threw open the prison door. The giant stared. Then with a roar, he rushed out and wrapped his arms around his benefactor in a rib-cracking hug.

'Hey!' cried Staines breathlessly. 'Forget it. You'd do the same for me. Aargh!'

'Do you have an appointment?'

Dunnett watched from an unobtrusive corner of the foyer as an attendant accosted Wallace. 'No,' he heard his captain reply, 'I'm afraid not. Could I make one for later today?'

The attendant shrugged, eyeing him curiously. 'Don't you find it awkward, with so many of your company coming on heat at once?'

'Well, it can't be helped,' said Wallace easily. 'And it gets it over with, doesn't it? Ha, ha!'

Dunnett shuddered and covered his eyes for a moment. He felt a sudden wave of homesickness.

The attendant's curiosity seemed satisfied. 'We always keep a few studs in reserve for emergencies,' she said. 'Would you like to come through now?'

Wallace's eyes flickered briefly towards Dunnett, then back to the woman. 'Yes, please,' he said. She led him away.

Dunnett looked around. There were about eight other attendants scattered through the foyer, mostly busy dealing with the women who were continually passing to and fro. As soon as Wallace had disappeared he slipped quietly along the wall, dropping a series of small canisters in his wake.

As the curls of smoke began to drift across the room, he ran out into the opening screaming: 'Fire! Fire! Help, help, fire! Help!'

Heads turned. Someone shouted. Then the whole room was in motion, women running everywhere, calling excitedly to one another. Hardly anyone made for the exits.

'Help! Help! Run for your lives!' he screamed hoarsely. Lines were forming and buckets appeared as if from nowhere. 'We'll all burn!' he cried. 'Save yourselves! Save yourselves!'

Hands grabbed his arms and he was propelled gently but firmly into a side room. 'It's all right, dear,' said a soothing voice in his ear. 'You just lie down here. Everything's going to be all right.'

He struggled against the gentle hands which bore him inexorably down onto a couch. 'You don't understand!' he cried. 'You have to get out of the building! You have to!'

The three women sprinted up to the clinic and pushed their way, panting, through the small crowd of curious onlookers. They stared in dismay at the clouds of smoke billowing out through the doors. A number of women were sprawled on the wide, shallow steps, coughing and retching. Marie gave a supressed shriek and grabbed Louise's arm. 'Richard's in there!'

'So are a lot of other people. What the hell have they done?'

Honna was trying to get some sense out of two smoke-blackened attendants who were gasping and choking, clutching each others' shoulders for support. 'It's all right,' she said at last. 'Nothing seems to be burning. Several of these were found where the smoke was thickest.'

She held out a sooty metal canister. Louise took it, and reflexively crushed it in her fist as she glared up the steps. 'Smoke bombs! They must have intended it as a diversion. Where are they?'

'One is being restrained in a side room,' said Honna. 'The attendants thought she – he – was panicking. I don't know about the others.'

'Come on,' said Louise. 'We have to find them.'

She ran up the steps and into the building, closely followed by Marie. The smoke closed in behind them and they found themselves suddenly plunged into near darkness. Acrid fumes caught at their throats, and they began to cough. Billows of smoke parted and closed, giving brief glimpses of a woman still pouring water onto the offending canisters, and of the women who blundered past, making for the exit now that the emergency was over. Louise stopped, disoriented.

A hand caught her shoulder and Marie shouted in her ear: 'This way!' She followed across the foyer, unable to see more than a few feet ahead. A corridor loomed suddenly to their right and they darted into it. The air was clearer here and they broke into a staggering run, gasping for breath.

Rounding a corner, they came upon the crumpled body of an attendant, breathing heavily. Wallace was bending over the catch which held the door into the pens closed. From behind it came a muffled shouting.

'Captain, don't!' Louise ran forward, but too late. With a yell of triumph, he flung the door open.

An immense figure charged out, flattening Wallace against the wall with a single blow of his fist. Then he stopped, and glowered at the two women.

The stud was huge, sweat glistening on his herculean chest. His nostrils flared as he scented them. His face was blank of all emotion except a savage lust.

'Oh, my God.' Louise began to back off, slowly. Marie

seemed mesmerized by the creature. 'Marie,' said Louise in a low voice. 'Walk towards me, slowly.'

'He's incredible!' Marie gasped.

'Marie!'

The stud reacted to the sharpness in her voice. His gaze focused on her, then swung back to Marie. He was getting an erection.

'Oh, shit.' Louise edged forward again, reaching for Marie's shoulder. 'Come on, Marie, it's just pheromones. Fight them. Think of Richard. You can do it.'

Marie shook her head, never taking her eyes from the beast-man before her. 'Piss off, Louise. You wouldn't understand.'

Louise hesitated, her hand only inches from Marie's shoulder. 'He'll kill you.'

'Leave me alone.'

'*Marie!*' cried a male voice.

The giant swung round, and Marie sagged into Louise's arms. Framed in the doorway to the pens stood Richard. He swayed a little on his feet and there was blood running freely from a cut over his right eye, but he was ready to fight for his woman.

Louise began to drag Marie towards safety. 'Men!' she exclaimed.

The giant lunged, but Richard was ready for him this time. He stepped neatly to the side and delivered a sharp blow just below his adversary's ear with the side of his hand. The stud collapsed, but almost immediately he pushed himself up again, shaking his head groggily. Richard closed in and kicked him in the kidneys. The giant howled and leapt convulsively to his feet. Richard hauled off and laid a right-arm hook into his face. Blood spurted. Louise looked away.

'Wait!' cried a voice. 'You'll damage him!'

Richard got in two more vicious punches before Honna reached him. She shoved him aside and stepped fearlessly up to the staggering stud. He lowered his head and stared at her. She pushed him in the chest, taking another step closer, and he began to turn back towards the pens. Then his knees buckled and he collapsed with a grunt, and lay still.

Richard stood panting for a couple of seconds, then he keeled over in a dead faint.

Marie shrieked and lapsed unconscious in Louise's arms.

Louise looked at Honna, who looked back at Louise. Louise closed her eyes and shook her head in despair. Honna started to laugh.

A huge crowd had gathered in Gaia Park. Almost the entire population had turned out to catch a glimpse of the three sentient males. Jirela and Areen, returning from a check-up at the clinic, were late on the scene and so found themselves at the very back of the crowd. They could see very little of the proceedings, and hear nothing, but they craned forward in hushed stillness nevertheless.

The crew stood in a group at the bottom of the ramp leading into their ship. Staines, bandaged and pale, was leaning heavily on Marie's shoulders, while Wallace and Dunnett shuffled their feet and stared at the ground a lot.

A short conversation ensued, in which Honna appeared to have distinctly the upper hand. The men nodded and squirmed and finally made their way hurriedly up the ramp, accompanied by Marie. At the top they paused and looked back, gesturing urgently. Some of the crowd afterwards insisted that Louise had then joined them, others that only four figures had been swallowed by the closing door. Everyone agreed that the egg had vanished silently and suddenly.

Jirela and Areen made their way against the crowd to the place where the egg had stood, but Honna was gone before they got there. Areen bent and touched the flattened grass. 'It really did happen then,' she said. 'Did *you* see if Louise stayed or went?'

Jirela smiled. 'Everything that can happen, does happen. Somewhere,' she murmured.

'What?'

'Nothing. Let's go home.'

They walked slowly from the park, and when they had gone there was nothing but the sun and the trees and the grass slowly straightening itself.

DAYS IN THE LIFE OF A GALACTIC EMPIRE

by
Brian W. Aldiss

Brian Aldiss is the godfather of British science fiction: author, critic, editor, essayist, anthologist, historian, reviewer, actor and trapeze artist. His achievements and awards could fill a page of this collection, a list of his novels and short stories even more pages: from his first SF book *Space, Time and Nathaniel* (Stan, for short) through to *Trillion Year Spree*, written with David Wingrove, which won the Science Fiction Achievement Award in 1987 (Hugo, for short).

Ibrox Villiers Cley remained entirely within his chambers while the Second Galactic War was waged. He saw few people.

His leisure time, which was ample, was spent mainly in aesthetic contemplation of the moral and social degeneration of which he considered himself a part, if apart.

Cley was ill, subtle, devious, sardonic, and a servant.

His manner was cheerful, even metallic, to cover his deep-rooted depression.

Cley served the Emperor of the Eternal Galaxy under the Banner of A Thousand Stars. He served the Emperor well by telling him the truth and by refusing to scheme against him. His distaste for other people kept him aloof from plots and treacheries.

The Emperor ruled over a million suns and three and a half million planets. Most of the planets were inhabited, by robot task forces if not by human beings.

The Emperor was himself a prisoner. The Emperor had been born and would die in what was called the Galactic Paradise. Guards never left his presence.

Every man and woman was his slave. And he was theirs. The Conventional Rules of Duty bound him as they bound his subjects.

The Conventional Rules of Duty constituted, or rather re-placed, all metaphysical systems within the Eternal Galaxy.

Ibrox Villiers Cley was almost as respected as the Emperor. His chambers were in the Galactic Paradise on the planet Voltai. His official title was Advisor of the Computers. He saw the Emperor in person every third day.

Those meetings were enclosed within a Fifth Force Field, so that no one ever knew what passed between the Emperor and his Advisor of the Computers. No note was taken, no record was made.

The edicts continued from the Throne Computer. The Galactic War continued, as it had for many generations.

The war was going well for the galactic empire. Twenty four solar systems held by the enemy had recently been destroyed. Countless populations were starving.

Whole armies fought and died under the Conventional Rules of Duty. They died without questioning the cause. The number of their deaths was reported to Ibrox Villiers Cley.

Cley's chambers were built of one of the new metals created through the exigencies of war. Cley himself had a sheen as of metal about him. His temples were palisades against the world of outside iniquity.

The perpetual light of Voltai came in through his long windows. Cley's chambers had no internal lighting. It was the fashion. He preferred to live in chiaroscuro.

His rooms differed little, one from another. In the sombre main chamber where most of his days were spent, there was no decoration, no contrasting texture. In a case along one wall were stored the six hundred and seventy seven volumes of the Eternal Galactic Encyclopedia, each cube awaiting activation.

Cley rarely referred to the encyclopedia.

His modest needs were served by an android called Marnya. Marnya had beauty of a severe kind. Her smiles were few and wintry. She had been designed by Cley's father, long ago.

Marnya was always about in Cley's chambers as a silent presence. She was a shadow within shadows. She was like an embodiment of the Conventional Rules of Duty. She provided most of the company that Cley needed. She was calm, loyal, without deceit, and self-lubricating.

Reports came to Cley on his desk screen of the numbers of men, women, and children who died every day for the sake of Empire. Sometimes he read these casualties aloud to Marnya.

'There are always more people,' she said.

He tapped the screen. 'These people are lost for ever.'

'But were they precious?'

'Not to me or you, Marnya, but to someone. And to themselves.'

'They became most precious when they fulfilled the Conventional Rules.'

'Certainly that is conventional wisdom.'

She sat down beside him and laid a velvety hand over his. 'They had no existence until the report showed on your screen, as far as you and I are concerned. Their existence was as brief as a phosphor dot.'

'They lived and died. No doubt in a brutish way.'

'It happened far away.'

'Yes, it was far away.'

Sometimes, Ibrox Villiers Cley had Marnya play him a piece of music composed long ago on a planet now forgotten in a remote galaxy. The music was written before the Conventional Rules were imposed on musicians. It was good, sensible, male music, without display, yet with a poignance of which Cley did not tire.

In a case beside the encyclopedia stood a solitary cube. Marnya occasionally activated it for Cley. The cube contained the works of a poet who had died in the distant town where Cley was born. On the last pages of the cube, the infant Cley had inscribed a map.

The map showed the kind of town which did not exist anywhere in the empire. It had not been formalized. The street system did not accord to a grid pattern. Roads ran here and there, houses were of various sizes. The house where the old poet died was marked.

The whole map spoke of a rampant but vanished individualism.

The cube was Cley's only personal possession.

Cley did not pretend to be, or aspire to be, a friend of the Emperor's. There was too much power, too many regulations, in the air for emotions to flourish. The Emperor merely consulted him. He was merely one of the Emperor's tools. This function he understood. It was reliable, as things go. Friendship he found more difficult to comprehend.

Nor did he cultivate relations with those on Voltai who admired him. They thought of Cley as a guru.

He mistrusted ravishment by charm, spiritual appeal, force, wit, or other blandishments.

Power favoured coldness, just as the empire favoured ruthlessness.

All empires are unscrupulous.

If Ibrox Villiers Cley was one thing, he was scrupulous.

Cley's closest acquaintance was Councillor Deems. Councillor Ardor Deems was Galactic Minister of the Arts.

Deems was a soft and highly coloured man who spoke always in a low voice. So low was Deems' voice that his auditors had to give it close attention. This habitual quietness had earned Deems the reputation for subtlety in his dealings. As he adapted himself to this reputation, Deems indeed grew subtle in his affairs, until man and reputation became one.

His gowns were always of softer material than the gowns of other ministers. His cheeks remained stubbornly rosy, even as his thought grew more pallid.

He came one day softly to see Cley, to discuss with him whether to ban, as it was in his power to do, a new play entitled, 'Forgotten Robe, Abyss, Glitter'.

'Certainly the play advocates a continuation of the war, as plays nowadays are required to do,' said Deems, folding his hands and placing them gently on the table before him, as if to show that he concealed nothing. 'But it also advocates extreme cruelty against animals as a matter of imperial policy, in order to dismay the enemy. Is that not obscenity?'

'The cruelty to which animals do you consider most obscene?'

'The play specifies long-drawn-out public torture for many animals, especially those the playwright deems most to offend against the Conventional Rules of Duty. To wit, cats, monkeys, meekrahs, jewkes, and miniature elephants.'

The fine lines of Cley's face could be studied as he gazed towards the ceiling before speaking again.

'You ask if this cruelty is obscene. The play's not a covert satire against the state, is it? It seems to me no more – and no less – obscene than the new Ministry of War headquarters just built on our satellite. We ban plays. No one bans architecture.'

'The rules for censorship of architecture might be difficult to draw up.'

'The Computers could do it without trouble. But humanity has a basic need for ugliness and brutality in its public buildings.'

'But not in its plays?'

'The majority of people do not care to hear of the torture of elephants. Except, of course, in our Eastern Region.'

Deems' eyes were soft, and did not rest long in one place, as if they sought something they feared to find. 'And the torture of children?'

'The majority do not mind that as much. We are accustomed, almost from birth, to hear of children being maltreated. Accounts of child abuse sell newsfulg.'

'If there is some hint of sexual abuse, certainly . . . Ibrox, I am a liberal man. I have wept to hear of children ill-treated. Even children on quite distant planets.'

'Congratulations. Your grief did you honour, as you know. You could relish both the pain of the children and your grief at the same time.'

'Oh, I am sincere.' He spoke without emphasis, and removed a white cloth from his collar with which to wipe his lips. 'Such crimes are common on Voltai. Other worlds, other mores . . .'

Although Deems spoke of other planets, Cley's chamber was perfectly prosaic, apart from its melancholy air. There was no sign that decisions were taken here which would affect populations on distantly scattered worlds. Cley's chambers suited the mentality of the entombed rather than the star-conscious.

After a pause, Deems said, 'I take it that you would not ban performances of "Forgotten Robe, Abyss, Glitter"?'

'Last galactic day, seven billion people were destroyed by a panthrax bomb on the planet Jubilloo. Do we ban panthrax bombs? Until we do, why bother about banning plays? They kill no one.'

Councillor Ardor Deems took a turn about the long room. His slender figure was plunged first into light then into shadow as he passed before the slitted windows.

Ibrox Villiers Cley did not stir in his seat. His gaze remained fixed on the polished surface of the table, which dimly reflected the glooms and gleams of the room.

The councillor approached nearer to Cley than custom demanded.

'I hate this war. I hate it as much as you do, Ibrox. It has become a part of life.'

'War has always been a part of man's life. Ever since the days when we were creatures of one world.'

Deems nodded. 'I heard just recently that a first cousin of mine was destroyed in the Battle of the Lesser Sack.'

'Did you love him?'

'I hated him. I hated his destruction more. There's the family to consider . . .'

Cley smiled and nodded. 'The Lesser Sack was a great victory for the empire.'

Deems' manner altered. He pulled his chair nearer to Cley's and spoke in his softest voice. 'You will be seeing the Emperor again tomorrow?' He then repeated the question with variations, as his custom was, as if unable to rely on the understanding of even his most intelligent listener. 'You have an audience with him at nine hours?'

When he received a glance of affirmation, he leaned forward, to speak even more quietly. 'The war must end, Ibrox. It must be terminated. We are destroying worlds we should be using. The Emperor will not consider proposals for peace. His will is set on continuous war.'

When Cley made no comment, Deems continued. 'As long as we are winning the war, and there are victory parades, and banners, and speeches, the vast majority of the population is also for the war. Their personal miseries become insignificant when compared with bloodthirsty accounts from our various war sectors. They can feel their petty lives caught up in great events. They forget they are mere statistics. Their psychic health –'

'I am Advisor of the Computers, Deems, not a rabble to be addressed.'

'Pardon me. I will approach the central question. Let us get to the point. Factions of the enemy hierarchy have made contact with me. They are prepared to sue for peace. Before peace can come about, something must be done about the Emperor.'

The steely profile of Ibrox Villiers Cley appeared not to be listening.

Deems' voice sank further. 'Something must be done about the Emperor. His mind must be changed. He must prefer peace. I have in my possession a new drug which will have the required effect upon him.'

He paused and then said, in a whisper, 'My party wishes that you will administer the drug to the Emperor during your audience tomorrow at nine.'

From his pocket Deems produced an object which resembled a short pencil. He laid it on the table halfway between him and Cley, his head on one side as he appeared to measure the distance precisely.

Cley did not touch the weapon.

'There are, I take it, inducements to – encourage me to use this drug against the Emperor?'

'Not "against", Ibrox. "On".'

'The inducements?'

'We do not put pressure on you. We believe that your own high intelligence will suffice to induce you to use such a weapon which will stop the war at last.'

'You think well of my intelligence.'

'Come, Ibrox, you are considered one of the most intelligent men who ever lived.' He allowed a whisper of reproach into his tone. 'Hence your position. You will do this thing, won't you? It is a noble undertaking, no less.'

The long room contained a long silence.

'How does the drug work?'

'It's name is mascinploxyrhanophyhaninide, or MPRP for short. It is delivered by aurasol. You have but to press a button. It sedates areas in the limbic brain from which the instincts of aggression rise. Permanently sedates them . . . You have but to press the button at nine, Ibrox, and at nine-five our beloved empire will be moving towards peace. Otherwise the drug is harmless, apart from some side effects.'

'What side effects?'

Deems eyed Cley narrowly, watching his response. 'Blindness.'

Cley made no response. After a moment, he said, 'An aggressive weapon is not the most promising way through which to try to achieve peace.'

'We all depend on you, Ibrox. Not to be melodramatic, but the empire awaits your decision. Your name will be imperishable if you do this thing in the name of peace. You must do it for humanity's sake.' He put a finger delicately on the MPRP weapon.

Cley rose to his feet and stood gazing down at the councillor. 'I want you to examine this act in which you propose we should conspire with the enemy against our emperor. Whatever its motives, it represents a physical attack. It is by physical attacks that battles and wars begin rather than end. Yet, as a preliminary to peace, you wish to make an attack.

'Do you not see that, over a million wearying years of galactic history, so-called peace has invariably had its prelude in attack, so that the seeds of further conflict were sown? You merely perpetuate a status quo of constant warfare.

'How can war be eradicated? It is a permanent human condition. The baby emerges from the womb crying anger. Even the excision of the entire limbic brain would not suffice

224

to remove aggression. This aggression of yours, represented by this MPRP weapon, springs not from the limbic brain but from the neocortex. It is an intellectual form of aggression, born of ambition, self-seeking.'

'I seek only peace.'

'Humanity is an aggressive species and no drug will alter those inherent characteristics.'

'You are being cynical and evasive.' As he spoke, Deems rose, clutching the MPRP weapon.

'I prefer my cynicism to your self-deceiving optimism.'

'Ibrox, my party wishes merely to see an end to conflict. We desire to finish with galactic war for ever. Is that self-deceiving?'

'It is nothing if not self-deceiving. Your party wishes to elevate itself. It would conduct conflict by means of backdoor dealing.'

'Backdoor! Our aspirations are of the loftiest.'

'This is what plotters always say. Deems, it happens that I have read this play which so disturbs you. It is written by a self-seeker. You should conscript him to your party. We do not have great writers any more, men to whom we can turn for enlightenment and discussion of the most engaging problems. The Conventional Rules of Duty have swept such men away. They languish in our reformatories. Those remaining seek fame or money, preferring trumpery things above such immovable integrity. Your play is written for a materialistic and spiritually bankrupt society – the people of Voltai. It is designed to shock and titillate them. It can do no harm since its audience is already corrupt. Any public which did not rise up in protest at the expense and ugliness of the Ministry of War edifice is corrupt.'

'But that magnificent building on which you pour such –'

Cley held up a commanding hand. 'Humankind condemned itself a long while ago to a perpetual diet of catastrophe. It burdens itself with the consequences of its own indifference to what is best. Go into a tavern tonight and listen to the music played there. What is of merit, what is not ephemeral, is shunned. The good in man is out of fashion. Mankind has chosen – or perhaps it was never a choice – a perpetual diet of catastrophe. Since it cannot and will not save itself, it cannot be saved by anything you or I might do. Not to mention your party. No, not even by killing the Emperor.'

Deems' voice barely reached Cley's ears. 'We have evidence that the Emperor is mad.'

'Then he represents the people well. People like mad rulers. They relish the rhetoric. Words like blood and loyalty and revenge and endurance awaken something primitive in their auditors, who enjoy the sensation of adrenalin coursing in their veins. They enjoy enmities.'

'They enjoy defending themselves against enemies. They are not cattle. The Emperor has become the enemy and must be destroyed.'

'For the sake of our enemies?' Cley folded his arms and stared at Deems. 'The Emperor is not your enemy, Deems, except insofar as he stands in the way of your advancement. He aids and abets you in the task of self-destruction. We have no real enemies. You realize that? We have no real enemies throughout the whole galaxy. Our battlefields were once a cathedral, silent until the congregation of mankind entered. Enemies are as much an ancient human invention as God.'

Deems made to speak but thought better of it.

'Mankind has always been alone, ever since it left Earth, millennia ago. Mankind had been unable to endure the – the purity of that situation. And the responsibility that situation brings. It has thought only about building 'empires', absurd, repressive, and unstable power-structures. Empires failed on our mother planet – how much more philosophically untenable are they across a dozen, a hundred, a thousand, a thousand thousand planets? Yet, rather than think out new and just ways of distributing the riches to which we have all fallen heir, it uses those riches as the basis for deadly quarrels.

'Mankind's real love is not of life, but of self-destruction.'

Deems raised the MPRP weapon and pointed it at Cley's face.

226

'We have to get you out of the way before we deal with the Emperor.'

Cley said, 'If that weapon kills aggression, as you claim, then it will have no effect on me. My cynicism, to which you have drawn my attention, prevents my aggression. I have never wished for power. I have no ambition. I am used. You have used me in the past. In order to enjoy solitude, I am prepared to be used. But I fancy MPRP is unlikely to change my character.'

He spoke easily, spinning out his words, until Marnya had come softly up behind Deems and taken the councillor in her grasp. The arms that always held Cley tenderly were strong.

As Deems struggled fruitlessly, the MPRP weapon fell from his grasp and rolled under the table.

'Even if you'd fired your drug at Marnya, Deems, it would not have harmed her. Androids have no limbic brain, and no desires.'

Deems was pale. His voice was husky. 'I'm sorry to have threatened you, Ibrox. My desires ran away with me. I cannot bear your diseased view of mankind.'

'How is that, when you are diseased yourself?'

'Is to desire change a disease in your eyes?'

'You don't desire change. You desire power. That's the disease.'

Deems was silent, hanging his head and then asking in a subdued voice, 'What will you do with me? Remember I am an old man.'

'You are free to leave. Everything that has transpired in this room has been recorded. Take your drug with you. It does not work.'

As Marnya released the councillor, the latter said, 'The drug does work.'

'You lie. I also know who sent you to me. You were ordered by the Emperor to test me. There is no wish for peace, on our side, even on the enemy's. Only I wish for peace.'

'It's useless talking to you.' As he made to leave the chamber, Deems said, 'If you perceive that the Emperor does not trust you, why continue faithful?'

Cley gestured with his left hand. 'Through cynicism. I like being tested. It interests me. One day in the future, the treacherous Deems-figure who arrives to make the test will employ an argument so sophisticated that I shall be convinced by it, and enter the Emperor's Council Room and kill him.'

'I will report on what you say. So you do still have hope, of a sort?'

'So does the Emperor, of a sort. He prays for the Deems-figure to win.' Ibrox Villiers Cley permitted himself a smile. 'I have no hope for humanity, if that's what you mean. Only for myself. Hope that the day may come when I am surprised by goodness.'

He crossed over to Marnya and took her patient arm.

'Goodbye, Deems,' he said.

Deems wiped his lips on his cloth. He left the chamber without answer, knowing the fate of those who failed on an imperial mission.

Cley was left once more in his chambers, in the shadowy silence which was now his greatest pleasure.

SKYRIDER

by
William King

William King lives in Stranraer, and has previously sold a short story to *Interzone*. If the relevant issue of *Interzone* doesn't appear before this anthology, then what follows is his first published story. Otherwise, it's his second. He also has a mysterious benefactor who allows him to write full-time, and he is currently at work on a novel or more.

1

After the crash he was finished. One night he went over the wall and fare-jumped the first mag-lev out of Paris. He sat with a group of Workfree headed south to find a place in the state Pensions.

In the seat across from him sat a small dark-haired girl. Her name was Rosa. She had failed to find work in the theatre and was returning to Marseilles. She did most of the talking. There was little he could tell her.

He was on the run and wired for combat in an aircraft he would never fly again. He had just turned twenty-three.

2

The Wing carried him out over the bay towards Chateau d'If. Below, he could see the tourist hovercraft. All around a flock of flyers banked and wheeled, crucified on the skeletal struts of their harnesses.

He pulled himself into a shallow bank, watching the digital readouts on the inside of his visor climb into the danger zones, feeling the cold tug of the wind on his body. It was a clumsy way to fly, a pale shadow of being integrated into an aircraft, but it was the only thing he had. The government provided a complement of recreational Wings to all Pensions.

On the roof of the arcology he could see Rosa. She was talking with someone. She seemed to be pointing at him.

He was at the wrong angle to use the normal approach to the Pension's landing ramp. Rather than try for a long, slow arc around the building he decided on the more direct method of descent.

He came in at a steep angle, bringing the Wing into stall configuration. The memory plastic of the harness whipped around until the Wing was almost a parachute. He absorbed the impact of landing with a flex of his knees, feeling the shock through the cushioned soles of his boots. A quick glance showed Rosa and another woman approaching.

The woman was tall and thin; taught muscles rippled under her tiger-stripe skinpaint. The only thing she wore was a Braun wrist-tag.

Her name was Monica. She was Rosa's supplier on the odd days Rosa supplemented her government money with a little dealing. Rosa said she was an old friend, moving up in the world. She didn't seem to like her much.

'Rosa said you were a pilot.' said Monica. 'I can believe it.'

He shot Rosa an angry glance. She looked away guiltily. Her movements had an electric energy, her pupils were the size of pin-points.

'What's it matter to you?' he said.

She stared at him. Their glances locked. 'Do you really want to discuss it out here?' she asked.

He looked into her cold, blue eyes then shook his head. 'Let's go downstairs.'

Discreetly, Rosa stayed on the roof. She was staring in fascination at the empty sky overhead.

3

The apartment was small but it had all the basic amenities. The tube clicked on as they entered, showing scenes from a Front National rally. The right-wing alliance were getting a lot of media coverage. They were expected to hold the balance of power in the Euro-Parliament after the elections. He hit the off switch on the console and the wall went blank.

He pulled the duvet over the futon then began to empty the ashtrays. After years of barracks living, Rosa's untidiness made him uncomfortable.

Monica swept the room with her tag. She was checking for bugs.

'My, aren't we the paranoid one?' he said.

She continued the sweep as if she hadn't heard. With a quick jerk, she yanked out the fibre-optic cable connecting the tube console to the wall.

'Fibre-optics are virtually untappable,' he said.

'Can't be too careful.'

'Get to the point.'

'Right. You don't officially exist, yet you're living in State housing reserved for the Workfree.'

'So what? I live with Rosa. I've dropped out of the social security network. I'm not unusual. There must be thousands of invisible people in Marseilles.'

'But you're a pilot.'

His sockets were like Rosa's scars. They could not be hidden in the intimacy of the bedroom. She had kept asking about them and one drunken night he had told her. He had never asked about the scars.

'It's strange that a man who can fly lives in a Pension. You have a skill. You could have a well-paid job if you wanted.'

'Maybe I can't fly. Maybe I only told Rosa that to impress her.'

'No. You can fly. We checked.' She told him his real name, his squadron, the name of the hospital where the motor and perceptual centres of his brain had been modified. While she spoke, he gazed past her.

'What do you want?' he asked, still not meeting her eyes.

'We want to give you a job. Pay you for what you were trained to do.'

He could see her striped back reflected in the wallscreen. She was offering him a chance to fly again in a proper aircraft. He had been remade by the military into a human component for a flying machine. He could only ever function fully in the air.

'You were trained to fly helicopters,' said Monica.

'Anything I can be hooked into.'

'You didn't get this in an army surplus store,' he told Monica, running his hands along the cool carbon-fibre flank of the Mitsubishi Skyrider. She laughed and turned to look up at the green slopes of the Atlas mountains.

His respect for Monica's connections had increased greatly. In its day, the Skyrider had been very near state-of-the-art. Probably some Third World dictator had boosted his coffers by selling this one.

'It's fucking beautiful.' He felt exultation well up in him as he gazed at his idea of perfection: the sleek propfan jet with reinforced rotors for near supersonic flight, streamlined as a shark, ominous bulges of weapons pods under each wing and a turret in its underbelly.

'It's radar invisible. We have the latest electronic counter measures systems on board. It's fuelled and ready to go.'

He looked back at the white painted mansion. Men in Bed-ouin robes and heavy, insulated gauntlets were carrying crates out from the house. They held them at arm's length. The metal boxes glistened with moisture, condensation from the cool of their cryogenic interiors. Men with submachine-guns watched from the roof.

'What are they?' he asked.

'Spare parts.' She studied him closely. 'Do you have a problem with that?'

He shivered a little. 'No,' he said, at last. 'No. They've got to come from somewhere.'

5

Overhead, the fixed stars of the orbital factory halo gleamed in the night sky. He climbed into the cockpit. Monica clambered in beside him. He noticed the bulge of a holster under her cutaway jacket. She was wearing the baroque multi-layered skirts and jackets fashionable with the Nova Rich this season.

She pulled on a mike and headset. 'Ready?'

He spooled out the fibre-optic cable, felt the click as he connected its jack-plug with his spinal socket. He leaned back and closed his eyes, feeling awareness of the onboard systems sweep over him in a familiar rush.

The Skyrider became his body, he became its brain. The engine throb was his heartbeat, complex detection systems were his senses.

After long abstinence the sudden flow of information was almost too much, an ecstatic experience more intense than any drug. He could perceive a new and larger universe through senses better and faster than human. His body was no longer a weak, pulpy envelope of flesh but a sleek, hard thing, knowing neither weakness nor desire. In that moment he felt like a god, ready to leap into the sky and hurtle through the vast African night.

With an effort he regained control, forced himself to monitor the incoming dataflow and begin the pre-flight checks. There came a thrill of recognition as he spotted what he had missed in the initial confusion of jacking in.

'New systems,' he said.

'Very new. But you should be used to them.'

The hardware was highly classified, cutting edge military gear, the kind he had been trained to use.

He reached out with radar fingers to probe the distant mountains. He took a deep breath. The readouts for fuel, airflow and temperature were superimposed on his sight. They all looked correct.

'You love this, don't you?' she said.

'Flying is better than anything.'

'You'll have to teach me sometime.'

He swivelled a microwave antenna, bringing it to bear on a comsat, unobtrusively patching himself into the air traffic control net. Reality melted into computer simulation, pumped directly into his brain through his modified nervous system. The land became a gunmetal grey sculpture in filled 3-D graphics.

He became a small point on a vast grid. Overhead passed the blue pulses of incoming planes, the white images of outgoing aircraft from Marrakech airport. Somewhere over Gibraltar, the flashing red arc of an emergency descent hurtled towards an ice-blue sea.

He added weather patterns and watched the dark lines of depressions sweep across the infinite plain of his awareness.

I'm adding the co-ordinates of our destination. Over the intercom circuit, Monica's voice sounded as though it came from light years away. The white tower representing their destination rose in the distance.

He asked the computer for the flight plan. Lines of light flashed out, weaving across the grid linking him to the distant tower. He merged into the systems until the Skyrider once more became an extension of his own body.

He fed fuel to the engines, feeling power build within his body. He rose over the simulated landscape as the Skyrider rose into the air.

He jacked into the weapon systems and wheeled the belly turret through 360 degrees. Through its camera, he saw the mansion retreat and watched the fields scroll by below him. If anyone looked up, they would only see a dark shadow against the black and hear the whisper of the muted engines.

Carrying a cargo of stolen eyes, he arced towards the Mediterranean.

6

'It's immoral,' said Rosa. Her speech was slightly slurred, her pupils were contracted. She had become her own best customer for Haze, the latest designer drug. 'How can you do it?'

'It's money and a new ID.'

'Do you know how they get those parts?' she said.

'No. And I don't care.'

'Harvesting, they call it. They find parents who are too poor to feed their children. They pay them for spare parts. An eye, a kidney. You know what the going rate was for a kidney, when I was a kid here in Marseilles?'

His eyes wandered to the wallscreen. On it was an advertisement for *Oui*, a new perfume. An idealized Rosa strolled on a beach with a handsome man. It was tailored advertising, personalized for each tube subscriber from their data-files, a blend of computer generated graphics and real footage.

Rosa failed to notice his lack of interest.

'Three hundred Euromarks. They sell them to private clinics because there's always a shortage of voluntary donors. Police came down on it here, so now they import.'

'I didn't make the world,' he said. 'I've got to live in it.'

'Sometimes they don't bother to bring the kids back, just break them up for spare parts. Who's going to complain?'

'What's that to you?'

She ran her finger over the scar on her back. It was a deep trench in the sea of blue bodypaint.

'I used to have a sister. She wasn't as lucky as I was. They let me go.' She stared at him expectantly. He touched the tube console, began cycling though the channels.

'You can't do this thing, you just can't.' She was almost crying. Behind her, images flickered: a soccer match, a soft drink, Charlie Chaplin.

'Who says I can't?'

'When they altered your brain to let you fly those copters, I think you lost something. Some part that lets you feel.'

She said it slowly, as if she were piecing the idea together as she spoke, as if she were seeing him truly for the first time.

'I don't think you're human anymore.' Her voice was chill and a little afraid

'That's not true,' he said, moving towards her.

'Keep away from me,' she said, the edge of drug-induced hysteria clear in her voice. 'I don't want you near me.'

Fifteen minutes later he was carrying his bag through the foyer of the Pension. He was surprised to see Monica waiting for him. How had she known? Then he remembered her sweeping the room for bugs during their first meeting. She had reconnected the tube cable afterwards.

'Bitch,' he said, as she moved to greet him.

The tiger mask formed a smile. 'Now who's the paranoid one,' she said. 'You've passed, by the way. You're into the big time. Next trip you'll fly solo, carry real weight.'

7

From the balcony of Monica's flat he could see the crowds on the promenade, a current of waxed paper umbrellas. Rosa had hated those parasols. She said skinpaint provided all the shielding needed from the ultraviolet rays flooding through the trashed ozone layer.

She wasn't answering his calls. A filter program blocked out all his attempts to contact her.

Restlessly, he prowled back into the living room. The angular Nova-Modernist furniture, grown from self-replicating crystal, contrasted starkly with the uniform fixtures of the Pension. It was a badge of wealth, like the private Intelligence who monitored the building or the uniformed guards at the doors.

Monica lay on a cushioned couch that resembled a block of onyx, an inhaler on the table in front of her. She offered it to him. He shook his head. She took a hit and turned her attention back to the tube. He closed the glass doors to the balcony.

The huge head of Juan Delgado, leader of the Spanish Socialist movement, filled the wall. He was talking about law and order; a linguistic Intelligence provided simultaneous translation. He referred to the growing drug problem among the Workfree on the south coast. He called for more action by the police. Monica seemed to find it all amusing.

'What will I be carrying?' he asked her.

'Haze. Several million tabs of it. We have the local concession. You'll bring it in from our Moroccan labs.'

'Who are we?'

'Local business. Marseilles has always been good for smuggling.'

'Organized crime, as Delgado calls it.'

She laughed. 'More like disorganized crime. This is the age of decentralization. There are lots of different gangs. Most of the time we're at war. Why do you think you're flying a gunship?'

'You're worried about being ripped.'

'It's dog eat dog. The big ones eat the little ones. So-called friends will sell you out to the law just to be rid of the competition.'

Behind Delagado, computer graphics displayed the drug routes out of Marseilles to the Riviera and the north.

That night he made the first of many trips. That summer he became a regular visitor to Monica's.

8

Outside, the streets of Vieux-Port were hot. In Giraud's, everything was cool. Huge rotating fans swirled the air. People danced to Eurobeat synthesized by the House Intelligence. Giant images of the patrons were projected on wall and ceiling screens. Giraud's computers distorted the images, mixed them against hallucinatory backgrounds, fragmented them and edited the pieces into new patterns. The dancers watched hypnotized, locked in the high energy promise of Haze.

On the floor a girl collapsed. Two bouncers went over to her. One had a bionic arm, long and skeletal, from which the carapace had been removed.

He watched as the exposed motors and cables moved silkily, lifting the girl with ease. At a nearby table, a man muttered about a bad batch of Haze, said people were going down across the city.

He looked across at Monica. She was back in skinpaint, local colour, camouflage. The paint contained some luminescent micro-organism which highlighted her bone structure, made her look skeletal. She sipped the drink.

'It's been a long and profitable summer. You've done well,' she said.

The House Intelligence picked the image of the girl as the most interesting thing on the dance-floor. A splintered pattern of images showed beads of sweat glisten on her crimson face-paint. One wall displayed only her eyes with their shrunken pupils.

He watched the twitching girl. She was back on her feet but starting to fall again. She couldn't seem to balance.

Monica noticed his interest. 'It sometimes happens. Haze affects the motor and speech sectors of the brain, produces a condition like Parkinson's disease. Long term exposure can do it, but a bad batch is the worst.'

'Our last batch was bad?'

She shrugged, looked meaningfully at the girl on the dance floor then turned back to him.

'This offends you?' she asked.

He sensed the subtle challenge in her voice. He stared at her for a long time. He could not match the vacuum coldness of her gaze. Eventually, he shook his head.

'Good boy,' she said. She fell silent for a time.

'You know, you and I are very alike,' she said.

'I'm beginning to see that,' he said.

On the floor, the girl continued to try to rise, limbs twitching uncoordinatedly, like a spider sprayed with insecticide. Her image filled the walls, sculpted in zoom and slo-mo.

9

That night he returned to the Pension for the first time in months. Many of the people he used to know looked ill. He made his way up to the flat he had shared with Rosa.

An Arab answered. He could hear the blare of the tube from within.

'Where is Rosa?' he asked.

'Who?'

'Rosa. She used to live here. Small dark girl.'

The Arab turned and shouted something into the room, and the noise from the tube descended. He turned back and said, 'She's gone.'

'Where?'

He shrugged and closed the door.

10

'I must warn you,' said the tired looking doctor, 'she is one of the worst cases. Her motor functions are so impaired that we had to operate, wire her into her wheel chair.'

'It's OK. I'd like to see her.'

'Very well.'

They moved through over-warm corridors. They had the empty, understaffed look of most Federal hospitals.

'Rosa,' said the doctor, ushering him in. 'We have a visitor for you.'

At first, he thought she was ignoring him, then he made out the tiny movements as she tried to turn her head. She was shockingly wasted and her hair had thinned. Fibre-optic cable ran from the chair to the top of her spine. Her face was lined. She looked like a woman of sixty. There was a whine of servomotors as the chair swivelled to face him.

'Hello,' she said, in a voice that was barely a whisper.

He looked around the little room. It was utterly neat. 'Hello, Rosa. How are you doing?'

'Gettin' betta.' The words were slurred. Her hands were twitching slightly in her lap as if she were struggling to move them. He reached out and took one. She looked at him gratefully. It was disorientating to see the intelligence in those eyes, trapped in that shrivelled body.

'Not fair,' she whispered. 'Not this. Wanted fun. Not this.'

'Christ, Rosa,' he said. 'I'm sorry.'

The silence in the room was like an accusation. He began to talk simply to fill it. He told her that she would soon be better

243

and then they could get out of Marseilles, now that he had money. He could tell by her eyes that she didn't believe him. The quiet seemed to swallow his words, reduce them to meaningless babble.

'I have to go,' he said, finally.

'Come back?' she asked with a hint of desperation. 'No visitors.'

'Yes,' he lied. 'I'll be back.'

At the door, he turned for a last look. Her right hand was twitching. He thought she was trying to wave.

II

He lay in bed and watched the desert sky. The stars gleamed frostily overhead; the air was cold. He could see dunes rolling away into the distance.

The illusion was spoiled by Monica's entrance. Light from the open door flooded into the room. She seemed to step out of a dune. Behind her he could see the hall. Warm air hit him.

She was naked. Without paint, her flesh gleamed whitely. She strolled across and climbed into the bed. Her skin was still warm from the hot-air dryer in the shower.

'This is the last job,' she said. 'We're moving out of Haze. Since the Parkinson scare, it's not selling.'

Political pressure over the casualties was making the police hungry for arrests. Monica probably wanted the money from this last consignment to make a run for it.

'What about me?'

She smiled, revealing small sharp teeth. She reached over to the side of the bed to touch the console. The walls returned to normal, the ceiling went dark. He felt the warm weight of her body press down as she moved to straddle him.

'Don't worry,' she said. 'You'll be taken care of.'

They were waiting for him at the rendezvous point.

In the clearing were two men and a Hyundai 4 × 4. They stood outside the circle of bio-luminescent tubing that marked the landing site. He hovered overhead, surveying the scene through the starlight scope of the turret camera, looking for Monica. He could see no sign of her. Everything appeared normal, but somehow the pattern was wrong.

One of the men beckoned for him to come down.

He trained the guns of the belly turret on them. He monitored the radio bands closely.

'He suspects something,' he heard someone say. 'Take him.' There was a crackle of static and then a message came at him over the radio. 'This is the police! We have you covered with ground-to-air missiles. Land now or we open fire!'

He tensed. He had been set up. With several hundred kilos of Haze in the back, they would have enough evidence to mindwipe him.

Information from the combat systems of the Skyrider pulsed through his mind. He hovered over the grey plain, suspended under the falling stars of civil airflights. He had already pinpointed the source of the radio call. In the distance, he could make out three insect-like shapes moving towards him. They skimmed over the radar map of the local terrain.

He fed the engine fuel and lifted off, drifted sideways into an evasive pattern and released a mix of chaff and incendiary flares from the tailgate of the Skyrider. He aimed the cannon of the belly turret at the source of the radio call and sent heavy slugs ripping through the trees towards it.

Bright diamonds of Nightowl missiles rose towards him from below. They flew into the glowing particles of chaff. One detonated, another arced away, pursuing the red glow of the flares.

He arched himself back into the sky, ignited the afterburners. He watched the fuel readouts sink as he pulled into a high G turn. More missile-diamonds leapt at him. He released more chaff, set his ECM systems for maximum coverage. The warning dots were resolving into three Firedrake gunships. The police must have known about the armament of the Skyrider. They were taking no chances.

'Surrender now!' came the command from a nearby gunship. He sensed the command programs from the radio link attempt to over-ride his controls. Protective software countered that.

He rocketed towards them. The perfect, crystal calm of being integrated in the ship's systems swept over him.

His swift mental impulse released two missiles at the leading enemy chopper. He felt the Skyrider shudder as they were unleashed. The target peeled off upwards, blanketing the area with chaff and flares and broadband static.

One Firedrake swept by below him, while the other veered above and to the right. He altered the pitch of the blades and swung leftward and downward on his rotor axis.

He willed a stream of bullets towards his victim. Tracer crackled through the night. The pilot realized what was happening and tried to turn. His flightpath intersected with the cannon shells.

For a second, the armoured hull of the craft reflected the heavy slugs, until they sought out the weak joint where rotor protruded from cowling. Sparks flew, then the Firedrake yawed wildly and began wobbling earthwards.

He became aware of the impact of shells on his own body and moved to avoid the irritation, pulling the nose up until he was flying backwards toward a long valley yawning darkly on his display.

Diamonds erupted from a pursuer. He swung the helicopter and sprayed chaff. A warning bleep reminded him that his supply was running low. He power-dived into the radar shadow of the valley. The Firedrake blips vanished, replaced by ghost images of their projected flight paths. He swept over the corrugated grey of the valley.

He was below line of sight and radar, flying using nape-of-the-Earth tactics. He tried to calculate where they would do an overfly, fed the details into the computer.

It was most likely that one would enter from each end of the valley. He moved towards the left and hovered there just above the trees. He heard someone break the radio silence to request backup. This gave away their position, but lent new urgency to his situation. He was wired faster than the police pilots, but he could not cope with the reinforcements they could command.

For a long tense moment he waited, then the monstrous insect image of the Firedrake moved over the edge of the valley. He let fly with his last two rockets. The distance was too short for evasive action or chaff release. The chopper disintegrated in a ball of flame.

Too late, he became aware of the other enemy moving across the edge of the valley. It had not come from the far end, but raced in at an angle from where the other one had been.

Slugs hammered into the body of the Skyrider. He felt searing pain as systems crashed. The grey graphics blurred and faded, the data-flow through the system diminished from a flood to a trickle. A shell had smashed through the scanners. He writhed to avoid the hail of bullets, not caring how danger-ous a manoeuvre this was so close to the ground.

Without the data provided by the Skyrider's external sen-sors, he was like a blind man. He cut in the backup systems and dropped back into his human body. He was momentarily disorientated by the blazing night sky seen through his visor.

Twin lines of tracer arced towards him. He knew that the Skyrider's armour was being chipped away. He brought his own guns to bear, willing them to fire. There was no response. The fire control systems were down.

He was going to die, but he intended to take the other craft with him. He opened up the engines and raced forward into the tracer. He watched his enemy loom larger in the darkness as he rocketed towards it. This was the way he wanted to die, hurtling like a meteor through the sky.

The Firedrake began to veer off, ducking sideways and down out of reach. Howling with frustrated rage, he turned around ready for another mad race towards collision.

Then he noticed the inferno below. The Firedrake had been too close to the ground. It had hit a tree and gone tumbling down the side of the valley. He could see its blazing carapace.

He turned the helicopter towards Marseilles, struggling to control a craft now barely airworthy. Nursing the crippled Skyrider home was a constant battle, the integration between human mind and airframe no longer complete. Parts of his extended awareness winked out as the systems went down. Soon he was reduced to flying on manual, by sight. Losing control of the helicopter was worse than losing control of his own body, it was a descent from godhood.

Monica would have to pay for this betrayal, even if he had to crash the Skyrider into her apartment block.

13

He could see the distant glow of light from Monica's apartment window. He made final adjustments to the Wing harness, pulling the straps tight, testing the hand controls for responsiveness.

He launched himself from the roof of the Pension, catching the updraft it created. He flew in low under the arc of the rooftop security cameras. His reflection loomed raptor-like in the darkened windows. He was buffeted by the turbulent air close to the building. He fought to keep control, balancing finely on currents that threatened to send him tumbling into the street, thirty storeys below.

He brought the Wing into a stall directly over Monica's balcony.

He fell, watching the visor readouts race into the red zones. The balcony grew rapidly in his field of vision. Waiting till the last possible moment, he snapped open the wings to break his descent. Impact jarred through his legs and he began to fall away from the balcony. Frantically, he fought to regain his balance, clutching at the railing with his gloved hands.

Heart pounding, he righted himself, removed the Wing and slipped over to the window. He peered inside. The walls were covered in soothing kaleidoscopic patterns of light. Monica lay slumped on the couch. On the table near her sat a drug inhaler. He tried the handle of the sliding glass window. It was unlocked. With a savage motion, he jerked it open and leapt into the room.

'What?' she said, staring at him uncomprehendingly.

He caught her body by the hair and raised her to her feet, grabbed her arm and forced it up behind her back. He began to push her towards the window. She struggled weakly.

'What are you doing? Let me go!'

He levered her arm further up her back until she moaned. On the balcony, he twisted her head around. She looked up at him. One side of her face was still illuminated by the lights from within.

'You shouldn't have set me up,' he said. 'Did they give you immunity for turning me and the others in?'

She shook her head. 'I don't know what you're talking about.'

He jerked her arm viciously. 'Don't lie.'

She took a deep breath, seemed to relax. Her eyes were bright and cold. 'It was business. Nothing personal.'

He laughed. 'It was very personal for me.'

'What do you want? Money? Negotiables? I could make you wealthy.' She fixed him with her hard stare.

He thought about his loss as the Skyrider crashed. He held her gaze, then slowly he shook his head.

'What are you going to do?'

'Teach you to fly,' he said.

He lifted her up. She screamed and kicked wildly as he threw her over the balcony. He watched her tumble down into the lighted street. He stood there until a crowd gathered and he could hear the distant wail of sirens.

He strapped himself back into the Wing and flung himself out into the sky. As he drifted upwards, he watched the tiny people below, his eyes as wild and predatory as a hawk's.

THE BRIDGE

by
Christopher Evans

Christopher Evans is the author of *Capella's Golden Eyes*, *The Insider* and *In Limbo*. He also purports to be co-editor of something called *Other Edens*, and like the other alleged editor he has written more pseudonymous novels than he hopes anyone remembers – he certainly doesn't remember them. His own name, however, is on the cover of his latest book, *Writing Science Fiction* (1988). In it, he analyses one of his own stories – a story in the same series as the one which follows, and for which he provides this introduction.

Introduction to *The Bridge*

The Bridge is chronologically the third in a series of stories following the life-history of a master-artist called Vendavo in a society where there exist invisible, ethereal creatures known as chimeras which can be brought into physical existence in any shape by artists whose minds are sufficiently well attuned to them. The world of the story is pre-technological in most respects, dominated by a dictatorship known as the Hierarchy. Vendavo, the child of a poor family, has become the most famous artist of his day, courted by the rich and the powerful. Promiscuous and opportunistic in the furtherance of his career, he nevertheless possesses great natural talent.

The air was alive with a flurry of unseen chimeras. Vendavo stood motionless at the centre of the stable, dusty sunlight slanting in through a broken shutter, the air rank with the smell of horses, even though the beasts had been removed days before. He closed his eyes, his mind filling with visions of barbarians — bearded and scarred men, red-eyed and yellow-toothed, lips cracked and bearskins muddy as they rode across an empty plain under a lowering sky. He could smell their sweat, their foul breath, feel the wind on their faces and the pounding of their horses' hoofs beneath them.

The chimeras pressed in more strongly, filling his head with a babble of whispers, imploring him to fashion them. He felt as if he were buffeted by winds, as if he stood on a mountaintop in the middle of an exhilarating gale. Grinning, he resisted their pressure, focusing on a rider at the head of the pack, a black-bearded man with piercing eyes and huge hands which whiplashed the leather reins across the neck of his mount. A thick scar split his right cheek, half his ear was missing and his nostrils were caked with blood. Yes, this one would be the legendary warlord who had swept down from the north, conquering Veridi-Almar and founding a dynasty.

There was a polite cough.

Instantly he let his vision dissipate. And instantly the chimeras retreated, their susurrus dwindling to a murmur.

Mersulis stood patiently, a slim figure in a tight black tunic, her indulgent smile a white arc in an ebony face. Her expression was one of polite boredom; as far as she was concerned, the stable had continued utterly silent and empty apart from the two of them.

'Will it suffice?' she asked.

'Indeed,' said Vendavo. 'It's ideal.'

Mersulis stared disapprovingly at the straw-strewn cobbles and the empty stalls. 'Rather bare and lacking in creature comforts, I'd have thought.'

'The space and solitude are exactly what I need.'

'You've told no one about the commission?'

'No.'

'Not even your wife?'

'I explained that I had important work to do, that's all.'

'Good.' Mersulis tapped the heel of her boot against the cobbles. 'Will you be sleeping here?'

Vendavo shook his head. 'My new-born daughter is sick, and I may be needed at home. I'll come before dawn and leave after sunset.'

'Be sure you carry your pass. The military have orders to arrest anyone on the streets after curfew without one. Even you.'

She began striding towards the door. Her cropped hair accentuated her long neck, the sweep of her shoulders. She looked more like the mistress of some exotic brothel than the third wife of the Hierarch. He followed her to the door.

'You realize you have ten days at most?'

He shrugged. 'It will be time enough.'

They stepped outside into the blinding sunlight. Four soldiers in the green uniforms of Jormalu's personal guard stood at the head of the alleyway which led to the stable. Like Mersulis, they were all dark-skinned Southerners. Mersulis handed Vendavo the key to the stable door.

'Do you have any message for the Hierarch?' she asked.

Vendavo was prepared for the question.

'Tell him he can have complete confidence in me,' he replied.

The sun hung low and red over the city as Ethoam hurried from the widow Bila's hut. He was late, having lingered too long at her bedside, trying to feed her thin soup and engage her in talk which would make her forget, however briefly, her sickness. He had succeeded in neither because she was too sunk in pain. Her ulcerated legs gave off the stink of death which made her heavily shaded room even more oppressive. Ethoam was ashamed of the relief he had felt on finally escaping into the street.

There was a stitch in his side, and sweat was trickling down his back under his robes. He passed a butcher's shop which had been gutted during the riots in the spring over the increase in food prices. Three months on, the foot patrols of Jormalu's soldiers remained ever-present on the streets.

The temple was a humble ochre-domed building close to the north bank of the Raimus. Just downriver was Jormalu's bridge, a soaring pillared arch of oatmeal stone. Gulls had already found nesting places on its parapets and ledges. Over twenty years in the building, it was soon to be opened by the Hierarch.

Nisbisi, the priestess, was standing just inside the arched door, placing a silver incense holder on a plinth. A stickler for punctuality, she frowned at him as he entered. Two novices in white were busy at the altar, arranging flowers for the evening devotionals.

Ethoam's cubicle was situated behind the altar, and he was relieved to see that only three petitioners sat waiting. The last of them was Tilarwa, and she smiled at him as he passed by.

The cubicle was small and windowless, a single candle burning in a bracket above his chair. Ethoam plumped the cushion at his feet before settling himself in the chair, adjusting his maroon robes over his ample belly. The first of the petitioners entered and knelt in front of him on the cushion.

Ethoam often felt that he was an utter fraud, and never more so than when he undertook his formal duties as a Comforter within the temple itself. The man before him, a smallholder, explained that he had lost half his pigs to swine fever and was threatened with ruin. What could he do? Ethoam went through the ritual of telling him to offer prayers to the Supreme Spirit and practise good works in the hope that his fortunes would improve. The advice sounded fatuous even to him, and the man only grudgingly dropped a handful of coins into the collection box before departing.

The second petitioner, a middle-aged woman, was engaged in a long-standing quarrel with her sister over the possession of an ornamental mirror left to them by their father. He had promised it to her on his deathbed, the woman claimed, but her sister refused to accept this. How could she make her see reason? Ethoam sighed as if in contemplation, recalling the same woman on a previous visit fretting over the ownership of the olives on a tree which overhung her garden. He suggested she tell her sister she had sought his advice and that he would be pleased if she too could visit him so that the matter could be fully explored. The woman looked pleased, scarcely listening, it seemed to him, as he also suggested a small donation to a charitable cause and quoted a pertinent passage from a holy text about the virtues of giving rather than receiving. As always, when he adjudicated in matters of material possession, Ethoam felt more like a lawyer than a spiritual counsellor.

The woman left, and Ethoam allowed himself a discreet belch. Before he had been ordained, he had always imagined that Comforters dealt constantly with matters of holiness and penitence, with questions of good and evil, life and death, salvation and damnation. But the temples catered chiefly to the comfortable and well-off, lulling them with their rituals, pandering to their prejudices and petty jealousies while the poor were left to rot in their hovels.

The curtain drew back, and Tilarwa stepped inside. 'You look as sour as a lemon,' she announced.

Ethoam smiled. At nineteen, she was eleven years his junior, yet she showed him no deference whatsoever. She wore a faded olive-green dress which hung on her slender body, and her arms and face were grimy. She made no move to kneel in front of him.

'What ails you today, my child?' he asked with mock formality.

'Nothing,' she said bluntly. 'I came in off the streets because it was cooler. Would you rather I found something to complain about?'

He shook his head, amused and somewhat in awe of her.

She had first come to him in the spring to complain that her father wanted to marry her to a man she despised, an undertaker three times her age with no teeth in his head. Ethoam advised her to resist the betrothal if she felt she could never be a dutiful wife to the man, and he also offered to speak to her father. But this had not proved necessary, because when she next came to the cubicle it was to inform him that the undertaker had abandoned his courtship after she flatly refused to marry him. Her left eye was bruised as if from a blow, but she made light of it, dismissing it as an accident.

Ethoam did not flatter himself that he had persuaded her to reject the undertaker, for it seemed to him that she was a strong-willed young woman who had already made up her mind before visiting him. She had never spoken of the matter again, even though she became a regular caller at his cubicle, often for no other apparent reason than to pass the time of day. Her father, a widower, was a tanner, and she was an only child.

Today she seemed somewhat subdued, watching him but saying nothing. Ethoam shifted in his seat, feeling self-conscious.

'Is there something you want to tell me?' he said finally.

'No. Is it against the law for me to come here for no reason?'

'Of course not. It's simply my duty to ask.'

'Why have you never married?'

Her sudden conversational forays always unsettled him, more than ever in this instance. He considered carefully before saying, 'Not many women want to be the wife of a Comforter.'

'Are you celibate?'

Her bluntness seemed artless rather than rude, and he could not bring himself to chastise her – or to refuse to answer her question.

'I don't visit whores, if that's what you mean.' She opened her mouth to say something, but Ethoam hurried on: 'There were women once, before I became a Comforter. Now my duties don't permit me the luxury of courtship.'

This sounded pompous – and also less than the truth. Women whom he found attractive tended to daunt him utterly so that he would never dare approach them.

Tilarwa continued to study him with her almond eyes. At times she seemed just like a child, at others – as now – very much the young woman approaching the prime of her urchin beauty.

'I must go,' she said abruptly, and she hurried out of the cubicle before Ethoam could say another word.

Vendavo stood under the central dome of the High Temple, drenched in the light which streamed through the Star Window. The faceted panes fractured the radiance into rainbow hues which splattered the white marble floor like multicoloured rain.

It was still early and the temple was not yet open to the public; but he had had no difficulty in gaining admission and being left alone so that he could pursue his calling. The Star Window had been created centuries before by an unknown artist whose work adorned many temples throughout the land. In those days, artists were thoroughly pious and utterly convinced that their gifts were directly inspired by the Supreme Spirit. The priesthood embraced them wholeheartedly, certain that the chimeras were not only supernatural but holy.

Vendavo climbed the altar steps, drinking in the cool solemnity of the place, the soaring curved spaces, the dark recesses in which multitudes of candles glittered. Chimeras flocked around him with a fury of whispers as he studied the figures and bas-reliefs of those who had preceded him. Above the altar, mounted on a pedestal, was the statue of the first woman Hierarch, an artist herself who had reputedly founded the religion of the land and raised the first temples after proclaiming the chimeras the Heavenly Host, the spirits of those who had departed the earth.

Anything fashioned from chimeras eventually decayed into inanimate stone, losing its vividness if not its form. The life-sized statue was pitted and worn, but its major features were still well-defined. It had been discovered half-buried in the garden of an abattoir razed to make way for the new road to Jormalu's bridge. It was popularly believed to be a self-portrait, a chimera wrought by the Hierarch herself, gaily coloured and lifelike when first fashioned.

Vendavo had never been a great frequenter of temples, and this was the first time he had studied the figure in any detail. By today's standards its execution was crude, and he found himself annoyed by the incongruously noble features, the air of serene gravity. The Hierarch had lived at a time when a ruler needed to be decisive and ruthless, and he had a vision of a domineering and fiery woman with the face of a termagant; nobility and serenity had no place in it. The statue could not possibly represent the real woman of history.

He descended the steps, satisfied that he would derive no inspiration from the works of other artists. He always gave of his best when he clung to the purity of his own vision and allowed nothing to dilute it.

In Temple Park, pedlars, beggars and lovers sat under the shade of flowering jacarandas, while street artists performed to small knots of people, just as he had done many years before. He hurried on, aware that he had spent longer in the temple than he had imagined; morning was well advanced.

On a cobbled lane, he entered a herbalist's; Nyssa had asked him to fetch an ointment for their new daughter's fever. The smells of camphor, aniseed and aromatic oils filled his nostrils. A woman sat at a table.

He passed her the slip of paper on which the doctor had written the ingredients for the ointment. As she studied it, she said, 'You're the artist, aren't you? Vendavo. I've seen you perform.'

She had hooded eyes, a chipped tooth at the front of her mouth, a tousled look. The top of her blouse was loosely tied, revealing the half-globe of a breast.

'I can sense your creatures,' she said.

He eyed her. Cautiously he asked, 'Do you create yourself?'

She shook her head, utterly dismissing the idea. Her

response pleased him; he was constantly being pestered by those who claimed to be 'sensitive' and wanted him to tell them the secret of how to fashion chimeras. The secret, he always told them, was to begin.

'Can the ointment be prepared immediately?' he asked.

'Of course.'

She retreated through a beaded curtain into a tiny room crammed with bottles, phials and jars. The curtain had a gap in it, and he watched her mixing the ointment in a mortar bowl, her every movement languid yet assured. She was a woman thoroughly at ease with herself, and there was no denying her rough handsomeness. Presently she emerged with a small glass jar which she laid on the counter.

He put a hand into his purse, but she shook her head.

'Create something for me.'

He smiled, and instantly a vision came to mind and a chimera rippled through him.

On the counter formed a miniature of the woman, the likeness at once flattering yet true. She lay on her back, naked, her arms outstretched as if awaiting the embrace of a lover.

Vendavo returned her smile.

'Are you alone here?' he asked.

She laughed.

Tilarwa entered the cubicle and surprised Ethoam by immediately kneeling on the cushion. Normally she did not visit him so frequently, and he had not noticed her in the temple when he had arrived earlier.

'What's happened to your hair?' he asked. It had been severely and crudely cut so that it now hung ragged about her ears.

'I did it myself.'

In her hands she held something wrapped in muslin. Head bowed, she thrust it at him.

'What is it?' he asked.

'A cake. I baked it for you.'

He opened it up. It was heavy and dark, redolent of treacle and vine fruits.

262

'I know you like cakes,' she said. 'I saw you on the street yesterday morning, buying sugared pastries at a stall.'

Ethoam knew she lived close by, but he had the uncomfortable feeling that she had been spying on him. In fact, he had bought the pastries for a blind veteran of Andrak's wars who was presently dying in one of the Comforters' retreats; all that was left to him was his sweet tooth. Ethoam was dismayed at the idea that Tilarwa would assume his corpulence was due to overindulgence in cakes; for years he had eaten like a sparrow, but his belly had not diminished one whit. Nevertheless, he was touched by the gift.

'It's very kind of you.'

'I burnt the first one I made. My father says I'm good for nothing.'

She spoke without self-pity, but her head remained bowed. Only now did Ethoam notice the graze on her chin. Gingerly, he reached down and put his hand under her jawbone.

'Did your father do that?' he asked.

She said nothing.

'Did he?'

'He has a new husband for me. A merchant who trades in cloth.'

Ethoam leaned forward, making a show of examining her face. 'Have you met him?'

'I cut my hair so I would look terrible. He has foul breath and the manners of a pig. I hate him more than the undertaker.'

'And no doubt you told your father as much.'

'I told him I intended to marry someone else.'

'Indeed? And is that true?'

'Yes.' There was a pause, and then she looked up at him. 'Can you guess who it might be?'

Ethoam was genuinely perplexed, and only when he saw the look of irritation on her face did realization dawn.

'I've told my father you'll visit us tomorrow evening.'

Ethoam was speechless.

'You must help me. He'll send the merchant packing if you do.'

Already she was on her feet. She gave him directions to her house, told him what time he was expected, then departed as suddenly as she had come.

Ethoam did not attempt to pursue her. He simply sat there for long moments afterwards, quite stunned, quite unable to decide whether she had been serious or not. No, it was impossible. Tilarwa was young and spirited, and it was simply ludicrous that she would want to spend the rest of her life with a fat and bumbling servant of the temple such as himself, even as a pretext to avoid marriage to the merchant.

The curtain opened and Nisbisi peeped into the cubicle. She frowned – her face seemed perfectly formed for it – and said, 'Have you finished your duties?'

'Indeed.'

'Isn't there other work for you to do on the streets?'

She disliked him lingering in the temple. In general the priesthood tolerated rather than welcomed Comforters, often deeming them insufficiently holy since they were not fully consecrated and spent much of their time in what were considered to be secular pursuits.

'I was thinking,' Ethoam told her. 'Meditating.'

'What's that?' she said. 'A cake?'

He was still holding it in his hands. 'It looks remarkably like one.'

'A gift from the girl?'

He thrust it at her, knowing he was obliged to hand over all offerings to the temples. No doubt she would scoff the lot at supper with her novices.

'That girl is becoming a frequent visitor,' she remarked. 'Is it wise to encourage her?'

'I'm surprised you noticed. Do you keep track of all my petitioners?'

It was unlike him to be so sharp, and he immediately felt abashed. Under her withering stare, he slipped past her and hurried out of the temple.

The streets were filled with evening shadows. Ethoam pushed all thoughts of Tilarwa from his mind, climbing a rutted track towards the old quarter of the city. He followed a circuitous route to the house, checking along the way to ensure he was not being followed. Such precautions made him feel foolish, but they were necessary.

Insaan the tailor had rooms above a disused warehouse in a secluded backstreet. The eight others were already present when Ethoam arrived – punctuality had never been his strongpoint – along with Melicort, one of the personal assistants to Alkanere, the leader that none of them had ever met.

'Have you heard the news?' Insaan said immediately, and with great excitement. 'The uprising will begin on the day the bridge is opened!'

Ethoam stood there, slack-mouthed, while the others hugged him and slapped his back. Unlike most of them, he was a relative newcomer to the group, having joined it only three years before. At their meetings, they constantly talked of overthrowing Jormalu and his government, but it was hard to believe that the uprising was actually now at hand.

Melicort was already preparing to leave, having other groups to address before sunset. A short, red-headed man, he had the intense eyes and brisk movements which Ethoam had observed in other deeply committed reformers; it was as if he couldn't wait to bring about the new order which he was always promising was at hand.

'You'll receive fuller instructions on the day,' he told them. But everyone pleaded for more details, and he paused at the door. 'There's going to be an entertainment on the bridge to mark its opening. The artist Vendavo is performing a pageant of some description. That's when we'll strike.'

And then he was gone, Insaan shepherding him out. Ethoam stared after him, stunned by the mention of Vendavo's name.

Perched on a low stool, Vendavo let the ghostly figures swim in the air while the chimeras seethed about him. He wore only a loose shirt and leggings, and he was soaked with sweat. Since dawn he had been summoning up figures of every shape and variety, examining and rejecting them, taking a feature here, a mannerism there, then combining them into something new, a phantom with the striking characteristics he needed. All the while he had to hold the chimeras at bay, resisting their urge to be made fully real. The preparation of the image, straining the imagination to conjure up all the details and idiosyncrasies that would make it vivid and memorable, was always the hardest part, like mining gold from thin air. Once done, bringing it to life was child's play.

At present he was working on Jormalu's great-grandfather, who had separated the Hierarchy from the temples by declaring himself a secular ruler and the chimeras natural creatures of the air, unconnected with the Supreme Spirit. By doing so, he had strengthened his own power while freeing artists from the constraints of piety. Traditionally he was portrayed as an ascetic and an intellectual, but he was also known to have been fond of oratory and of the sport of wrestling, in which he often participated himself. Considering this, Vendavo suddenly found his representation of a lean and cadaverous figure in white robes utterly inadequate and inapt.

With a fury of exasperation, he dissolved everything. Around him the chimeras recoiled and retreated, their hectic inarticulate babble fading to a murmur. Vendavo let out a great sigh, clearing both his lungs and his head.

Slowly the chimeras began to flitter back into his vicinity, their manner hesitant, querulous. Already he had begun to revise his image. Yesterday, in the park, he had seen a burly beggar accosting passers-by, vehemently demanding coins. With robes instead of rags, a sceptre in place of a walking stick, rings on manicured fingers, the beggar could be transformed –

'I hope you'll excuse the intrusion.'

Vendavo spun around. Mersulis was standing there, as black as a shadow. He had not even heard the stable door open.

'I hope you don't mind me visiting,' she said. 'I simply wondered how you were progressing.'

Normally nothing could distract him when he was working; he could create anywhere. But this was a particularly difficult and ambitious undertaking, and Mersulis had disturbed him at a crucial moment.

He summoned up his new vision of Jormalu's great-grandfather, sending it racing towards Mersulis, its arms outstretched menacingly.

To her credit, Mersulis did not scream, though her surprise and alarm were evident. She simply took a step back, far too late to prevent the hands from closing around her throat . . .

But of course they passed harmlessly through her, as insubstantial as the figure itself was. Even if he had made it fully solid, it could not have harmed her. There was something about chimeras which made them shy from human contact during their summoning. They could never be made to actively injure living things.

Vendavo allowed the figure to dissolve away while Mersulis recovered her composure. At length she said, 'Who was it?'

He told her.

'Ah,' she said. 'Interesting. I'd always imagined him differently.'

'We each have our own image of things.'

She ran a finger under the collar of her tunic. A mist of sweat had formed on her face and neck.

'Are you basing your work on the Chronicles?' she asked.

He nodded. 'They're the only source we have.'

'But there's very little physical description in them.'

'To my mind, that's a freedom rather than a restriction. One has, inevitably, to interpret. I've assumed that I would be allowed complete freedom in this respect.'

'Oh, perfect freedom, have no fears on that score. But you won't forget that Jormalu will want to see . . .' she hesitated, choosing her words, '. . . a progression of nobility and achievement up to our own time.'

'Of course. The display will emphasize that.'

Mersulis leaned against a stall-post, undoing the top button of her tunic. She was much taller than most Southerners, and in certain lights her skin looked like black suede. She radiated an utter confidence in both her status and her beauty.

'How do you credit the Chronicles?' she asked.

Vendavo eyed her. By all accounts, Jormalu trusted her implicitly and frequently took her advice on matters of state. She had lasted far longer than his two previous wives, and his affection for her was apparently undiminished.

'In what sense?' he said.

'In the sense in which we read them. As history.'

Vendavo affected to consider. 'I'm no historian. They certainly tell a vivid story.'

'Of that there's no doubt. Today's historians will tell you that their chronology is doubtful and their genealogies certainly spurious. But they will only say so in private.'

She was smiling, as though challenging him to comment. Of course he knew that the Chronicles, written by a variety of hands over the course of several hundred years, often reported events decades or centuries after they had happened and usually presented them in a manner designed to flatter the ruler of the day.

'I'm no expert on these matters,' he said. 'I read the words and bring my imagination to bear.'

Mersulis nodded, still smiling. 'And so do we all. We each create history in our own image, wouldn't you say?'

It was such a smile: teasing, enigmatic, nothing whatever to do with humour or good-will.

Ethoam sat opposite Tilarwa at the dinner table, telling her of his strained relationship with Nisbisi and his belief that the priesthood was in general idle and self-satisfied, their attitude towards Comforters high-handed. True, he was not as devoted in a religious sense as someone like Nisbisi was – in fact, if he was honest with himself, he had long ceased to believe that there really was a Supreme Spirit directing their destinies, irrespective of the existence of the chimeras. He was an agent of the temple who counselled prayer without faith in its usefulness, an apostate who only continued to practise his calling for the practical good it did.

Throughout all this, Tilarwa listened while clearing dishes, pouring more wine and serving fried bananas in a creamy sauce. Ethoam felt positively indulged, the meal far finer than any he had eaten in a long time; surely it spoke of her affection for him to have gone to such trouble.

She wore a lilac dress that was obviously her best. Between them on the table was a small urn containing the widow Bila's ashes which he had given her on his arrival. Earlier he had officiated at Bila's cremation, and there were no relatives present to receive her earthly remains. The gift of a departed spirit's ashes was considered by many to be the profoundest token of esteem and affection.

Before arriving, he had imagined Tilarwa's house as a cramped hovel in some dingy alley, or a cluttered room in a tenement, the stairs rank with rotting food and dogs' droppings. He had spent his childhood in such a tenement, though he and his brothers and sisters played outside in the street whenever they could, escaping both the fetid atmosphere and the squabbling of their shrewish mother and drunken father. It pained him to think so uncharitably of his parents, but they had never shown him any guidance or love, and he, the youngest, had been forced to rely on his elder brothers until a priest, assuming his timidness was something holy, had taken him into the temple at the age of ten. Only then had his education begun.

Tilarwa's house turned out to be a small but sturdy building at the corner of a street down which Ethoam had passed many times. Her father was not present, having gone to visit a cousin because, Tilarwa said, he was ashamed to meet his daughter's spiritual counsellor. This development unduly flustered Ethoam at first, and he tried to leave. But Tilarwa had cooked plantains and sweet potatoes with scraps of pork bought with money filched from a hoard her father kept hidden. There was also home-made apricot wine, which Ethoam began drinking freely to embolden himself. He now informed Tilarwa that Comforters were encouraged to marry since a settled family life was deemed to improve their ability to minister to others. He talked of his desire to have children, something which had never crossed his mind until now.

The wine was making him garrulous and indiscreet, but for some reason he did not want to stop talking; he wanted Tilarwa to know how he felt about such things so that, he reasoned, she would understand just what sort of man she intended to marry – if, indeed, she did intend it. A detached part of himself was aware that he was being foolish, undignified, possibly blasphemous. But the world and all its considerations had faded into the background; all that mattered, all he was aware of, was the dinner table and Tilarwa sitting opposite in her lilac dress. He might have talked all night had she not finally whispered, 'Hush.'

He stopped. She was smiling at him, the way an indulgent mother might smile at the excesses of a precocious child. Only then did he actually wonder how long he had been talking, and how much of what he had said was of any interest to her at all. With a crushing sense of embarrassment, he felt as if he had overstayed his welcome, strained her hospitality to breaking point, ruined the whole evening.

'Forgive me,' he spluttered. 'I didn't mean ... I should leave now.'

He lurched up from his chair. The room slewed, and he would have fallen had not Tilarwa reached across the table to steady his arm.

He blubbered more apologies as she led him across to the armchair beside the hearth and ordered him to sit down.

'I must go,' he insisted. 'I must.'

She pointed to the window: the sky beyond was a deep blue. 'It's past sunset. You'll have to say here.'

'No. I can't ... Your father ...'

'He won't be back tonight. No one need know. You can't go home like that.'

'I must.'

Then he began to hiccup. Bile rose in his throat. He swallowed air, held it down for as long as he could, exhaled it in a great blast. Miraculously, the hiccups ceased. He felt a great weariness, but became aware that Tilarwa was laughing at him. Then she was hauling him up from the armchair, leading him towards the stairs, telling him firmly she intended to put him to bed.

Again he protested that he preferred to risk the curfew than compromise her. Again she laughed and thrust him towards the stairs.

It was an arduous, humiliating business, with him panting and grunting like a sow. Finally they crawled into the attic room. Tilarwa pushed him on to a mattress covered with a worn patchwork quilt. She wrenched off his sandals. Then he felt her tugging at his robes.

'No,' he murmured, striving to sit upright, to force her hands away. The feather pillows suddenly set off a violent bout of sneezing. He found his handkerchief, blew his nose copiously. He felt ridiculous.

Again Tilarwa seemed to be laughing at him.

'Were you serious,' he said, 'about wanting to marry me?'

'It's hardly a joking matter, is it?'

'I've got nothing to offer you. Not even pleasing looks.'

She made a scoffing sound. 'Who are you to judge what I see in you? You're a good man – you have a good heart. When you spoke of how you hated the way the poor are treated, of how you want to fight for a better life for them – well, I feel the same. I'd like to be part of that fight.'

Suddenly she seemed so composed and adult. His memory of the evening was already hazy, but he had no recollection of saying any such thing.

'I'm just a Comforter. I do what I can.'

'Oh no,' she replied. 'I think you're much more than that. Let me help you, Ethoam. You can trust me.'

Another sneeze overtook him. He heaved himself off the bed, snatched up his sandals and began stumbling down the stairs. He heard her calling after him, but he was determined to brave the streets. Barefooted, he hurried to the door, wrenched it open, and fled into the night.

Their daughter had cried throughout the night, and the doctor had arrived early that morning and promptly announced that the crisis was coming. Vendavo sat in the anteroom with his five older children and their governess, listening to the child's whimpering, to Nyssa's exhausted words of comfort, to the physician's utter silence. He had little faith in doctors, for Nyssa herself had almost been killed by one when carrying Leshtu, their eldest. He was now a strapping boy of fifteen who sat, restless and bored, watching his younger brothers and sisters play with the miniature landscape and soldiers which Vendavo had created for them.

Sunshine poured into the room like something liquid and sweet. The day was well advanced, and Vendavo found it increasingly difficult to suppress his frustration. He wanted it to be over, one way or another. Their daughter was only a month old, and she had been sickly since birth. Because of this, they had not named her, for it was easier to lose a child that had no name. Of course he hoped she would survive, but he could not countenance many more broken nights or precious hours away from his work. Even now, the chimeras pestered him with their silvery babbling, despite all his efforts to banish them.

Not for the first time, the children began squabbling over the possession of a soldier. The governess tried to intervene, but her shrill voice only added to the noise. She was a thin-faced woman who wore sack-like dresses and stank of liniment. Vendavo's patience was exhausted. 'Enough!' he shouted. 'Take them outside.'

There were no protests, and the governess was soon bustling the children through the door. Only Shubi, his eldest daughter, lingered.

'Can I stay, father?' she asked in her quiet voice. 'I won't be a nuisance.'

She was a blonde nine-year-old, a reflective, self-contained child with Nyssa's warm brown eyes. Vendavo had to admit she was his favourite, and he was seldom able to refuse her anything.

'Go and sit by the window,' he said.

With the others gone and the room reduced to silence, Vendavo became aware that in Nyssa's bedroom all was quiet too. Was their daughter finally asleep? Or had she given up the struggle to cling to life? He rose, intending to open the door and go in. But he did not take a step forward. Better to leave them alone. Better to wait. Sooner or later he would know, for good or ill.

He paced the room in slow strides, wanting the solitude of the stable and the imperatives of his vision. Again the chimeras thickened about him as he began contemplating his pageant. Though often irritated by their ceaseless, wordless demands, he did not feel truly alive without them.

'Father!'

Shubi spoke in an urgent whisper. She was sitting on the window-ledge, peering down into the street.

'Father!' she said again. 'Look!'

He crossed to the window. Three soldiers were dragging a young man into a narrow alleyway opposite the house. The man was fighting with them, flailing and kicking in their grasp, until one of the three elbowed him hard in the stomach. As he slumped, they dragged him deeper into the alley and flung him into a tangle of weeds. Clouds of dandelion seed rose as they kicked him about the body and head.

Finally the man lay still. One of the soldiers withdrew his sword and placed the tip on the man's abdomen. Leaning on the hilt, he drove it under the ribcage. The body spasmed then went still. The soldier withdrew his sword and wiped the blade on the dead man's leggings before he and his two companions returned to the street and resumed their patrol.

Vendavo swept Shubi up in his arms, taking her away from the window.

'Why did they –' she began, but he put a finger to her lips. Staring hard into her serious eyes, he smiled.

'I did it. It was just a creation.'

She looked back at him. Plainly she did not believe him. 'Is the baby going to die?' she said.

'Let's hope not,' he said. 'Shall I conjure something else for you?'

'I want to go and see.'

273

'No,' he said firmly, unsure of what exactly she meant. 'We have to wait here. Be patient.'

But at that moment the bedroom door opened and the doctor stepped out.

Ethoam lingered on the corner of the street, filled with indecision. Above him, pigeons were roosting in the eaves of a house, their cooing like a conspiracy in code.

Evening had lengthened the shadows, but dusk would not fall for some time yet. He watched children splashing in a horse trough, a woman putting a dish of rice in a small street shrine, a hooded widow hurrying by with a wicker basket of asparagus. Everything continued as normal, yet it was far from normal. He had gone about his duties as usual, uttering his vain litanies of comfort to the sick and the helpless, but his mind was entirely elsewhere. And so he had finished his work early and taken a barge across the river. The house fronted the waterside, and the windows which faced the street were small and narrow, giving it a slightly forbidding aspect.

Still he did not move, still he was uncertain of what to do. It was all a question of loyalty and of trust, that most unreliable of human virtues.

A group of soldiers entered the street and began to walk in his direction. This hastened his decision. He strode across to the door and tugged on the bell-pull.

The woman who answered was the stern-featured governess; Ethoam could not remember her name. She did not recognize him instantly, which did not surprise him; over two years had passed since his last visit.

'I'm here to see Vendavo,' he announced.

It was only then that recognition seemed to dawn in her face. She gave a curt bow of the head. 'Of course. Come in.'

Inside, it was cool, the evening sunlight mellowing the austere white walls and marble of the reception hall. She led him through into the main room, where Nyssa sat with a baby cradled in her arms while the rest of the children played at her feet. On seeing him, she smiled and said his name.

She rose, still holding the baby, came across and kissed him on the cheek.

'Another one?' he said, peering at the sleeping child.

Nyssa nodded. 'A daughter. You came at a good time because she needs a blessing. She's only just recovered from a fever which almost killed her.'

Nyssa looked haggard, her eyes sunk in grey hollows, her hair lank and tousled. The children were watching him, and he realized he had never seen the youngest boy before.

'It's been too long since you last visited us,' Nyssa was saying to him. 'Have you been keeping well?'

'Well enough,' he said, studying the children. 'They've all grown.'

'Time slips by.'

'Is Vendavo here?'

'He's taking a nap. I'll wake him.'

'There's no need. I can wait.'

'Nonsense. He'll be pleased to see you.'

She went through into the study, leaving Ethoam to the attentions of the children.

'You're Uncle Ethoam, aren't you?' said one of the girls.

'I'm pleased you remember me.'

'The last time you came you brought us toffee.'

'You *do* have a good memory. I'm sorry to say I've got nothing for you today.'

'You can name the baby. None of us can decide.'

There was a hearty cry of 'Biru!' and Vendavo appeared, striding over and embracing him warmly.

Only Vendavo called him by his old name, but he did not object since he often thought of his brother as Neni; his fame as an artist belonged indeed to Vendavo, who was somehow another person from the elder brother who had taught him how to steal melons from market stalls, how to shin up walls, catch moths with candles and glass jars, the brother who had shepherded him through the hazardous streets of their youth and entertained him with gaudy displays of his talent.

Ethoam noted that his brother was thicker around the waist

and wore his hair longer than before. He was unshaven and looked dishevelled with sleep. But he still had his good looks, his ease of manner, his powerful physical presence.

'Did you come to see our newest one?' he asked.

'That was fortunate,' Ethoam admitted. 'She's as lovely as her mother. It's as well you can support your ever-growing brood.'

Ethoam spoke good-naturedly. He had never envied Vendavo, despite his gifts, and never advertised the fact that he was his younger brother. Not even Nisbisi knew. If anything, he had sought more anonymity as his brother's fame had grown. Their lives were very different, and it was not always easy to approve of his activities. But there was a blood bond to be honoured, past loyalties to be repaid.

'So,' Vendavo said, 'what brings you here today, if it's not simply good fortune?'

'A matter of some importance.' Ethoam turned to Nyssa. 'Would you mind if we spoke alone?'

'Of course not,' Nyssa said.

Vendavo exchanged the briefest of glances with her.

'Come through into the study,' he said, taking Ethoam by the arm.

The study was a big room whose wide balcony overlooked the river. A sofa and several floorcushions were the only furniture apart from crude wooden shelves on which stood an infinite variety of small stone chimeras – figures, animals, flowers, trees, houses, even miniature landscapes.

Ethoam paused at the centre of the study, trying to sense the presence of unformed chimeras. But he could hear nothing, feel nothing. It had always been that way, even when they were small boys and Neni used to tell him of how the chimeras assailed his mind, of their ceaseless urge to be shaped. He was deaf and insensate to them.

From a shelf Vendavo produced a bottle of wine and two cups.

'Refreshment for honoured guests,' he said, and led Ethoam out on to the balcony.

They sat down. Red wine lolloped into the cups. Ethoam watched his brother, feeling a strong sense of both kinship and estrangement. They were the only two of seven children who had escaped the poverty and disease of the streets. The rest of the family – their parents and all their brothers and sisters – had succumbed to sickness and neglect while he was still a young apprentice at the temple.

Ethoam essayed only a small sip of wine before setting it down on the floor. The sun burnished the river and lit the pale blue triangular sail of a fishing boat that was returning from the sea. Smoke rose from chimneys as ovens were stoked for evening meals.

'Well, Biru,' Vendavo said, 'what is this matter you wish to discuss?'

'A matter of violence in Veridi-Almar.'

Vendavo turned his head to face him.

'Before I say any more, I must have your promise as a brother that you will say nothing of what I'm going to tell you to anyone else. Not even Nyssa.'

'It sounds like a serious business.'

'It is. And you are involved in it, whether you like it or not.'

Now the blue eyes were filled with an avid curiosity. 'Involved? Involved in what?'

'First I must have your promise that you will say nothing to anyone.'

'I promise. What have I to do with this business, Biru?'

Ethoam could hear the sailors on the fishing boat calling to one another. At that moment he became convinced that he was making a grave mistake. But it was too late to stop now.

'There's going to be an uprising on the day the bridge is opened. We aim to overthrow Jormalu.'

Vendavo was silent for a moment. Then he raised his cup to his lips. 'We?'

'I'm one of those who opposes the Hierarchy.'

'You?' Vendavo sat up, genuinely surprised. 'You, Biru? For how long?'

'For some time.'

'But why?'

'Because I want to see justice for all our people.'

'You amaze me. I never thought – well, you hardly seem the firebrand.'

'I believe we have a duty to those less fortunate than us.'

He could see his brother beginning to think furiously. He had always been quick-witted, rescuing Ethoam on many occasions from the attentions of bullies and irate stallholders with smooth words or startling chimeras. Memories came to him of white mice, voluptuous nudes, sudden snow flurries, a scattering of silver coins. But that was long ago.

'Do you want a donation for your cause?' Vendavo asked. 'Is that why you're here?'

'There will be a rising on the day the bridge is opened,' Ethoam repeated. 'I'm not here for money.'

'Then I can't see why this should concern me.'

'We know you're planning some display for the Hierarch's benefit. You'll be caught in the middle of the fighting.'

Now there was a long silence. Below them, the twilit river slid past, heavy, unstoppable. At night, Jormalu's soldiers dumped the bodies of his enemies into its waters. Most of them were cast back up on its muddy banks long before it reached the sea, their eyes pecked out by gulls, their limbs gnawed by rats.

'If you tell anyone about this,' Ethoam said, 'then I and perhaps hundreds of others may die before –'

'I'm well aware of that!' Vendavo snapped. He stood up, began pacing the balcony. 'The question is – why have you told me, and what am I supposed to do about it?'

Ethoam knew he was angry because now he had been placed in a dilemma, something which he disliked unless it was a practical matter of his art.

'I've told you because I'm your brother and I want you to save yourself. I don't want to see Nyssa a widow, your children fatherless.'

Vendavo was gripping the balcony rail with both hands. Lights had begun to shine in the houses on the north bank as the twilight deepened. Without turning, he said, 'What am I to do?'

'There is only one thing to do. You must find a pretext to cancel the performance.'

A veil of cloud had coated the sky, and lightning flickered within it. The sun was like a gold coin drowned under milky water. There was no rain, and the air was still, as thick as syrup.

Vendavo sat with Mersulis and Jormalu's two young children in a palace courtyard, watching striped fish drift through the dull water of an ornamental pool. Dragonflies hovered over magnolia waterlilies, snapping up the insects which darted on the surface of the water.

Mersulis waved a black lace fan in front of her face while Vendavo watched the two children play with the fanciful galleons he had created for them, tentatively launching them from the edge of the pool. The boy was twelve, the girl ten, both offspring of the Hierarch's second wife. They were silent and serious-faced children, their manners impeccable.

'Sometimes he makes unexpected visitors wait all day,' Mersulis remarked. 'Sometimes they have to wait even longer. You should have told me you wanted an audience with him.'

'It was a sudden decision.'

'I hope it's nothing too serious. Nothing that will affect your performance tomorrow.'

Vendavo made a noncommittal sound. Mersulis had been pressing him to tell her the reason for his visit ever since he had arrived at the palace, but he was determined to say nothing until he was in Jormalu's presence.

Thunder growled in the distance, and a thin heat-haze blurred the horizon. Everything seemed utterly motionless, any sound swiftly swallowed up by the heavy air.

The fan moved silently in Mersulis's hand. She wore a tight-fitting sheathed gown of black silk which left her shoulders bare. It flared below the knees, revealing her slim yet muscular legs. Black slippers were loosely strapped to her ankles.

'It's the rainy season in the south,' she observed. 'When I was a child, I used to sail boats made of bark down the main street of our village during the flood.'

'You were born in a village?'

'We lived there for part of the summer. It was quite large. My father always liked the jungle.' She kicked off a slipper and stretched out her leg to dip her toes in the water of the pool. 'Did you know I was responsible for his death?'

Her father had been the ruler of the southern peoples until the armies of Jormalu's father had subjugated them. Later he had been installed as a puppet governor before an attempted rebellion during the early years of Jormalu's reign led to his execution. Mersulis's survival – and her present status – were all the more remarkable as a result.

'I always hated him,' she said in the same conversational tone as before. 'He had many nasty habits, especially his determination to take me into his bed as soon as I was old enough. Shall I tell you how I revenged myself on him?'

Vendavo watched the ripples spread from her foot. She wanted no reply.

'You may recall that several years ago the province was restive. Chiefly it was due to my father's poor governorship and the corruption of officials who worked under him. He was negligent and lazy rather than corrupt himself, but the unrest became so serious that Jormalu himself came south at the head of an army.'

She paused, and glanced across at the children. They were out of earshot.

'Jormalu had tired of his wife, and was already planning to have her executed. I saw my opportunity. I made myself fully available to him, offering not only the kind of comforts which all men desire from women but also good counsel. There was serious danger of a full-scale revolt which would require considerable force to suppress. By taking my advice, Jormalu was able to avoid any great bloodshed. He denounced my father as the source of the people's troubles, had him publicly executed and promised immediate reforms. Then, with his wife disposed of, he married me as a gesture of his good-will and affection towards the province.'

The boats had begun to bobble in the water as Mersulis created waves with her foot. Vendavo did not dare look at her.

'Don't misunderstand me,' she said. 'I acted expediently because I knew it would benefit not only myself but also the people of my province. *Anything* is better than death.'

He wondered what she was trying to tell him. Jormalu's promised reforms in the south had never been implemented, and the province was once more restive.

On the pool, both boats capsized. Within moments they had sunk. The children watched the bubbling water, showing neither alarm nor disappointment but simply a grave scrutiny.

'Give them new ones,' Mersulis whispered to him.

As always, he was attended by chimeras, and it was a simple matter to do as he was ordered. He conjured a pair of galleons even finer than before, placing them on the water where their predecessors had sunk. Only the briefest of glances at Vendavo betrayed the children's pleasure.

'Take them out of the water,' Mersulis called to them. 'Then you can go inside.'

The children obeyed, hurrying off through one of the arched entranceways.

'They're well behaved,' Vendavo said. 'Mine squabble like crows.'

'They were made aware from an early age of the need for dignity. Jormalu is a strict father.'

'You seem to have a good bond with them.'

'Considering that I was instrumental in the death of their mother, you mean?'

He stole a look at her. If anything, she appeared amused.

'I think we are alike, you and I,' she said. 'We do what is necessary in the circumstances while giving ourselves room for manoeuvre. I think we understand one another perfectly.'

He had begun to wonder why she had spoken so freely about herself. The answer became strikingly obvious as she gazed at him with candid eyes. She was binding him to her, making sure he owned a secret whose selling-price would be his death, because she desired him. And though he understood the dangers, he was also aroused. Chimeras thickened invisibly around him as he imagined Mersulis submitting to him in some private chamber, a black amazon on a battleground of white sheets, a formidable and demanding lover who would test his mettle.

At that moment, one of the household guard appeared, marching briskly forward.

'The Hierarch will see you now.'

Accompanied by Mersulis, Vendavo was led along a labyrinth of marbled corridors to another courtyard where Jormalu, a dumpy figure in purple robes, stood stroking the flank of a white horse while a retainer held its reins.

Middle-age had made the Hierarch look bloated, but there was still a youthfulness, almost an adolescence, about his features. In recent years he had developed a passion for horse-racing and was having the palace gardens modified so that a track could be made through them.

'Well?' he said, his back to Vendavo. 'How does your work progress?'

Vendavo hesitated before saying, 'It progresses well, my lord.'

'Then what are you doing here?'

The Hierarch spoke with patent irritation. Once more, Mersulis looked amused, and only then did Vendavo appreciate the full extent of her ruthlessness.

'I have something to tell you,' he said.

Ethoam was shaving by candlelight when he heard the knock on the door. He froze, staring at his startled face in the mirror. Dawn had not yet broken, and he was expecting no visitors.

He snuffed out the candle. The knock came again. Creeping over to the window, he peeked out through a gap in the shutter. He could see nothing.

His house was a small single-roomed stone building with only one door. There was nowhere for him to hide. For the past few days he had dreaded that the soldiers would come. He was not a brave man, and he knew only too well that he would be tortured if he was arrested. And the arrest itself would be a likely sign that the uprising had failed even before it had begun.

Again the knock. But it was not brutal and peremptory, the heavy hand of the military, but urgent and impatient, a brisk rapping. Still he waited, hoping that he might succeed in persuading his caller that the house was empty.

'Ethoam!' came a voice. 'I know you're there.'

He pulled the bolts on the door, swung it open. Tilarwa stood alone on his doorstep.

'What are you doing on the streets at this hour?' he said to her. 'You'll be arrested.'

'All the more reason for letting me in.'

He did not want to court the attention of any dawn patrols, so he ushered her inside and closed the door. Then he had to fumble in the dark for a match to relight the candle.

The room filled with a shadowy yellow light.

'One of the novices at the temple told me where you lived,' Tilarwa said. 'You haven't been to your cubicle in days.'

'I've had other things to attend to.'

Unexpectedly, her face broke into a grin. Ethoam realized that he was standing there is his undershift, his face patched with shaving soap. He went back to the basin and put a towel to his cheeks before reaching for his robes.

'Why are you here?' he said. 'What do you want?'

'I want to help.'

'Help? Help in what?'

'You know what. The rising. I want to be a part of it.'

He began to search the floor for his sandals. 'I know nothing about that.'

'The city's filled with rumours. It's today, isn't it?'

He tugged hard on his buckles. 'I've told you I know nothing about that.'

'You think I'm stupid, don't you? A stupid girl.'

'Oh no,' he said softly. 'Not at all.'

'Then let me help.' She came forward, touched his arm.

Birds had begun to sing in the fields which bordered his house. He threw open a window. The sky was lightening, and the air was heavy with the promise of a storm.

'Let me help,' Tilarwa said again. 'Let me be at your side when the fighting starts. That's all I ask.'

He wanted so much to believe her. 'I have duties I must attend to this morning. Alone.'

'Then tell me where I can meet you later.'

She looked so pretty in the candlelight, her eyes dark and wide. Sighing, he said, 'Very well . . .'

Soon after dawn, the storm finally broke. All morning the downpour continued unabated while thunder resonated over the city and lightning veined the livid clouds. In the streets, swelling streams of water began to carry the detritus of the city – rags, papers, rotting food, dead rats and ordure. Everyone huddled in their houses, with not even a soldier to be seen. The only sound was the hammering of the rain.

Towards noon, the storm ended as abruptly as it had begun, the cloud dissolving away as the sun burned through again. Soon it was as hot as before and there was little trace of the rain except for caked rivulets of mud in the gutters.

Soldiers were the first to emerge, some on horseback, others on foot, all heavily armed. They manned the corners of all the main thoroughfares and massed at both ends of the bridge. Vendavo watched from his window, the house utterly silent around him. He had sent Nyssa and the children to their home in the mountains – ostensibly for Nyssa and the baby to recuperate. Nyssa had wanted to stay and see his pageant, but he was adamant she leave. She had not pressed him to tell her what was wrong.

Silence. And stillness. There was scarcely a trace of a chimera, and never had he felt more alone, more at the mercy of imponderables. Already nobles and dignitaries had gathered on the bridge, arrayed in all their finery. Then the Hierarch's golden carriage, drawn by four white horses, made its stately progress to the centre while soldiers massed along the parapet walls. Now musicians, acrobats and mime artists were performing as a prelude to the climax of the opening ceremony – his pageant. Afterwards there was to be a great feast at the palace where he would be guest-of-honour.

His mouth was dry, his stomach knotted. Presently a troupe of six soldiers came marching down the street. They stopped outside his front door. Then they knocked.

Vendavo did his best to compose himself. He had decided against wearing the new white tunic which had been tailored for the occasion, and was instead garbed in sober greys and browns which would make him less readily distinguishable in a crowd. He draped his cloak over one shoulder and opened the door.

Without a word, he accompanied the guards down the street towards the bridge. A scattering of commoners watched as he went by, some offering words of encouragement and good luck, others saying nothing at all. Overhead, the sun shone fierce in a limpid blue sky.

Near the bridge, the crowds were thicker. Footsoldiers were massed in ranks, keeping them at bay. A uniformed avenue opened up for him as he marched forward with his guard of honour. A few cheers went up, but not many. The crowd seemed subdued, as if expectant of something other than entertainment.

More soldiers stood at the prows of vessels which filled the waters of the Raimus on both sides of the bridge. Never had he seen so many boats – barges, sailing craft, sloops, trawlers, caravels. They rang bells normally used only in fog.

At its midpoint the bridge bulged outwards, and tiered steps descended from the heightened parapets. Here the rich and respectable were thronged – merchants, bankers, the priesthood and the lesser and greater lords. In the centre of the open space a single huge block of masonry was missing. Originally Jormalu had intended to end the opening ceremony by lowering the final slab of stone into the hole by means of a windlass; but at the last moment Vendavo had presented him with a far more palatable alternative.

He had gone to the palace intending to tell the Hierarch of the plot against him. But something about his conversation with Mersulis prior to his audience – he could not say what it was – made him decide otherwise. And so instead he asked Jormalu for permission to end his pageant with the most dramatic creation of all – a statue of Jormalu himself, astride a miniature version of the bridge, which he would then place as the final stone in the structure, a permanent memorial to its creator. As he had anticipated, Jormalu readily gave his approval to the scheme.

The Hierarch sat with Mersulis and his two children on a red velvet sofa under a tasselled awning. His green-uniformed household guard surrounded him. As he was led forward, Vendavo tried to concentrate his mind on the pageant he intended to create – a visual history of the Hierarchy from its beginnings to the present. He had laboured long and hard to make each chapter in the pageant spectacular in every respect, but for the first time he could bring no images to mind. His head was empty and the chimeras had deserted him utterly. Despite the crowds and the noise, he was engulfed in silence and solitude.

Vendavo bowed before the Hierarch. Jormalu flicked a fly-whisk in front of his face; he looked hot, peevish. Mersulis, strikingly dressed for once in white, favoured him with one of her ambiguous smiles, while the two children sat with their hands folded in their laps and their faces composed in expressions of virtuous forbearance.

Jormalu eyed him without favour.

'Your audience awaits you,' he said. 'Are you ready?'

He had never been more unready, but he nodded. Jormalu rose and addressed the crowd: 'The artist Vendavo will now perform for us.'

Vendavo turned, all eyes on him. The sun beat down, and he felt as if he was shrivelling under it, as if he might faint. The larger silence which now emanated from his audience – an expectant, demanding silence – was the mirror-image of the blankness in his mind. He scanned the crowd, the soldiers, searching for the merest hint that the rebellion was about to begin. He looked for a sword slowly being drawn, a surreptitious signal between two men, the silent flight of an arrow, a movement on the waterfront. But there was nothing, and he could not keep his audience waiting any longer.

Panic began to well up in him. And then, just as he felt that he was going to be overwhelmed by it, as if he would never create again, a seething rush enveloped him, a host of babbling creatures demanding his attentions as the barbarian warlord sprang to life in his mind, a yellow-eyed savage on a foam-streaked horse, shouting oaths of triumph as he rode through the blazing city . . .

Ethoam stood at the rear of the crowd, trying hard to stop himself sneezing as the fox-fur on the edges of Nisbisi's gown made his nostrils peppery.

He had to admit that Vendavo was not failing the crowd, producing tableau after tableau of startling force – images of invaders razing cities, storming fortresses, handing down laws, making treaties with other rulers, even giving bread to the poor in the depths of a snowy winter. The tableaux were taken from the Chronicles, but Vendavo had instilled his own special vision and power into them. In every scene the ordinary people featured in some way, not always as victims of great events but an appreciative audience to them, so that the message was ambiguous, a glorification of the Hierarchy but also an affirmation of the dignity and steadfastness of those who were ruled, an acknowledgement of their importance in the scheme of things.

It was clever, but then Vendavo had always been clever. Ethoam was surprised when he had discovered that the display was going ahead as planned, but then the day had been full of surprises. In the teeming rain, he had gone to Insaan's house to receive instructions for his part in the uprising, only to discover that Melicort had left orders that he was to return to the temple and conduct his duties as normal. The others in the group regarded him with a mixture of pity and suspicion, and he suddenly felt like an outcast, someone whom they no longer trusted. No explanation was offered for Melicort's decision, and he was not made privy to the plan of action for the day.

Rebuffed, he went to the temple as instructed and found Nisbisi full of high-minded anticipation. She had been invited to the opening ceremony, and it was she who confirmed that Vendavo was performing as planned. At this news, Ethoam was determined not to spend his day skulking in the temple or wandering the streets, so he announced that he was Vendavo's brother and begged her to let him accompany her to the ceremony. At first she would not believe him, so he fetched from his house a figurine which he normally kept locked in a chest. It was inscribed TO BIRU, WITH BROTHERLY LOVE, and the craftsmanship was unmistakable. Nisbisi knew that Biru was his old name, and he had gambled that she was enough of a snob to relish the prospect of having the artist's brother at her side during the opening ceremony, even if he was only a humble Comforter. And so it proved. Ethoam had spent much of the morning going through interminable introductions to eminent members of the priesthood while they waited for his brother to arrive.

Now Vendavo paced about, while the latest of his creations solidified close to the missing square of masonry at the centre of the arena. An almost complete circle of figures now surrounded the hole, all remarkably detailed and vividly coloured, monuments of genius to rulers wholly unworthy of them. No artist before his brother had ever had such control over his creations; no one could twist them so effortlessly into whatever shape he chose.

A chimera of Andrak, Jormalu's father, appeared. He was presiding over the trial of a peasant who, it was clear from a mime, had been accused of theft. Six men just like the accused sat under Andrak's pedestal, and it was they who consulted each other before one of them whispered into the Hierarch's ear. Andrak listened, then nodded, before emphatically motioning that the man was to be freed.

The watching Jormalu began to clap, and the rest of the audience quickly joined in. Ethoam took the opportunity to blow his nose, reflecting that while Andrak had indeed introduced trial by jury, he had chiefly used it to eliminate all his rivals on trumped-up charges.

A hush fell once more as Andrak's chimera congealed into solidity. The circle was now complete. Ethoam kept glancing around. Ever since arriving on the bridge, he had been waiting for the fighting to break out, but there was no sign of it. The crowd remained orderly, and the guards lolled against the walls of the bridge, looking hot and bored.

At the centre of the circle, a chimera of Jormalu now shimmered into existence, above a diminutive replica of the bridge. It was a convincing rendition, even if the figure was rather taller and less plump than in real life, its features more finely cast. As the crowd burst into applause, a fit of sneezing overtook Ethoam. In response to Nisbisi's furious stare – he had sprayed her in the process – Ethoam backed away up the steps, escaping the press of bodies.

On the river, the barges and boats had closed around the bridge. Rope-ladders were trailing down to them and men were clambering frantically up, actively assisted by the guards on the walls. It was a moment before Ethoam realized what was happening: the ferrymen had no love of the bridge and must have easily been enlisted into the uprising. Everyone in the audience was enrapt with the display, and no one seemed to notice as the first of the armed men began scrambling over the walls on both sides.

Hurriedly Ethoam returned to the embrace of the crowd. Below, the household guard suddenly swarmed around Jormalu and his family, submerging them in green. Ethoam assumed they meant to protect the Hierarch, but when they drew their swords, they directed them inwards. Screams burst out, and a section of the crowd surged forward.

Vendavo's chimera bridge erupted into white flames which swiftly consumed the figure of the Hierarch. At the same time the flames seemed to turn solid and crystalline so that the whole representation was swiftly encased in a transparent block. It tilted over and dropped neatly into the hole at the centre of the arena.

Now the air was filled with screams, and the entire crowd began to panic. Ethoam was knocked to the ground in the rush to escape, his head hitting the edge of a granite step.

Someone was humming tunelessly in the darkness. The air stank with all the odours of the human body, and the heat was suffocating, life-denying.

Vendavo lay on the cobbled floor, unsure of whether he had just awoken from a doze or whether he had been half-conscious for hours. He and a host of other prisoners had been locked in the cavernous wine-cellar three days ago, fed slop by guards who would not acknowledge any of them. By day, a watery light filtered through a narrow window high in the wall at street-level, but it only turned darkness into a deep twilight so that what could be seen were huddled shadows but not recognizable human beings.

Still, there were voices, and at first many of the prisoners – chiefly the high-ranking ones – had been eager to identify themselves. Vendavo knew many of them – a lord whose banquets he had attended, a military commander who frequented a bathhouse he sometimes visited, a priest for whom he had composed religious statuary. He remained silent, sensing that there was safety in anonymity. Two or three times a day the guards came to the cellar and took away many of the most eminent prisoners. None returned.

Rumours were rife in the cellar. The Hierarchy had been overthrown, and it was said that every lord and every member of the priesthood was being executed as a matter of principle. It was said that prisoners were put in stocks to be pelted by the crowd before they were tortured and their throats slit. It was said that the bodies were cut up and fed to the poor.

Vendavo listened, but he did nothing to attract attention to himself. His bones ached from sleeping on the cobbled floor, and it was only a matter of time before he came down with one of the sicknesses that were already afflicting many of the prisoners – dysentery, fevers, wracking coughs. Assuming, of course, that he wasn't put out of his misery by execution first.

He drifted in and out of sleep, his dreams muddled and alarming. At length he was woken by bright lights in the cellar which made huge shadows move on the walls. A trio of guards with lanterns were wandering amongst them, calling out names and peering hard at faces as they walked roughshod over the huddled forms on the floor. Vendavo heard his own name being called.

Terror seized him. He contemplated saying nothing, pretending that he was not present. But the guards were already hauling a reluctant prisoner to his feet, ignoring his protestations. The previous day, another prisoner had resisted so fiercely he had ended up with a knife in his belly.

Unsteadily Vendavo rose and began clambering over the motionless bodies of his fellow captives, not daring to look at any of them. He identified himself to one of the guards, and was promptly ordered to stand in line with the others whose names had been called. Then they were marched up the stairs and out into a small empty courtyard. The blinding sunlight speared his eyes, and he staggered under it. He was pushed forward towards an open doorway.

Inside again, they were led along a carpeted corridor, then up several flights of stairs before being ordered to enter a small bare room with bars on its windows. Vendavo, the last in line, was about to go inside when one of the guards took his arm and said, 'You're first. Come with me.'

He was certain he would faint from hunger and wretchedness. The guard led him up more stairs, along another corridor and into a large room with a big lace-hung window at its farthest end. At a desk flanked by four more guards sat two men. One was a stranger; the other, Biru.

He rose immediately, came forward, hugged Vendavo. He smelt of soap and cleanliness, was as soft and flabby as civilization itself. Vendavo caught a glimpse of his own face in a mirror on the wall, and he recoiled with shock: his hair had turned white.

'Shall we proceed?' said the man who was still seated.

Reluctantly, it seemed to Vendavo, his brother disengaged himself and returned to his seat. The other man was small, middle-aged, with thinning hair and the pinched expression of a minor cleric.

'This is Alkanere,' Biru said. 'He is the People's Arbiter.'

The title meant nothing to him, but the name was vaguely familiar. Vendavo strained to remember, then recalled the name being frequently mentioned by others in the cellar. Alkanere was the shadowy rebel leader, the very man who had masterminded the overthrow of the Hierarchy.

'Your brother speaks highly of you,' he said.

'I explained how I took you into my confidence,' Biru said hastily. 'And that you agreed to go ahead with the performance for Jormalu so that he would suspect nothing.'

Alkanere put a finger to his lips, and Biru fell silent. Vendavo saw that his brother had a gash on his forehead, a deep but already healing wound. He could not think of what to say.

'They tell me your display was impressive,' Alkanere remarked. 'Though somewhat ambiguous.'

Vendavo opened his mouth to speak, but he could summon no words.

'Fitting that the Hierarch – or at least a representation of him – should be entombed in a bridge built on the backs of our people. And how well it matched the mood of the moment.'

The moment seemed a lifetime ago, the pageant itself a distant thing, only dimly remembered. But the final flourish – yes, it was coming back to him now – had been prompted by Biru's warning. He had built it into his conception as a precaution. Would it save him?

The nets on the window were luminous with sunlight. Biru, backdropped by them, looked at once dark and faded, a dim figure with no power to speak or influence events. Alkanere leafed through some documents in front of him, turning each page slowly.

'There is no reason why we should not have you executed,'

he said matter-of-factly. 'Do you have anything to say in your favour?'

Vendavo looked at his brother, who mouthed the word: 'Speak.'

'My work has always been popular with all the people,' Vendavo heard himself saying. 'I've always given public performances, free of charge. I was raised in poverty myself. I know as well as anyone the harshness of people's lives.'

He wanted to say more, to smother the situation with words and justifications; but again some instinct made him hold back.

'Memory is one thing,' Alkanere said dryly. 'Active sympathy quite another. But let us not quibble, or delay matters longer than we must. Executing you would serve no useful purpose, whereas keeping you alive may.' He paused. 'We shall need artists who will be ready to celebrate our achievements, and we already know how capably you can rise to such a challenge. Do you understand me?'

Vendavo nodded.

'You must be prepared to serve us as well as you served the Hierarchy.'

'I'll do whatever is required of me.'

Alkanere gave him a long appraising stare before motioning to Biru.

'Take him home,' he said.

Ethoam knocked on the door and waited, huddling into his robes. Overnight it had turned cold, and a thin mist shrouded the city, presaging autumn.

It was dark behind the shuttered windows, and he was surprised when bolts began to rattle on the door. It opened.

The man was bunched up in a grubby robe, his grey-streaked hair unkempt, his expression disgruntled. Ethoam had obviously woken him.

'What is it?' he asked.

'Tilarwa. Is she here?'

'The man cleared his throat and spat at Ethoam's feet. 'She's dead,' he said.

Ethoam stepped back. 'Dead?'

'She was killed in the fighting at Temple Park.' The man watched him, and now there was hatred in his eyes.

'You're the priest, aren't you? That priest she was seeing.'

Ethoam wanted to say that he was no priest, but the man gave him no chance.

'Damn you all,' he shouted, and then he slammed the door in his face. Ethoam stood there, listening to the bolts being rammed home. He wanted to knock again, to make the man – her father, presumably – tell him what had happened. But he could not face his anger and disgust, so he turned and stumbled blindly away.

Dead. Killed in the fighting at Temple Park. And it was his fault. He had been certain she was a spy of the Hierarchy under orders to seduce him into betraying the uprising. And so, when she had come to him on the final morning, he had told her to meet him in the park, where there was to be a mass gathering before they marched on Jormalu's palace. He had never imagined that the park would indeed prove to be one of the battlegrounds in the fight for the city. Alkanere had admitted that he had not been allowed a part in the uprising because of continued doubts about his undeclared relationship with Vendavo. Various stories had been circulated about the planned revolt in order to confuse Jormalu's spies, and Mersulis had kept them informed of the Hierach's intelligence so that they could choose the least expected strategy on the day. It was ill fortune, but he was still to blame. Tilarwa was dead because he had not trusted her.

He hurried on, consumed with guilt and grief. If Tilarwa was innocent of any intrigue, then she might have been sincere in her desire to marry him. Which meant that he had betrayed not only a friend but someone who might have become far more to him. Never had he felt more contemptible.

'What are you doing on the streets?'

It was a patrol of four soldiers. All wore the old uniform of the Hierarchy, though now they served Alkanere and his assembly of advisors. Since the uprising, the curfew had been extended.

Ethoam reached into the robes and produced a pass. It was signed by Alkanere himself. The soldiers gave it the briefest of scrutinies before marching on.

Only now did Ethoam register his surroundings. He had reached the avenue leading down to the bridge. It was lined on both sides with gibbets on which hung those executed as traitors. There were perhaps a hundred, and every night the bodies were changed.

He began walking down the avenue, gazing over the jumble of rooftops to the dome of the temple. He had not gone near it since the uprising. Apparently Nisbisi had survived after opening its doors to the homeless and destitute. In general the priesthood had fared better than the nobility in the aftermath of the fighting, Alkanere and his assembly sparing anyone who had committed no blatant crimes. They would be needed, it was now being said, to help the people in the difficult times which lay ahead.

Ethoam averted his eyes from the corpses, with their bulging eyes and soiled leggings, their protruding tongues. Such public deaths appalled him, because they turned even the most hated enemy into a travesty that was to be pitied. He had refused to serve as an examiner in the treason inquests, even after Alkanere had pronounced him eminently qualified. Judicial slaughter was just as abhorrent to him as any other kind of killing. He had always known that his commitment to the overthrow of the Hierarchy might eventually lead him to be a party to violence and death, but he had never imagined it would come to such a brutal, uncompromising end.

He was a fool. A fool and hypocrite. The air stank of death, and he was as much to blame for it as anyone else.

At the head of the bridge a line of soldiers stood on guard. Dawn had broken, but the curfew was not yet over. Ethoam paused to look back, for he had the sensation that someone was following him. But the avenue was filled only with corpses.

He showed his pass to the soldiers and asked for permission

to go on to the bridge. To his surprise, he was allowed through.

The rising sun had banished the mist, and the bridge soared across the Raimus in all its splendour. It had been opened two days before, despite the original promise to the ferrymen that it would be demolished stone by stone. The assembly had decreed that it was needed to encourage trade and prosperity for everyone.

All of Vendavo's chimeras had been removed from the arena except for the crystalline block encasing Jormalu. The figure lay face-up, its arms at its side, its eyes open. It looked quite dead. The entombment of the chimera had probably saved his brother's life. Vendavo was one of the few prisoners to be freed, and he had hastily departed the city to join his family in the quietude of their mountain retreat. His reprieve would be popular with the people, who cared nothing for his indiscretions. The Hierach's wife, by contrast, had not survived, despite having been highly instrumental in ensuring the success of the uprising by persuading Jormalu's household guard to support the revolt. She had been killed close to where he now stood, as had Jormalu's children, whose lives she had tried to bargain for. The betrayal had not ended there, because the household guard themselves were now imprisoned, awaiting a trial from which they could not expect to emerge alive.

The curfew was over, and a crowd had already started to gather at the entrance to the bridge. There were families with children, traders with mules, young men and widows carrying sacks and baskets, all waiting to be allowed to cross. A slim figure passed through the line of soldiers and began walking towards him. Ethoam recognized her immediately, and he felt a surge of shock and joy.

Involuntarily, he began to adjust his robes over his belly. She wore a dun-coloured linen dress, and her hair was cropped even shorter than before. As she came close, she smiled at him.

Ethoam swallowed. 'He told me you were dead.'

'I asked him to. Then I changed my mind.'

She had been allowed through the cordon without difficulty, and so presumably she had a pass just like his.

'Is he really your father?'

'Yes.'

'You followed me here.'

'Yes.'

'Why?'

'Why do you think? I wanted to see you.'

She looked even more youthful with her hair cropped, but at the same time she was very much more composed. A stranger.

'I thought you were one of Jormalu's spies.'

'No, not his.'

He gave an empty laugh, because now he understood.

'Was it you who advised I shouldn't be trusted?'

She shook her head. 'I told them I thought your loyalty was genuine. But they preferred to take no risks. They had to be sure you kept out of mischief.'

There was an attempt at her old impudence in her expression, but he remained unmoved. She was no waif, no hot-headed temptress, or even an opportunist in the pay of the Hierarchy. It was all far more devious than that. Doubtless she had been sent to him on the final morning to keep him under scrutiny, and doubtless he had been followed throughout the day. A part of him relished the knowledge that while they had known of his visit to Vendavo, they did not suspect he had actually warned his brother. It was a small miracle the two of them had survived his indiscretion.

The guards at the entrance to the bridge were letting the crowd through. In a disorderly fashion they hurried forward, wheeling their carts and barrows, herding their animals, helping aged relatives along.

'Did you cut your head in the fighting?' Tilarwa asked.

'I did no fighting. I tripped.'

An old woman at the head of the crowd was pushing her handcart straight down the centre of the bridge. She ground its wheels over the block of crystal holding the chimera of Jormalu, then hurried on.

'Perhaps,' Tilarwa said, 'when things have settled down, we might meet again. Perhaps I'll come to your cubicle.'

Ethoam was silent. He had finished with the temple, if not with his work. He intended to find a post at a retreat, caring for the sick in more sheltered surroundings. It was time to withdraw and take stock.

'Or perhaps you'll come to my house again. My father isn't such an ogre, and I owe you a proper introduction.'

'What do you want of me?' he cried. 'I've got nothing to give you.'

She looked taken aback for a moment. 'I'm very fond of you, Ethoam. I hope you believe that.'

He was still a Comforter, used to keeping his own feelings in check. He suppressed his anger and gave a smile of tolerance and forbearance. Then he pushed past her, disappearing into the tide of people which flowed in the opposite direction to the bridge's farther shore.